Time For You

Sunny Brook Farms, Book One

USA TODAY bestselling author

RENEE HARLESS

All rights reserved.

ISBN: 978-1-7362591-8-4
Imprint: Independently published

Copyright ©2023 Renee Harless
This work is one of fiction. Any resemblance of characters to persons, living or deceased, is purely coincidental. Names, places, and characters are figments of the author's imagination. All trademarked items included in this novel have been recognized as so by the author. The author holds exclusive rights to this work. Unauthorized duplication is prohibited and this includes the use of artificial programs to mimic and reproduce like works.
All rights reserved
Image: Wander Aguiar
Models: Lucas Loyola and Natasha Kirby
Cover design by Porcelain Paper Designs
Editor: Virginia Tesi Carey
Proofreader: Crystal Clear Author Services
Paperback Edition

Time For You

Sunny Brook Farms, Book One

USA TODAY bestselling author
RENEE HARLESS

I had big plans when I returned home to my small town, but they didn't include a retired hot-shot hockey player getting in my way.

The last person I wanted to fix up my historic dream home with was the handsome older man, with money to burn, who bought it right out from under me.

But thanks to my father, that's exactly what happened. Colton Crawford was making my house a home, and I was back in my childhood room, trying not to think of the towering, gorgeous Adonis with a killer smile… and how much I hated him.

Or at least that's what I tried to tell myself.

Because the more time we were forced to spend together in the dust and debris, the less our age-gap mattered.

And the more the sparks flew.

Colton was used to scoring on the ice, and after a freak storm left us sharing one tiny bed in his metal camper, the heat smoldering between us was hot enough to burn us both.

But just when I thought my sexy, new neighbor might not be so bad, real-life came knocking, reminding us what we walked away from.

Dedicated to the girls that had to forge a new path to make their dreams reality.

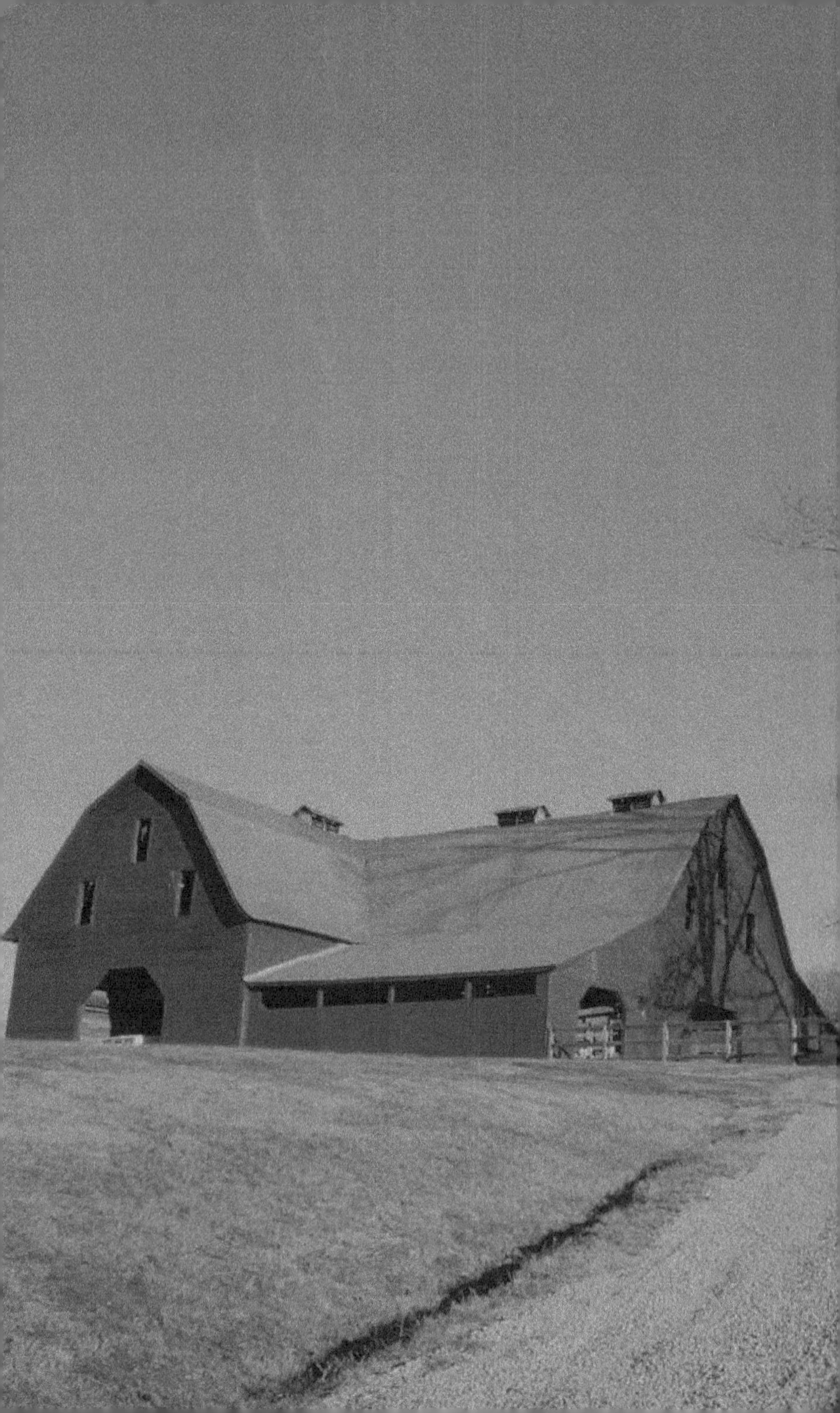

Chapter One

Autumn

"And then she asked if we had any larger eggplants just as she was making eyes at Coach Chisolm."

"She said what?" I asked my sister Rory just as I set my oversized shopping bag at my feet, gently pushing the material with the toe of my boot to tuck it under the wooden table that made up my family's vegetable stand. The farmer's market stood in an open field in the middle of our town's main thoroughfare and had been a staple of the community for decades. There were even pictures of my great-great-grandparents standing in the same spot as my sisters and I currently found ourselves.

Rory squealed, her eyes lit like a child watching fireworks when she realized I had snuck my way to the market. Alex quickly joined in. And as a trio, we rocked back and forth ignoring the looks of the people milling about.

I spoke with my sisters frequently, but there was something different about being in their presence. They had a calming effect on my ambition. The same ambition that had me leaving town six years ago without a backward glance.

It wasn't until I was in their company that I remembered how much I missed and loved them.

They were also never sure when I would follow through on a promise and return home for more than a weekend. This time had been out of my hands, which left me a bit more bereft about my current situation. But I didn't want my amazing sisters to think it was because of them. They'd always championed for me.

After consolidating years worth of embraces into a solid minute, I asked Rory, my innocent school teacher sister, to continue.

"Old Mrs. Hensen stood at our booth, stroking an eggplant, asking if we had any that were larger just as Coach Chisolm and his wife Lily walked by. Then that crazy spinster asked if we could try to grow them bigger next season because she liked the size of our cucumbers from the summer. Autumn, I was mortified."

Alex stepped from around Rory and tossed her arm haphazardly across my shoulders while saying, "See what you missed all these years?"

"It's definitely good to be back," I replied as I squeezed her hand.

Rory chimed in again as Alex released me. "That wasn't even the best part. Lily, being the badass that she is, walked over to Mrs. Hensen, inspected the eggplant, and agreed that we need to have bigger ones next season."

"She did not!" Alex exclaimed.

"Oh, she definitely did. Most of the people here heard her."

"Well, at least we know what coach keeps in his Wranglers."

"Ew," Rory cried out, scrunching her perfect button nose in the process. "He's like. . .older than our brother."

"Doesn't mean we can't admire him. Isn't that right, Autumn?" Alex asked with a cunning slit to her eyes as she looked over at me where I was unabashedly examining the eggplants. Considering the direction of my love life, perhaps Mrs. Hensen was onto something. But Alex was right. It was no secret that I'd crushed on the high school and minor league hockey coach when I was younger. I'd always been attracted to older men. As the eldest of our parents' four children, I always felt older than my twenty-four years. My grandfather used to say I had an old soul. Whatever that meant.

As my sisters went back and forth nagging each other just as they always had growing up, I took a moment to look around the market. It had grown exponentially in the years since I'd left Ashfield. Booths not only lined the open field, but they curved around the sidewalks and alleys.

Turning my back toward the crowd, I inhaled the thick mountain air as I stared at the Great Smoky Mountains off in the distance. There was something about their grandeur that always left me feeling lost. That I'd never know my place in the world. I'd always felt so minuscule in their shadow.

At one point, I thought I'd find my place in the bustling City of New York working for one of the top event planners in the nation only to learn that I was as expendable as a penny. Easily lost and forgotten.

Especially when the man who promised you the world, and signed your paycheck, left you for his newest client. Taking your self-esteem and apartment with him.

Talk about a blow to my confidence.

Turning back around to look at my sisters, I couldn't regret rushing back to Ashfield. I had wanted out of this small town when I was younger. It wasn't that I disliked it here. I just thought I was destined for bigger and better things. I was the ambitious Easterly daughter. So arriving back at my family's farm with my tail tucked between my legs wasn't the way I had wanted to prove myself to everyone. I worried everyone would think that I'd chased my dream and failed. It wasn't in my plan to return so soon.

"When did you get back to town?" Alex asked as I rejoined my sisters as they greeted customers and waved at the people walking past. "You should have called us."

"Last night, just after dinner," I mumbled as I snagged a carrot from the stack at the top of the vegetable display.

Our family farm functioned as corn growers, but my sisters and I carried on my grandmother's penchant for gardening. Even as little girls, we kept up with her vegetable garden that had expanded from a small plot of land to two and a half acres of seasonal vegetables. The market stand that my family used in the past for homemade sauces and jams (which my mother still made in small batches to sell) transitioned to a booth for us. It made just enough to keep the garden growing, but I wasn't sure how much longer my sisters could keep it up. We all had regular non-farming jobs that required a lot of time. I hoped to return to event planning, Alex managed a local bar, and Rory was a first-grade teacher. Only our youngest sister, Aspen, still worked at the farm with my father. Collectively, we had a friend of the family that ran the stand if we were absent, but typically my sisters and I rotated shifts. That was all before I moved away. I had a feeling that as we got older and busier, we'd come out less and less and would need more help with the stand. Who knew what would happen when we started our own families?

"Did you see Dad at all?" Alex asked.

"No, but Mom was up with Aspen."

"That's good," she murmured under her breath the way she did when we were teens and she had more she wanted to say. I couldn't help but notice how her knuckles whitened as her fingers bit into her palms. I got along with all of my sisters, but Alexandra and

Aspen fought like caged animals. They were truly like the summer and winter. Two polar opposites.

I wanted to ask more, but I noticed a crowd was growing across the way and I wondered what had captured everyone's attention. The nosiness of small-town living was in our blood from birth and there was little any of us could do to fight it off.

"What do you think is going on over there?" I asked no one in particular as I grabbed another carrot to munch on.

"Oh! Coach Chisolm was talking to some of his players about his protégé coming into town to visit for a while. It's the biggest thing to happen to Ashfield since we heard you were coming back." The petite blonde standing across from me stared with wide eyes as if she would blink and I'd disappear. There was a look of both mystery and envy in her gaze, and it left me feeling. . .lacking.

"Well, that's something," I said, munching on the orange veggie.

The girl stared for a second longer, then leaned closer toward me over the display as if she was about to tell me all of the world's secrets. Her eyes glistened with excitement and the corners of her mouth tipped up in suppressed joy.

"What's it like? New York? Is it just as beautiful as all the movies make it out to be?"

This girl could be no more than fourteen, fifteen at most, and I didn't have the desire to burst her bubble and tell her that New York was both beautiful and lonely. For every shining beacon, there was a shadowing hole ready to envelop you. But I remembered the excitement and thrill of imagining such a glamorous place and I would have sneered at anyone telling me differently.

I opted for the closest truth I could muster. "It is beautiful and when they say no one ever sleeps, they mean it. But you know what?" I told her, watching as her chest puffed out, holding in her exhale with bated breath. "I missed home. There is nothing quite like it." While it was true, it was definitely a stretch. While Ashfield was my birthplace, I grew up thinking the place was holding me back. There was nothing besides family that ever made me want to stay.

"Wow," she exhaled with a whoosh, the hair surrounding her shoulders moving with the air.

I responded with a simple smile, hoping that I placated her dreams while internally I felt shame from the lie.

"It sounds so amazing. I don't know why anyone would ever come back. Nothing exciting ever happens in this town."

Internally, I agreed with the teen and my inner self was nodding her head enthusiastically, but externally, I continued to smile politely with a tilted head. My dad always called it my "you're not right, but I'll let you think you are" look.

"Well, never say never," Alex said with her signature sneer. For someone named after the birthstone of June, she had the cold temperament of the winter. Another reason she and Aspen rarely got along.

The teen trotted off, not nearly as affected by my sister's proclamation as I was.

"You shouldn't dismiss her hopes and dreams like that. Maybe she'll actually get out and find her way."

"Yeah, her way back home. Everyone always comes back. . .usually," Alex said as she began placing the vegetable trays in the back of her vintage pickup.

I knew what she meant. Everyone came back except for Rory's childhood friend and our neighbor. It was a sore subject with our sister and we rarely spoke about it, but I knew that was what Alex was implying.

They weren't surprised when I called up last Sunday and said I had packed all my belongings and would be home the following weekend. It had offended me they weren't bowled over to hear the news, but Mom asked at the end of every phone call when I was going to move back home. To them, I was living some childhood fantasy and needed to get my head on straight.

But until my ex had destroyed everything, I had been happy. I'd loved my life.

Right?

I remembered the perfect little apartment we'd leased on the Upper East Side. It had been in his family for years and was rent controlled. We would have never been able to afford it any other way. I'd adored the apartment and thought of how we could raise a family in the three-bedroom space. I'd even hoped that he was going to propose the exact night he dumped me.

It was the same tragic tale that I'd seen in movies countless times. I just never expected it to happen to me.

Fired and dumped in the middle of our living room, surrounded by hundreds of candles. I'd set up the room for our anniversary, expecting something else entirely.

Heaving a sigh, I lifted one of the trays and placed it in Alex's truck.

"What's the matter?" Rory questioned. She'd always been the most intuitive of the sisters. We could usually speak without saying a word.

"Nothing," I said with a chipper edge I knew wasn't going to fool anyone.

"Liar, but I'll let it slide this time," she added as she joined us to load the truck with the food left from the stand. If it wasn't something we could use within the week or pickle, we donated it to the local church, which distributed them to families in need. It was a way for us to help the community.

Silently we loaded the rest of the empty trays into the truck and then broke down the items used at the stand. Rory and I both jumped when Alex slammed the tailgate of the cargo bed. She shrugged her shoulders in a silent apology as she made her way back to us.

"What are your plans today?" Rory asked us both as she counted the money in the metal box.

Alex replied as she opened her door. "I need to do inventory at the bar."

"I need to hit up the grocery store. Mom and Dad are making my favorite since I'm home. You both will be there, right?"

"Of course. We never miss Saturday dinners if we can help it. Is that why you were here today? I loved having you, but it was a surprise for sure."

My sisters stared at me with rapt attention, which made me feel like I was back in college public speaking, standing in front of an auditorium full of my peers giving a speech.

"Well, I felt antsy being at home, so I thought I'd go out for a drive and run some errands for Mom."

"Oh, yeah?" Alex said with a smirk. "There was no pit stop or drive that you detoured?"

"Alex," Rory scolded.

"It's fine, Rory. Yes, I drove by the house. It looks so sad just sitting there on that hill. It needs so much love. I just wish there was something more I could do."

The house sat on a plot of land in the middle of our family's farm. It used to belong to our great-great-grandfather and was the original farmhouse, but when he passed away, he left it to his youngest son who had a penchant for gambling.

The story goes he lost the title to the house and the hundred acres of surrounding land in a bad poker hand. My great-grandmother had tried her hardest to get the property back into our name whenever it would go for sale, but she was always outbid. It had sat vacant for as long as my family could remember.

Last I'd heard, it was still in the name of the previous owner, but it was at the point I wouldn't be stunned to find it condemned. Dad did his best to check on the property when he would inspect the adjacent land and would board up windows and holes. He'd even laid a tarp on the roof when a tree branch fell through ten years prior. But there was nothing more we could do but sit and wait.

It felt like it was what I'd been doing my whole life. The house was a fairytale to me, just like my previous job. All of it now out of reach and feeling more like a pipedream with every passing day.

"Have you thought about reaching out to the owners?" Rory questioned.

"Only every day. But all I have is my piddly savings and who would sell their home to someone without a job or any job prospects? It's not like Ashfield has a need for an event planner or someone with a degree in hospitality. Hell, there isn't even a hotel close by.

"And by the time I could probably afford the down payment, the developers that keep bugging Dad for some of his land will most likely have swooped in. I'm actually surprised they haven't already," I said exasperatedly. It was the same argument I had with myself whenever I drove by the two-story farmhouse.

I could close my eyes and see myself on the upper porch looking over the front yard where my kids would play on the wooden swing dangling from one of the centuries-old oak trees. My husband would stand behind them, pushing them with each passing. It was all so clear in my mind that sometimes I felt bereft realizing that it was all in my head.

It was also no secret in town how much I loved that house; which made it all the more upsetting that the owners didn't even reside in our town. My nails bit into my palms at my sides and my gut churned just thinking about it.

My sisters must have noticed how I'd grown rigid and tense as they quickly apologized for bringing up the subject at all.

"It's okay. It's not like it's a big secret. I just hate that the town can't do anything about it."

I did have some research in my back pocket, though. It was something I wanted to share with my dad first, and I wasn't ready to divulge it to anyone else.

"I'm heading out," Alex said as she stepped back from the truck. Rory and I stepped away from the tailgate and watched as Alex jumped into the cab of her vehicle.

"See you guys tonight?" she called out and we both nodded in unison, my arms wrapped around my waist in a protective gesture. Being around my entire family was overwhelming and I didn't always know how to act. I wasn't slim and petite like my sisters. My body had curves that mimicked the natural waves in my hair. But I'd also been the only Easterly to ever leave the homestead, something none of them ever let me forget. Tonight I was going to feel more than just a disappointment, I was going to feel like a failure. They wouldn't do it intentionally, but it would feel that way regardless.

Once Alex's truck sputtered away, the dark clouds puffing from her exhaust finally clearing in the air, Rory turned and asked if I was parked nearby. We'd both left our cars in the public parking lot by the town bakery and we opted to walk together.

Rory was a good buffer for the townspeople when they'd stopped and waved. Despite them asking her if she was ready for a new school year as a first-grade teacher for our local elementary school, I noticed how their eyebrows raised in surprise when they realized I was her companion. It seemed the confirmation of my return hadn't begun spreading yet.

"Don't let them get to you, Autumn. Everyone is really excited to see that you're back."

"Yeah, right. They probably think I'm a joke."

"Well...um...no, but you're the town sweetheart. They were all devastated when you left."

"Yes. The once valedictorian has returned uninspired, unattached, and unemployed. What a sad story they're going to paint of me."

"Don't think like that," she scolded as she followed me to my small red two-door coupe. "Have you thought about speaking to Dad about using the old barn on the outskirts of the west field as a wedding venue? That was always your backup plan if the internship after college didn't work out."

In fact, I hadn't thought about it. The prospect hadn't crossed my mind once. I'd been wallowing in an Olympic-sized pool of self-pity that I hadn't even considered any other options than to start sending out resumes. But Rory was right. And thank goodness she had the memory of an elephant.

"Maybe I'll speak to him tonight about it. I'm not sure how open he'd be to the suggestion, though. You know how he feels about tourists and that is mainly who we would target."

"Well, I'll back you up. I think it's a great idea and think about how much revenue that could bring to the farm. And you could probably look at partnering with the bed-and- breakfasts in town for sleeping arrangements. The possibility is there."

Turning around, I looked at my little sister. There was a hopefulness in her enthusiasm that I couldn't deny. Her eyes glistened in the early afternoon light like sun rays on a pond and the corners of her mouth reached upward in an encouraging grin.

"You're excited," I teased her as I shifted my bag from my shoulder down to my waiting hand and began searching for my car keys.

"I'm excited to have you home. And if I can find a way for you to stay, I'll do whatever it takes. Besides, I think Jeremy may propose soon."

Her high school boyfriend was a sleazebag to the first degree, but Rory would hear none of it.

"Ulterior motives, I see." With the key fob in hand, I pressed the button to unlock my car doors. The resounding beep and flash of yellow startled the couple crossing the lot in front of my car and I winced when they sneered at me.

Replying with a quick one-armed hug across my shoulders, Rory replied, "Always. See you tonight."

Chapter Two

Colton

I knew my old minors coach lived in a small town, but as I drove down the winding single lane road, I felt like I'd been transported back in time. There was nothing but fields of grass and flowers, rolling hills, and towering mountains on either side of me. I feared I was lost and was about to end up in a real-life version of *Texas Chainsaw Massacre* if the cell reception hadn't been outstanding.

When I reached out to Brett, my old coach when I played for the farm team before getting in the NHL, he had offered me a place of solace, a respite to get my head on straight. The last two years had been anything but calm. A career-changing injury sent me for a whirlwind both physically and mentally. At my age, I wasn't even sure I'd be able to return to the game. A torn ACL was an ender in most sports. But my issue ended up having more to do with my love of the game than with the injury.

I fought tooth and nail to heal and get back on the ice, but by the time I'd returned, I felt like an old man compared to the newbies on the ice. That was the life of a retiring player.

It was more than all of that, of course, but that's the story I gave to the press, and they ate it right up. I hoped that while I was here, Brett and I could get some time on the ice.

At least that gave me something to look forward to. I hadn't discussed a concrete amount of time with my agent, but I knew he was in the mindset that I'd grow tired of small-town living and I'd want something bigger and brighter in a few weeks.

Little did he know that my favorite childhood memories were made in a small town.

Maybe not this small, I thought to myself.

Franklin, Illinois, was outside of Chicago and where I had learned to play hockey, but it had a few big box stores and its own sign off the interstate.

When Coach Chisolm sent me the address to his house, he informed me I had an hour drive on a single lane road once I left the interstate. He'd even attached a map because the satellite navigation never could "get it quite right."

I peered down at the map as I crossed paths with another road and checked the directions to confirm I was still headed in the right direction. Out of the corner of my eye something black caught my attention and I slammed on the brakes, thankful I had been driving well below the speed limit on the tiny, unfamiliar road.

My shoulders rose to my ears as the truck screeched to a stop before it collided with a herd of cattle. My hands gripped the steering wheel so tightly that the whites of my knuckles showed through the skin appearing as if they were ready to pop through the covering. My breath came out in heavy pants at the same rate as my racing heart.

"Fucking hell," I heaved.

Taking a moment, I let myself calm down, using the breathing techniques that the team therapist taught us on how to control our anger. This time I used it to knock back the adrenaline coursing through my veins.

When I was finally able to pry my fingers from the steering wheel, the noise causing my body to cringe, I popped open the door and jumped down from the truck. I needed to catch my breath. My body hunched over itself. My hands firmly gripped my knees as I hauled in tremendous pulls of air to fill my lungs. Closing my eyes, I removed myself from the moment and settled back into my body.

"Are you okay there, son?" a gravelly voice filled with concern called out from the distance.

I glanced up, not sure what I'd find, but a man sitting on the back of a brown and white horse wasn't even in the realm of possibilities.

When I didn't give a response, the man added, "I'm sure these here gave you quite a fright. It's not every day you see a hundred cows hanging out on the asphalt."

The horse trotted closer, bringing the man within a few feet from where I stood.

"Yeah, I definitely wasn't expecting it. That's for sure."

"Best things in life are unexpected," he added cryptically.

Standing to my full height, the adrenaline slowly dissipated from my veins and my body immediately grew tired. Something I was going to have to fight through the rest of the trip. I always felt the same after every game except this time I didn't have a bus or airplane to doze in.

"What are they all doing out here?" I asked as the stallion drew next to me, its curious eyes taking me in. The large animal whinnied as its rider stroked his neck.

"Well, see, this here road runs between my land. I was moving them to the field across the way. Bet ya scared them just as much as they scared you."

Making eyes back at the large black heifer that was staring at me, I grunted. I'm pretty sure if she could laugh, she would.

"Doesn't seem that way to me."

The man had the decency to stifle his chuckle, but his chest moved all the same.

"I'll get these girls moving so you can be on your way."

"Thanks," I said as I moved to get back in my truck, but a thought glued me in place. "Hey, I don't suppose you know how much longer it is until I reach Ashfield, do you?"

"Well, now, I do. I thought I recognized you."

Immediately, my hackles rose. I was famous in the sports world, but I spent most of my days covered in twenty-five pounds of gear and a helmet. My chances of being recognized prior to my retirement were slim, but with the news outlets having me on for sports interviews, my face had been front and center.

The last thing I wanted was to be recognized here.

"Oh. If you could. . ." I began trying to barter with the man to keep my identity a secret, at least for now. Once I left, he could blab all he wanted. I'd buy this man five more of those stallions if he'd keep quiet.

"Good ole coach said he was expecting someone."

"Coach?" I asked, perplexed. My head tilted as if that would help me understand the man better. It didn't.

"Yes, sir. Coach Chisolm. Those kids at the high school love him. Damn good coach. You know he took our hockey kids to the state championships this year? Man, it was something. Anyway. We don't get people here quite your height. I figured you must have been that hockey player he was going on about at the market this morning. Had the town in a frenzy."

Ah, so it seemed Brett had been telling people I was coming.

"Yes, sir. That's me, but if you could keep my arrival quiet, I think that would be best for everyone. I don't want any press knowing my whereabouts. If you know what I mean."

"Yeah, I heard something about your injury and nasty breakup. Don't you worry, son. We ain't got no reason to bring those camera people round here. Got enough to worry about ourselves, if ya know what I mean."

I didn't, but I nodded and smiled just the same. I'm pretty sure he didn't have nudes of himself doctored and made to look like I was in bed with a well-known female escort and those images plastered across every tabloid in the nation.

Maybe they didn't even get those glossy magazines here. Wouldn't that be something? This town was sounding better and better the more I thought about it.

"I'm headed in the right direction?" I asked as I began moving again and stepped inside my truck.

"Yes, sir. You've got about another fifteen-minute drive down this road, then you'll hit the town square. It's about another twenty minutes from there. Can't miss it."

I was pretty certain I could, indeed, miss it.

"Thank you, sir," I called out after I slammed my truck door and rolled down the window.

"Give me just a few minutes and I'll get these here cattle out of your way."

"Thank you. It was nice to meet you."

"You too, son."

Son. That must be a southern thing, I thought to myself. It was as unfamiliar to me as an I love you. But it was nice to hear, even if it wasn't more than a term of endearment.

It took the man exactly five minutes to get all of the cows across the street. The one that had eyed me earlier had been the last to leave the path and I could tell she was angry about it. I had the sneaking suspicion that she was up to no good and was planning her vengeance just as I sped past.

And just as he said, fifteen minutes passed when I came across a sign for the town of Ashfield. I slowed as I approached and took in the grandeur of the picturesque town nestled in the valley between the rolling hills. The Smoky Mountains set the perfect background for the town. I could see why Brett found it so charming and made it his home.

A horn sounded from behind me and I was stunned to see a fairly new BMW in my rearview mirror. My instinct wanted me to throw up a single finger at the driver for honking at me and interrupting the moment of silence as I took in the land before me, but I was in a different place now and needed to remember that. I tended to do things first and then think about the consequences later.

Pressing the accelerator, I brought the truck back up to speed and made my way to the town center, wondering in my head where the car had come from. I hadn't seen any roads since the interstate, but I hadn't been paying a lot of attention either.

The streets were full once I got closer. People milling about, cars lining the roads, and canopies on every free surface of the sidewalk. A banner hung high in the air, draped between two buildings on either side of the road.

FARMER'S MARKET
EVERY SATURDAY
8AM-12PM

Well, that at least explained the dispersing crowd.

Glancing at the dash, I noted that the time was around three in the afternoon, so the farmer's market was long over. I wanted to get something for Lily, Brett's wife, as a thanks for allowing me to stay with them for a short time. The market would have been a great place, now I'd have to find something, and fast.

Luck must have been on my side because a sign for Chuck's Grocery Store stood out like a beacon in the middle of a hurricane.

Pulling my truck into the lot, I parked a good distance from the entrance, not that the parking lot was huge. There were only a handful of other vehicles in the lot, one being a little red car parked across from me a lane over.

Approaching the store, I gave myself a pep talk and tried to remember that this was not the big city. Things were going to be different. Not bad, but different.

I passed by the shopping cart area and paused a few feet inside the store. There weren't many aisles to choose from, but there was a decent floral area and from what I could tell, a remarkable bakery section. The scent of fresh bread and chocolate had my stomach growling the second the smells wafted across my nose.

Immediately, my body began moving toward the intoxicating fragrance on its own accord. I was just a passenger along for the ride. My feet were moving and before I knew it, I was standing in front of the bakery stand without any knowledge of how I'd come to be there.

"Can I help you, sir?"

There were so many choices. More than I'd ever seen at a small grocery store, which New York had plenty of. The options were endless. Breads, cakes, and pies. I wanted it all.

"I don't suppose you know which dessert Lily Chisolm likes the best, do you?"

"Well, now. You must be the hockey player coming to stay with her and Mr. Chisolm," the older lady said with a sweet southern drawl. She had kind eyes that reminded me of a grandmother. The type you'd see in the movies since I'd never had one myself.

"Apparently word gets around."

She had the decency to laugh as her cheeks reddened. Those same kind eyes twinkled in amusement.

"Sorry, ma'am," I said. "I didn't mean anything by it. It's just been a long drive."

"It's nothing, young man. I apologize for saying it out loud. You're pretty popular around these parts. Coach's protégé and all that jazz. We're just excited to have you in our town.

"Now, to answer your question. Mrs. Lily likes anything with custard or cherries. I have a Boston cream pie that she would absolutely love. If you want to look around the store, I'll get that all set up for you in a few minutes."

"Thank you. . ."

"You can call me Betsy."

"Well, Betsy, I'm sure you'll be seeing me plenty. Got to find a way to stay on Lily's good side while I overcrowd their home."

She laughed genuinely that time. Those eyes crinkling at the corners, the valleys growing deeper with time. "Well, you're absolutely headed in the right direction."

Leaving the bakery stand, I searched around for a bathroom to clean myself up a bit after the long drive. I was surprised to find it immaculately tidy. I'm not sure why I expected anything different. The entire store was neat and polished from top to bottom. The owner must have taken great pride in his business.

Something I understood.

When I finished, I took a few minutes to walk around the store, watching a few people grab their canned goods and local meats. A magazine rack near the entrance caught my eye and I glanced over the selections. They were over a week old, except for the hottest tabloid fodder.

Quickly, I grabbed a copy and scoured through the pages. I wasn't front news anymore since my ex, Nina, sank her claws into someone else and she settled the lawsuit I had against her, but when it was a slow news week in the sports world something about me always popped up.

It was times like that I was glad I didn't know my parents. I'd hate to know the embarrassment I would have caused them, even though none of it was my fault. I would have disgraced them either way.

I returned the magazine back to the rack when a couple started ushering their brood over to the single register. Moseying back to the entrance, I stopped at the floral stand.

Flowers were always a nice gesture. But I was completely overwhelmed as I took in the selection.

Maybe just a pie would be fine.

Chapter Three

Autumn

Quickly, I slid onto the driver's seat of my car and tossed my bag on the floor of the passenger side. The ignition rumbled as it came alive after I pressed the start button. I stared at my rearview mirror watching protectively for Rory to get into her car. It may be the middle of the day in an overall safe town, but I'd spent too many days and nights in New York looking over my shoulder to do anything less.

Once I saw her brake lights turn on, I backed out of the parking spot and turned the vehicle out of the lot heading for the store at the edge of town. The drive was no more than five minutes since only a handful of lights existed down the main thoroughfare and they were all green. Apparently today was my lucky day.

Once I parked the car, I dug into the bag and retrieved my wallet and the list of groceries Mom had requested. All of the ingredients for chicken korma graced the white paper in my mom's delicate cursive handwriting. Her penmanship was something I'd always been jealous of.

Inside the store, it didn't take long for me to find what I needed. The layout hadn't changed in the six years since I left and I doubted it would in the next sixty. Unlike the big grocery chains, Chuck's Grocery didn't have the latest technology where you could scan your items as you went and then pay via a mobile app. They were old school and still tagged each individual item with the price tag. There wasn't even a self-checkout to be found.

Mr. Granger stood at the register, his face wrinkled with smile and laugh lines. The kind you hope for as you age. The kind that showed you lived a good life. He waved at the family that had just finished checking out before turning back to the register. His eyes shot up when he noticed me standing there.

"Well, if it isn't Miss Autumn Easterly," he said as I began placing my items on his tiny conveyor belt. "I'd heard you were back in town, but I learned long ago not to believe everything you hear."

I didn't have to force a smile for Mr. Granger. My happiness to see him was honest and sincere. It helped that I used to work part time in the grocery store when I was in high school to help buy my first laptop and he'd paid me a little extra under the table when I'd tutored his grandson.

"It's the truth this time. Mark that one in the history books," I said and admired his gravely chuckle. I'd missed that sound.

"I can only hope the reason for your visit is nothing more than the telephone game then." He started sliding my goods across the scanner as I narrowed my eyes at him shrewdly.

"What are they saying?" I said apprehensively. It wasn't that I cared what the town said about my return. I knew how Ashfield gossip worked. But I didn't want to cause any damage to my parents or their reputation, especially if it wasn't within miles of the truth.

Mr. Granger had the decency to blush as he released a nervous chortle under his breath. The type where you're embarrassed for someone else, but you aren't quite sure how to tell them.

"Well, you and I both know it wasn't anything salacious. So, you might as well spill the beans."

I listened as he loudly whispered what some rumors were of my return. If I were in a lesser frame of mind, I would retreat to the only home I'd known with my tail tucked between my legs, but it was all too sensational to give it more than a giggle in passing.

Once Mr. Granger had finished bagging the items and I'd paid with my card instead of Mom's cash, surprised to see he had finally upgraded to a credit card reader, I left him with a smile and a wave. I couldn't help the snicker as I turned to exit. His old cheeks were still a ruddy, blotched mess from our conversation.

I was too busy looking over my shoulder at my old employer to notice the solid wall of muscle in my pathway.

"Oomph," I mumbled as I impulsively pressed a hand to the mass as I took a step back. Luckily, I held the bag of groceries in my other or else there would have been a mess to clean up on aisle three.

But as I turned my gaze from Mr. Granger to the form I'd bounced off of, I realized there was still a chance for a mess on aisle three. I wasn't sure if it was pure unadulterated lust or just my synapses not firing on all cylinders, but my hand clenched the stranger's white t-shirt in my fist as I stared up at him slack-jawed. Maybe I had been gone too long and I was seeing a mirage, as if I'd been lost in the desert searching for water. And he was certainly a tall drink of water.

Double my height and a wall of pure muscle, the man before me lifted the edge of his mouth in a smirk as I blinked uncontrollably. I didn't recall seeing him before, but again, I had been gone for long enough that new residents made Ashfield their home.

"Um. . .sorry," I said, reluctantly unclenching my hand and releasing his shirt. I winced at the clump of wrinkles I left behind. "I wasn't looking where I was going."

"That's okay. No harm done."

"Well, I'll let you get back to choosing a flower arrangement." I was already overstaying my welcome, and as he turned his attention back to the display, it was clear that he didn't need me lingering.

But obviously my brain was still a muddled mess and I asked, "Need any help?" I may not be a botanist, but with my event planner job, I'd put together a few floral arrangements in my day.

He huffed out a laugh and it wrapped around me like a warm, heavy blanket. I wanted nothing more than to lose myself in its comfort.

"Is it that obvious?" The stranger turned his dark brown eyes to me again and I felt myself melting beneath their gaze. I returned a soft smile, noticing that the temples of his wavy, dark brown hair were slightly gray. Which left me realizing that he was older than I originally thought, but a lot of men grayed earlier due to stress or life in general. Hell, there was a girl in my high school that started getting gray hair at sixteen. I always had a thing for the George Clooney type anyway.

"You do seem a little lost. But I've put together a few arrangements in my time. What occasion are they for?" I asked as I skimmed across the display. I knew the flowers were local and there was a wide array of choices, but I'd always been drawn to seasonal arrangements.

"Dinner." He'd said it without a second thought, which effectively poured cold water over my entire body. Of course, a man like him would be taken. It was stupid to think otherwise. He was the most attractive man I'd ever seen in Ashfield or New York for that matter. He almost had a familiarity about him, but I couldn't place it. Not that it would matter now. He was buying flowers for his date or girlfriend. I'd already searched for a wedding band and found him lacking. At least I was able to narrow that down. I wasn't a homewrecker like my ex.

Wordlessly, I grabbed the display I thought was the most beautiful. And was probably the most expensive, but by the watch he wore and the name brand sunglasses dangling from the collar of his crewneck, I knew that he most likely had the money to spend.

"These. I'm sure she'll be impressed," I said as I not so gently shoved the cellophane wrapped bouquet at his chest. Luckily, he grabbed it as I released my hold and shifted my grocery bag into the other hand. He was too busy adjusting the flowers in his grip to notice that I'd moved past him to the exit.

"Thanks!" he called out after me, but I continued walking like I hadn't heard him. I'd embarrassed myself enough for one day. I needed to head home before I did any more personal damage.

With regret, I stomped toward the back of the lot where I parked, wishing I'd parked closer so I could make a quicker getaway.

Finally, I made it to my car and I popped the trunk with my keys and stored the bag inside, slamming the trunk closed when I finished. I dove into the driver's seat, heaving a deep breath once I was safe inside only to scream when a knock sounded on my window.

Twisting my head, it shocked me to find the stranger standing on the other side of my vehicle.

"Can I help you?" I asked hesitantly as I pressed the button to slide down the window.

Holding out one of the sunflowers from the bouquet, he said, "Here, to thank you for your help."

There was no way he could know that sunflowers were my favorite and as much as I wanted to tell him that it wasn't necessary, I reached out to grab the stem, making sure our fingers didn't touch in the process.

"Thank you."

"Maybe I'll see you soon?"

I sure hoped not.

"It *is* a small town."

The man laughed as he stepped back and the window ascended. I gently laid the sunflower on my passenger seat before exiting the parking lot.

I told myself not to look back, to forget the interaction, but the pitter-patter of my heart forced my eyes to the rearview mirror where I saw him standing beside an oversized black truck with one hand tucked in his jeans pockets and the other grasping the arrangement and a bakery box at his hips. He had the same smirk on his lips while his head shook side to side like a boat on the ocean.

I really was going to have to find a way out of this town sooner rather than later.

On the drive back to my family's ranch, I forced myself to forget about the man in the store. Instead, I focused on my sisters. I was excited to spend time with them again. We rarely saw each other in the years since I'd moved away. They only visited New York once and never returned, saying it was too jarring for them. And I understood, but it still hurt knowing that they couldn't appreciate the place I loved.

After that visit, I came home on the occasional weekend and for birthdays. Holidays were always iffy, and that was when my job hadn't scheduled us for an event. I was also a workaholic, spending more time on jobs than in my own apartment.

My sisters and I did make a point to video call weekly and there was a group chat where we messaged each other constantly.

I'd never admitted to them how much I'd missed them in the previous years.

But now we had time to make up for it.

Then Rory's words flitted through my mind. The barn on the west field of my parents' farm was old and decrepit, just like the house I loved so much, but I saw the potential.

Hell, I saw the potential in every trainwreck I came across. Mom said I was a fixer. I wanted to fix every person, place, or thing. And I could do it too, in most cases. I'd helped reconstruct houses with charity and fix up a community garden in the city. People fixing, I hadn't quite got right. I tended to make someone better. . .for the next person that came along.

Bringing the west field barn back to life was an idea that I'd had in high school – my backup plan. I had a vision of fixing it up and making it less rustic than what was expected and enclosing it all. We'd have to add a kitchen and bring it up to standard fire codes, but all of that was doable. The problem was getting my father's approval. He cared for change about as much as

I wanted to go crawling back to my ex, Max. The cheating bastard.

But what if he agreed? What if he said yes?

I could see my sisters and me working on the project together. That had always been the subplot to my journey into that brainchild. There were so many things that they were good at and I could see each of them excelling at them. Alex could do all things with beverages and food. Everyone loved Rory and she had a knack for people and could easily convince potential clients to use the space and see the overall vision. And Aspen, though young, knew all of our family's history. That would absolutely be part of the experience of the space. And I would be the planner and overseer.

It all played out in my mind like a movie. I could see it clearer than daylight.

Unfortunately for me, things never seemed to work out the way that I wanted.

On instinct, I let off the gas and the car slowed down. I was coming up on the turn in the road where my dream house resided. There was no one behind me as I got closer and I pulled to a stop to take it all in again.

She stood majestically at the top of a hill overlooking the large span of acres below. The once light tan hued brick was now an ashen gray, weathered by the heat and sun of summer and the cold, brutal winters. Her roof dawned large blue tarps placed there by my father. Most of her shutters had been removed. The majority lost or broken during storms. I'd seen pictures where they were a darker color, probably black, in contrast to the weathered brick exterior walls. But I always envisioned them as a royal blue.

Her porches had seen better days, though my dad assured us they were solid, just needed some tender loving care. The entire house needed it.

And I wanted to be the one to give it to her.

The inside was barren, a few sheets draped over the antique mantles surrounding the fireplaces, and across the counters in the kitchen and butler's pantry. When we were younger my sisters and I used to sneak up to the back windows and look inside, but my father put a kibosh on that by having a cop come by and scare the piss out of us. Literally, Aspen peed her pants she was so petrified. She'd only been five at the time, but we still pick on her for it.

"I'm going to figure out how to save you, pretty girl," I said in my car speaking to the house.

There had to be a way to get in touch with the owners. But I know my father had tried in the past to no avail. It seemed like a hopeless cause.

"I'll be back," I said as a goodbye and moved my car down the road again.

Pulling up to the ranch, I noted a few things that needed some fixing up around the entrance. The sign needed a fresh coat of paint and the stone columns desperately needed to be pressure washed. All things I could do for my dad while I stayed at the farm.

I parked my car along the side of the house, in the same spot I used to when I was in high school. It all felt so familiar and strange at the same time. Almost like déjà vu, except I knew that I'd experienced it.

I was going to walk up to the house and it was going to wrap me in its comforting arms like a warm hug and I'll remember how much I love that part of being home. Each time I stepped over that threshold, it made it that much harder to want to leave. I'd forget how much I wanted to be something more than one of the Easterly daughters.

There was more for me out there.

Right?

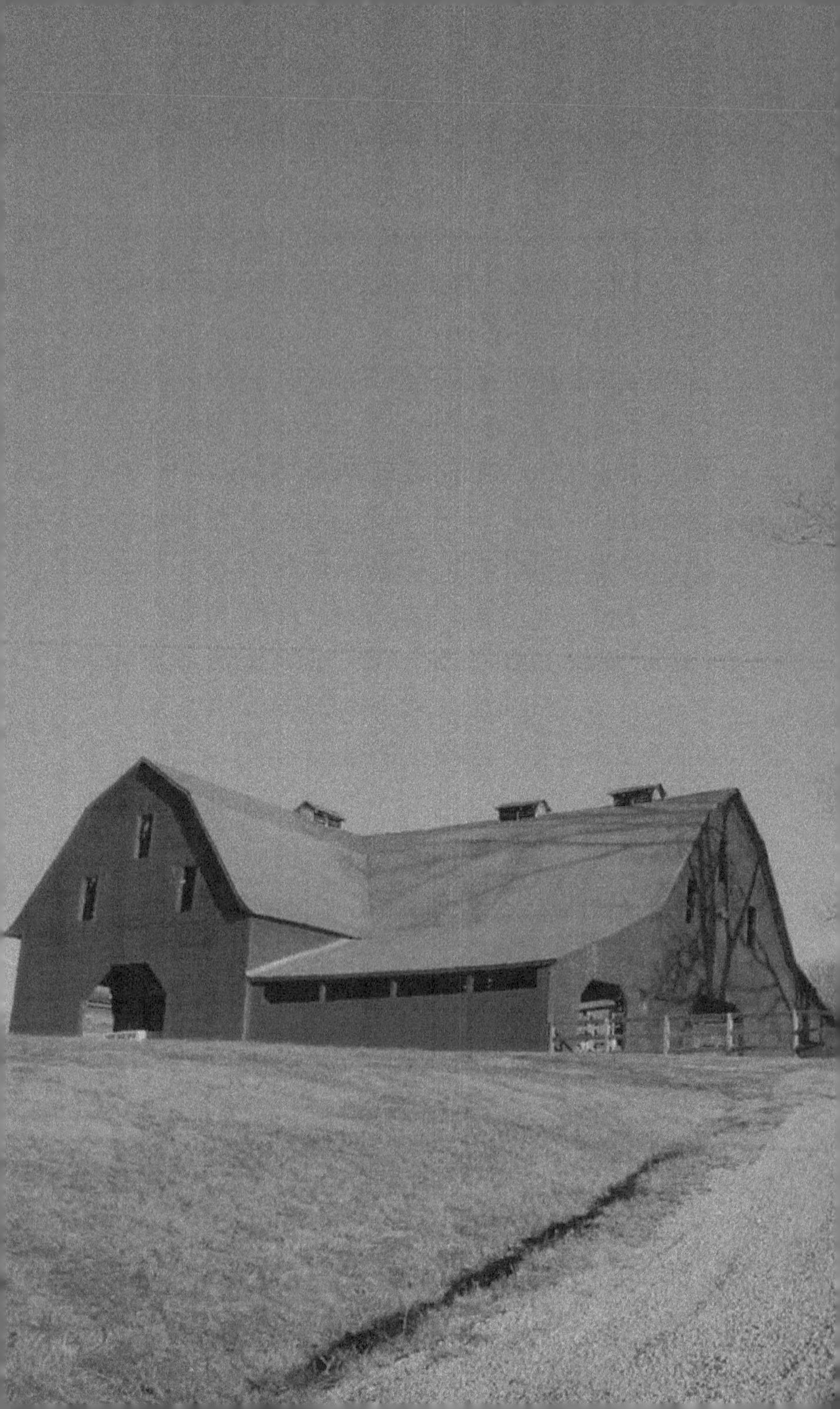

Chapter Four

Autumn

"Hey, Daddy," I said as I stepped into the kitchen and wrapped my arms around my father's neck. It wasn't often we found him in the house during the day, but since he'd reached retirement age, my mother pressed him to take weekends off. She knew his heart lay in the fields and it was always going to be his first love, but she pleaded with him to take some time to relax on the weekends. She wanted to spend more time with him.

It was sweet when I thought about it.

They were always affectionate around us when we were growing up. It used to gross us all out, but now I realize how special that was. It was what I wanted for myself and thought I'd had.

"Hi, darlin'. Have a good time in town?"

Setting the bags on the kitchen counter, I went in search of a small vase to place the dwarf sunflower in.

"It was the same as always," I replied as I tugged a barstool over to the fridge so I could search the upper cabinets.

I was perched on top when a screech sounded below.

"Ah!"

I had to grip the sides of the fridge to keep from falling off the stool.

"Mom!"

"Get down from there this instant. You're going to fall and break your neck."

"I am not. Stop exaggerating."

Opening the cabinets, I huffed when I came up empty-handed. Climbing back down, I returned the stool back to its spot under the kitchen island and began rooting inside the lower cabinets.

"What are we looking for?" my mother said from beside me on her hands and knees as if we were in search of hidden treasure.

Rolling my eyes at her antics, I explained, "I'm looking for a small vase to place a flower someone gave me."

Immediately I knew I said too much as my mother's eyes widened in delight and she sat back on her haunches.

"Someone gave you a flower?" It was less of a question and more of her excitedly repeating it back to make sure that she heard me right.

"Who was just handing out single flowers?" my father questioned from his seat at the table, where he continued to play a game of sudoku.

Ignoring them both, I continued to browse the lower cabinets until I reached the one in the farthest corner. I blindly moved my fingers around until I felt something like glass and shaped familiar. Gripping it in my hand, I pulled it free and smiled when it happened to be the vase I was looking for. White milk glass with cute little knobs. It was a favorite of mine.

Stepping over to the sink, I filled it halfway with water, then took it over to the island and set the stem of the pretty flower inside. I knew it wouldn't live long, but I wanted to admire it while I could.

"It was just a stranger looking for a flower arrangement for his dinner date. I happened to be leaving the store at the same time and helped him pick one. It was his thank you, I guess. Don't read too much into it."

Of course, I didn't tell them how I made a complete fool of myself and how I hoped to steer clear of him for the unforeseeable future.

"Oh! I'll have to call Betsy to see if she saw any of it. She has a direct view of that area from the bakery. I know she'll have the scoop on who he is. I can get you all of his information before sunset."

"Mom," I said gently as I placed my hand on her arm. She was practically shaking with excitement. I hated to disappoint her. "It was nothing. Okay? I was simply helping someone out. Don't bother Betsy."

"Fine. If you say so." My mother frowned like a disciplined child who was told no. I moved over to the grocery bag and began unloading the contents from her list.

"It's okay, dear. We'll find someone for you. We've had a bunch of new people your age move to town. I'll keep my eyes and ears out for any single men."

I glanced up at her in confusion. *What new people?*

"Don't look so surprised. They sold and developed two of the farms on the east side of town into neighborhoods. We've added a new school and up the interstate about twenty minutes is a new manufacturing plant. That's where the new transplants work."

"Huh. How come no one mentioned it before? I speak to you guys on the phone all the time."

"We did, sweetie," Mom said as she brushed past me, patting my cheek along the way, just as she did when I was a child and she was placating me. "You heard us, but you were sort of in your own little world with work going on in the background."

I hated when she called me out like that. I did have a hard time paying attention to the conversation when it focused on the town and there was a work event I was focused on. It wasn't that I didn't care about what she was telling me, or about the town as a whole. I had just mentally removed myself from the entire foundation of Ashfield on my journey to find my own path in life.

"I'm sorry, Momma," I told her as I went up behind her and wrapped my arms around her waist as she was reaching in the pantry. "I'll try to do better."

"I know, baby. You have the biggest heart I know."

"Can I help with dinner?" I asked her, knowing that was the way to mend any fences in our house when it came to our mother. She loved to cook and was always willing to share that love with us. Only Alex inherited her culinary talents. I was lucky that take-out was the go-to in New York.

If there was anything that I missed when I left, it was my mother's cooking. And my father's hugs, but he was well-versed in that fact. It was no secret that I'd always been a daddy's girl.

Mother and I went to work preparing the korma sauce I loved so dearly and had never found another Indian restaurant that served anything quite like it.

It always baffled people when I moved to the big city and they learned that an Indian dish was my favorite. They always assumed there wasn't much variety in small town living. And sometimes there wasn't, but we had all different cultures that took up roots in Ashfield. It also helped that my mother had spent her college years in Boston. Despite her always asking when I'd return home, she'd always been my biggest advocate for leaving. And made sure I knew that I always had a place to come home to.

My mom cheated a bit with the jarred sauce, but by the time she added all her own ingredients, it looked and tasted nothing like what was served in the glass jar. It was a trick she learned from one of her college roommates.

While the sauce cooked, mom went to work on the naan using the dough she started this morning.

"Hey, Dad. Do you have a minute?" I asked him and he pushed the sudoku aside without a backward glance, giving me his full attention. His blond hair had started to turn grayer over the years and the blue in his eyes was grayer too, something I hadn't noticed before. But he was still just as handsome to me. Those eyes twinkled with knowledge and mischief, both of which my father carried in spades.

"Pull up a chair and tell me what's on your mind."

"How'd you know I have something on my mind?"

"You're giving me that same look you did when you were twelve and wanted to install a pool in the backyard. I'm just surprised you don't have your trusty notebook in hand to make sure you don't miss any points."

I glanced over my shoulder and eyed the pool with the cover draped over the water for the colder weather. My parents had caved and installed it a year after my talk. I didn't believe for a second that it was because of my well-planned and thought-out pitch, but that my sisters and I begged non-stop for a year. Our half-brother even told Mom he thought it would be a cool place to hang out in the summer. And they were willing to do anything to keep my brother close to home. He loved us all but he felt as suffocated by Ashfield as I did, though Aspen said he'd been hanging around the farm more and more.

Turning back to my father, I said, "Yes, well. I keep my notebook all up here now." I pointed to my head. "Anyway. I wanted to talk to you about the farm on the west field."

"Oh, are you asking Dad about the barn?" a voice chimed in from the hallway before Aspen appeared. She was covered in dirt from head to toe and Mother called out her name the moment she placed her foot in the kitchen.

"I'm going, Mom. My room's upstairs, remember? Did you want me to walk in here naked?"

"No, I want you to use the mudroom, put your nasty clothes in the basket in there and switch into the clothes I specifically laid out for you for when you came in. Just like I told you this morning."

"Fine." As Aspen stomped away, I turned my attention back to my dad, who was shaking his head in amusement.

"Like I was saying. I wanted to speak with you about the old barn in the west field."

"Sweetie, are you trying to ask your father about turning the old barn into a wedding venue?"

I swiveled on my chair and pinned my gaze on my mother. How did she know about that idea? I only ever mentioned it to my sisters.

"Don't look so surprised. Nothing is sacred in this house. Remember how I told you the walls have ears? Well, those ears lead straight back to me."

I didn't want to think about the things she might have heard. All those times Alex and I snuck out when we were in high school and then the nights the girls and I spent gossiping about boys. My inner teen cringed.

"Is that it, Autumn?" my father asked and I spun back to face him. "You want to know if you can turn the old barn into an event venue?"

"Well, it's more of a backup plan. I want to apply for some jobs but if say, in six months or so nothing pans out, maybe I could do that. If you'd allow me to, of course."

"I thought you wanted to be in the big city?"

"I did. I mean, I do. But my prospects aren't looking too good right now. And I have missed you guys."

"And what would happen if we get this all up and ready to go and you get a job offer in one of those bustling cities you're fond of?"

"I. . .I don't know, Dad. It was just a thought. Something that I think would be good for the farm and good for us."

"How about I make you a deal?"

My ears perked up at that. I was always willing to take a gamble. It ran in our blood, after all. That's how we lost the house on the hill.

"I'm listening." I immediately raised my voice so my mother could hear me. "I really am listening this time."

"Shush," she mumbled and I bit my lip as I giggled.

"Okay, Dad. What's your bargain?"

"Spend the next month here. Really take it all in. The town, the farm, the life. Remember how it felt to grow up here before you knew there was anything more outside of the county lines. And if, after a month, you still have the itch to leave Ashfield, then we'll continue to support you as you search for a job. But, if you have the slightest longing to stay, I'll let you follow through on the wedding venue. But you have to make an effort, Autumn. That's a lot of time and money for all of us. You have to promise to at least give the town a try again."

"I feel like you're pressuring me to stay if I want to do the venue."

"I'd never pressure you to do anything. We'll always support you, but if we get it started and then you up and leave, who would run it? We could hire someone, sure, but the love behind it would be gone. Do you see what I'm saying?"

I did. It all made sense. We were both taking a gamble on this venture. And it wasn't that I hated being in this small town. I remembered how the townspeople always rallied around each other. Like when Alex had her tonsils removed, the town brought ice cream to the house for weeks. I had nothing against it and it had been a great place to grow up. I just had aspirations that didn't exist here.

"I do, Daddy."

"Do it. Autumn," Aspen commanded, as she stepped back into the room wearing gray sweatpants and a pink t-shirt. "You have nothing to lose. Stay here for a month, which is inevitable if you think about it, and then decide what you want to do."

I thought about what they were both saying. A month wouldn't kill me. And there were things I could do to occupy my time. I had the information regarding the dream house to delve deeper into as well.

"Fine. You're right. You're both right. Okay, Daddy. I agree. One month, and pretty much I'll make my decision." Holding out my hand, I expected him to shake it like we were in a board meeting, but he brushed it aside, stood to his full height, then leaned down to hug me.

"I can't wait to see what you have planned for that hunk of wood," he whispered in my ear.

"What makes you so sure I'm staying?" I joked.

Pulling back, he held my shoulders in both of his hands as he gazed down lovingly. I wish I could bottle up that feeling. It would sell like hotcakes.

"Not sure. Just hopeful."

A commotion sounded from the side door and I stood from the table at the same time my father rushed forward toward my mother.

"Autumn! Autumn!" the voice called out as it grew louder and louder. Suddenly, an out of breath Alex stood at the doorway of the kitchen. One hand gripped a stack of what looked like newspapers, while the other grasped the doorjamb as Alex bent over, her back lurching as she gasped for air.

"Is everything okay?" I asked as I rushed to her side. "Why are you out of breath? Didn't you drive?"

She lived in an apartment in town above the bar she worked at. Her only way to the farm was in her truck.

"Of course, I drove. I just. . .the excitement. . .you know how I get."

"What's going on, Alexandra?" Mother's voice seemed to calm Alex and she straightened, then immediately headed for the large kitchen island.

We all followed suit.

My nerves were getting the better of me as I watched Alex line up the papers, then rearrange them again. The marble was cold beneath my palms, but it did little to settle me.

"Alex, get on with it," Aspen said impatiently from her perch on a barstool.

"I wish Rory was here for this. I'm not sure she got my text," Alex murmured, just as someone called out from the front of the house. "I'm here!"

"Aurora! Get in here. Your sister has something important to tell us." Mother's voice carried throughout the large house without the use of an intercom. She was her own personal megaphone.

"Sorry. What's going on?" Rory asked as she settled on another barstool beside Aspen, placing her large bag at her feet with a plop.

"Ok," Alex said, as she rearranged two more papers and then stepped back. "Do you see it?" she asked excitedly.

I stepped into her vacated spot, but I saw nothing in the hundreds of articles. "What am I looking for, exactly?"

"Here. Let me help. Rory, do you have a pen?" In a split second, a pen appeared from Rory's hand as if she called it from thin air and she handed it over to Alex, who circled one of the articles in the first paper.

I moved and leaned over the counter, mouthing the words as I read. Tax lien. State to sell. Fifty acres and property. 130 Easterly Lane.

"OH MY GOSH!" I shouted as I skimmed over each of the Knoxville papers where the article resided. The last three weeks posted the same article.

"Oh, my gosh. Oh, my gosh. Oh, my gosh," I repeated as I grabbed the last paper and held it to my chest and turned toward Alex.

"And I checked. It still has a tax lien."

"Will someone please tell us what's going on?" Father demanded.

I was too stunned to speak. Luckily, Alex had calmed down enough to explain that the house I'd dreamed of, and used to belong to our family, was now owned by the state because of unpaid taxes for the last few years.

"What does that mean?" Aspen asked, and the rest of us mumbled the same assessment.

"It means that it's going to be sold at auction." Alex turned to face me directly and placed her hands on my shoulders. "Autumn, it's going up at auction on Monday."

"I. . .I. . ." The words lodged themselves in my throat and I had to pause for a moment to collect myself or I was going to become a sobbing mess on the floor. "I can't afford it, you guys. I just lost my job. I can't cash in my savings for something like this. It was always a pipe dream. Something I could bring back to our family. I never thought it would actually happen. I gave up on that fantasy."

"If you had access to the money, what would your plans be for the house?" my mother asked, as if she hadn't a clue. I was most certain that she knew exactly what I wanted to do with the property.

"I'd fix it up to how it would have been in its glory days. Restore all the hand-crafted woodwork. Things like that. And I wanted to submit it to the National Register of Historic Places so that it would be protected.

"And I wanted to turn it into a bed-and-breakfast. It was always something I thought would be fun."

"Then we'll get you the money. That's our heritage, after all," my mother said like I was asking for a copy of a recipe.

"What?" my sisters and I asked in unison. My father stood there proudly as if it had been his plan all along. "Why don't you all just buy it instead of giving the money to Autumn?" Rory chimed in.

"That. . . all of it. . .was what she's meant to do. Autumn, you lit up when you spoke about it. That's your dream and I'm going to make sure that you have it. I'd do it for any of you," she emphasized as she gave a look at each of us. "So, let's all cross our fingers that it pans out the way we hope.

"Now, tell us more about the bed-and-breakfast idea," Mom added as she began swooping up the papers, settling the vase with the single sunflower back into the center from where Alex had nonchalantly moved it out of the way in her haste.

I still didn't understand her reasoning, but knowing my parents, they probably had something up their sleeves.

"Where did this flower come from?" Aspen asked curiously, her fingers reaching out to touch the delicate petals.

Mom chimed in before I could respond. "Autumn met a man in town today and he gave it to her."

In less than two seconds, the house filled with the chatter of four girls bickering and nagging each other like we had when we were teens.

"I will say it one more time!" I shouted to be heard above everyone. They kept prattling away, ignoring me. "He is not my boyfriend!"

"Autumn and mystery man sitting in a tree. K-I-S-S-I-N-G," they sang at my expense. I was surprised my ears didn't bleed from how off-key they sounded.

That was my parents' plan all along. . .to fill the house with the sound of love.

Chapter Five

Colton

Glancing over at the bouquet of flowers nestled on the leather of my passenger seat, I huffed out a chuckle and shook my head, remembering the interaction with the woman at the store. At first, I thought she'd recognized me and it put me on edge. It wouldn't have been the first time someone faked running in to me to get my attention. Hell, it was how my last girlfriend and I met. Only difference was we were at a coffee shop and she spilled her piping hot liquid down my shirt and pants, which she thoroughly patted dry. She was now dating the newest captain of the New York Renegades. Once I announced my retirement, she went in search of the newest and brightest star with the biggest bank account. But that was after she tried to take me to the cleaners with fake news stories about infidelity and a penchant for prostitutes.

Maybe it was me. Maybe I caused women to trip over themselves to get my attention.

"Yeah, right," I mumbled under my breath.

Not a single woman gave me the time of day until I hit college, when I finally grew into my long limbs and packed on fifty pounds of muscle. Hockey required a lot of energy and muscle. Growing up, I had the energy in spades and I used that to my advantage because I was lacking extra muscles. The foster mom that introduced me to the sport of hockey said I looked like a walking stick bug on blades. But she'd also said I was a natural on the ice and that I had the spirit of a player.

Moving around the way that I did, there were years I missed being a part of a team, but when I tried out in college as a red shirt, without ever playing a single official game, I made the second string. And earned a scholarship for my remaining years.

The rest was history.

I wondered what the history was of the woman that ran into me. She gave off a very confident and self-assured air, but when she looked up at me, I saw that it was just that – a façade. There was a girl underneath that seemed just as lost as I was. A girl that seemed to spark something inside me I hadn't felt before. She was an enigma that I wanted to solve and keep for myself. I already felt protective of her and I didn't know her from the man working the register. And I could see the hint of attraction in her gaze as her eyes swept over me.

The feeling was mutual.

When I tracked her down and handed her the flower, I considered asking for her number as well, but she'd been spooked enough. I knew coming on strong, as I was known to do, would be too overwhelming.

Maybe I'd see her again in this Podunk town. That was something I could look forward to at least.

I glanced down at the directions again, refreshing my memory before pulling out of the parking lot and finishing the remainder of my journey to Brett's house. People still milled about the town, walking in and out of shops. I noticed a couple of bars and signs for restaurants across the fifteen or so blocks on Main Street. There were clearly more businesses between the alleys and within the second and third rows of buildings.

They seemed more eclectic than I originally thought. I saw signs for every kind of ethnic food I could imagine, and stores ranged from yarn and books to crystals and, I had to do a double take as I passed, witchcraft.

Well, I wasn't going to be bored, that was for sure. I'd have to check out the bookstore the next time I came to town. Despite what people thought about athletes, a lot of us had the brains to back up the brawn. Reading was one of my favorite ways to relax.

The truck continued on its way, leaving the nestled confines of the town and back into the wide expanse of fields and mountains. As we proceeded, the road wound more than it had when we were closer to the interstate. I slowed down since I was unfamiliar with the area and didn't want to cut a turn too sharply.

Just as another right angle turn came up on the road, a truck drove into view. Its large frame was coming toward me and taking on the entire lane. As quickly as I could muster, I pulled off into the ditch to give the approaching vehicle ample room.

"Shit," I cursed as the driver barely missed clipping my own truck.

"Sorry!" the voice called out from their window as they passed with a friendly hand wave.

My fingers shook as I shoved them through the strands of my hair while I took deep, heaving breaths. This drive was going to be the death of me.

I maneuvered the truck back onto the road and took the turn as slowly as possible. Someone really needed to come out and straighten that turn, or at least cut back the hill obstructing the view. I wondered how many accidents occurred in that same spot.

Just as I came around the bend, my eyes fixated on a stately home perched on the top of a hill in disrepair. It was in dire need of someone to bring it back to life. I slowed as I approached the home and turned onto the dirt path that seemed to lead toward it.

The truck ambled along, jostling with every pothole and divot that the tires sank into. It was bouncing uncontrollably by the time I reached the front yard of the place.

Leaving the ignition running, I stepped out and looked up at the front fascia. There was something familiar, but I couldn't quite put my finger on it. I stared up at her rotting columns and then stepped closer to the front. The main porch was in good shape. It appeared that someone had replaced the boards in the last ten years or so. They were weathered, but not warped. I glanced up toward the bottom of the second-story porch and made the same assessment.

The windows on the first floor were all boarded up, and when I delicately stepped across the porch, the doorknob didn't budge. Locked.

Twisting to look over my shoulder, I made sure no one was watching. I didn't want to be front page news for trespassing on abandoned property.

Casually, I made my way around to the back of the house, surprised to find a sunroom that was also boarded up just like the remaining windows. At a closer inspection, I could tell that the plywood was fairly new, as in the last year or so. It was clear someone came by frequently to check on the building.

From the top step leading to the sunroom, I gazed out at the expansive yard. It was a gorgeous landscape that needed just as much love as the home, but the potential was there. It was clear a garden sat along the eastern side of the property and there was enough room for a personal skating rink or a large pool along the backside of the flat space. Further than that the land sloped down to the rest of the field.

The house sat on a natural pedestal overlooking the property. It was obvious the home was old and most likely built by hand. Why would someone abandon such an impressive home?

I walked around the other side of the house, moving tree limbs out of my way as I went. The old oak trees surrounding the property reminded me of New York.

That was when it struck me. The house was familiar because it resembled the first foster home I moved to. The one where I learned to play hockey. It wasn't nearly as large, but it had the two porches and similar features.

What I wouldn't give to fix up this house and see it brought back to life. This house deserved a family living within its walls. I'd spend my entire savings to bring this house back from the ruins and make it my own. It may be the closest thing to feeling like I'd done right by Ms. Cathy, the foster mom that introduced me to the game I loved.

"I'll be back," I said to the house as I turned around to return to my truck. A breeze whipped up around me and I took that as a positive sign that the house wanted me there.

The remaining drive to Brett's continued without incident. I was too geared up to pay much more attention than to keep the truck on the pavement.

I recalled a few farm signs on my journey. One read Sunny Brook Farms and was the closest to the house I was interested in. I wondered if the owner knew anything about the home.

Both Brett and Lily Chisolm were waiting on a porch swing when I pulled into their driveway.

I exited the truck with the pie in one hand and the flowers in the other, my mind immediately floating back to the woman that had selected the bouquet.

"Colton, glad you made it," Brett said as he came close and retrieved the pie from my grip. "We were afraid you got lost."

We exchanged a one arm hug just as Lily joined us.

"I made a detour along the way. These are for you," I stated, as I held the flowers out for Brett's wife. She gleefully accepted and raved about the arrangement.

That woman from earlier definitely knew what she was doing.

I followed both of them into their ranch style home. Their two kids left the nest and were off with their own families. So I wasn't going to be bothered non-stop while I stayed in their home.

The house smelled amazing, a mix of freshly cut grass and Italian food.

"Brett can show you to your room. We're having lasagna for dinner. Obviously, you don't have to join us, but we'd love to hear what you've been up to all these years. It's not often one of our favorite players comes to visit," Lily said as she moved further into the house, to where I expected was the kitchen, leaving me and Brett in the hall.

Sometimes it was strange to call my old coach and mentor by his first name, but he insisted. He was pushing his mid-sixties but didn't look a day over forty. He and his wife had the market on an incredible gene pool. Lily looked no older than the first time I met her.

"You're in here." Brett opened the door and ushered me inside. "We weren't sure how long you were staying, but you know our house is yours."

"I don't want to be in the way. I just need to figure out a few things and lie low." With the settlement fresh off the printing press, the false claims made against me were still hot news. And the official mention of my retirement only added fuel to the fire. There were also a few personal things I needed to discuss with Brett, but I wasn't ready to delve into any of it yet. I wanted to pretend I had no worries for at least a few days.

"You do what you have to. Lily is thrilled to have someone to cook for. I'm usually holed up in my office or on the road. She always thought of you like another son."

That's what I loved most about making this trip. Both Brett and Lily treated me like they did their natural-born children. I was just another addition to their brood. We talked every week like a real family or at least the kind I imagined growing up.

"The feeling is mutual." Eyeing the room, I wondered if there would be enough space for some workout equipment. But it was too small. At most, I could add some dumbbells. The town was sure to have a gym, though.

"You actually gave me an excuse to install a gym in one of the kid's bedrooms. Lily finally caved when I told her you would probably want to continue your workouts."

"That was really nice of both of you. But I'm not sure I need to keep up with my old routine."

"Sure, you do. Just because you have considered no longer playing doesn't mean that's the final straw for you. Once a hockey player, always a hockey player. It's in our blood."

The coach stood just inside the room, leaning against the threshold. His impressive arms bulged against the thin material of his shirt. I sent a silent prayer out into the universe that I have his physique when I reach his age.

I homed in on his eyes. They were staring at me with worry and intrigue. Like he wasn't quite sure what to make of me and the situation.

"You have something up your sleeve."

Standing to his full height, just a few inches shy of my six-foot-six, Brett released his arms and rubbed his hand nervously along the back of his neck.

"Maybe."

Chuckling, I tossed my phone onto the bed, then settled next to it to listen to his proposition.

"Get on with it, old man."

"Old man? I could still kick your ass if I had to."

"No doubt."

"Fine. You know we have a recreational hockey team. All different ages from little ones just learning to skate up to old men, like me. And if you're interested, I'd love to have you join us. Even if it's not to play, I'm sure all the players could use some words of wisdom."

I didn't want to make any promises, especially if I didn't stay long in Ashfield. The house I saw earlier was the only thing that sparked my interest in the small town. But I wanted back in the game, somehow. My agent emailed this morning stating that I impressed a few news agencies with my guest spots and they were considering bringing me on full time. They also wanted to try me as a host of a baking and cooking show. I just wanted to do something to keep myself busy. I didn't do well with idle time and this town had it in spades.

I thought back to the woman from the store. She was also an intriguing option to spend my time with here. That is, if I could find her.

"I'll think about it. My agent sent me some things to consider. I need to return to New York in a couple of weeks for some test spots, but I'll be back. I just don't want to make any promises, you know?"

"I know, kid. I always admired that about you. Can't break a promise if you never made it in the first place. Anyway, I'll help you with your bags and let you relax for a bit. Later I can take you to the high school if you're up for watching some unruly teens practice."

"Sure thing, Coach," I replied as I stood from the bed and followed him back out of the house toward my truck.

It didn't take us long to bring the few bags inside. I never needed much. Something I learned as a foster kid. Another point of contention between myself and Nina. She wanted the world to know how much she had and could afford.

I unpacked what I could into the dresser the Chisolm's provided, then scrolled on my phone for a bit before deciding to reply to my agent. I let him know I had found a place to lie low and to send over any potential contracts that came his way. In the meantime, I would read over the scripts he provided in his email this morning.

But that wasn't going to be today.

Ducking out of my room, I noticed the bedroom across the hall had been converted into a gym with all the equipment I'd need to stay in shape. I bet if I asked Brett, they'd let me use the rink at the high school when I needed to be on the ice. Which was something that was a necessity almost daily.

"Hi, Lily. I'm going to walk around and check things out if that's okay," I said to Brett's wife as I walked through the kitchen toward the back door.

"Sure thing, Colton. I'll holler for you when dinner's ready if you're not back before then. Make sure to go to the farthest part of the yard. I know Brett is waiting for you. Just past the tree line."

"Thanks, Mrs. Chisolm." She shook her head at my response. I knew she hated when I called her by that name. That Mrs. Chisolm was her mother-in-law was always her response. But the manners remained.

I strode through the back door and onto the porch that filled the expanse of the back of the house. Last year, Brett had installed a fire pit in the center surrounded by built-in benches. It was a place for him and Lily to relax with their grandkids. He'd sent me the mock-ups in a text a year prior as a surprise for his wife.

Stepping off the deck, I crossed the large backyard. A new swing set sat in the same place as the older one that I remembered from a video call with them a few years ago. Seems they sprung for another gift for their grandchildren. Next, I expected they'd have a pool.

Brett and Lily were suckers for their grandkids.

If I ever had a family, I wished my kids would have relatives like those two. Instead, they would be stuck with me and whatever family their mother had. The closest thing I had beside the Chisolms, the foster mom that taught me hockey, had passed away when I was in high school at sixteen. I may not have lived with her any longer, but I tried to contact her as much as I was allowed.

Or I'd remain single the rest of my life, just like Nina had threatened. Apparently, my heart was as cold as the ice I skated on. Lily said differently when I retold them the story over the phone, but the mental and emotional damage had been done. I had a fairly hefty ego, but it was fragile just the same.

I continued my trek through the meticulously cut lawn, piles of leaves surrounding the parameter under the tree line. The smell of fall was in the air. Sometimes it just smelled like cold and wood. And the season was approaching fast.

Finally, I came to the part of Brett's lawn that Lily had mentioned. Beyond the farthest corner, about twenty yards through the forest, there was an opening where an old pond sat. I knew it wasn't forgotten as a brand-new deck jutted out into the water with a tackle box and fishing pole resting on the slats.

"Figured you'd make it out here soon," Brett's deep voice called out from my right. He sat on a bench with a beer in his hand and a cooler at his feet.

It was colder in this part of his property, most of the treetops shading the land below, and the sun rarely shone through. But enough of the lingering day lit up the water on the pond.

"She made it no secret that I would enjoy this area." It surprised me he had never mentioned the quiet spot before.

"I just had her restocked, too. For your visit."

I shuffled over to the bench to sit by my friend and the closest thing I had to a father figure. The denim of my pants felt cool against my thigh as I sat down.

"You didn't have to do that."

"Like I said earlier," Brett began, as he reached down into the bright red cooler with the white top and handed me a beer. "You're just the excuse to get some of the manly things updated around here. If it were just for me, Lily would have nixed it immediately. But for you, I got the go ahead."

"Go figure," I mumbled as I took my first sip of the chilled beverage. The heavy wheat beer tasted thick on my tongue, but it wasn't unpleasant.

"Have a few tosses while the sun is still shining. Once it goes down, it gets mighty dark back here. I still need to install a light across the way for some night fishing."

Nodding, I collected my beer and headed toward the dock where I baited my hook and tossed out the line like it was second nature. Muscle memory is what Brett used to call it. We stayed silent, me throwing out my line every couple of minutes and Brett watching. Occasionally I'd snag a fish and he'd take a picture with his phone before I lobbed it back into the water.

We stayed out in the woods for about an hour before Brett's phone rang.

"The missus says dinner is ready if we could head on back."

"Sure. Let me just get this all put away," I said of the tackle box and the pole.

"We can take it back in the UTV. Much easier on my knees than walking all the way out here. You can use it too if I'm at work."

"What's a UTV?" I asked as I gathered everything and met him at the bench.

"It's like a two-seater all-terrain vehicle. Follow me," he explained as he led me to an opening on the other side of the field where a black and blue vehicle sat.

He placed the cooler in the back area, then grabbed the tackle box and fishing pole from me, doing the same.

Together we rode back to the house, our bodies rocking back and forth with the jerky terrain, as I tried to come up with a way to ask them about the property I saw earlier in the day. I didn't want them to get their hopes up in me staying in the town permanently. But I saw the house as a nice investment property if I could get it up to livable standards. I could rent it or sell it when I was finished. Or keep it as a vacation home for myself.

Now that was an idea.

Once we returned to the house, Lily immediately directed us to the sink to wash up before we could eat dinner. Not that I needed to be told. I had no desire to eat with my hands smelling of fish.

When we were seated, she served the homemade lasagna and my mouth watered at the sight over the heaping plate. I couldn't recall the last time I had a home-cooked meal like this one.

Unless it could be cooked in the microwave, I was hopeless. Which baffled me that a cooking channel wanted me to be the face of a new show. But I was willing to learn. And I had high hopes that Lily could teach me a few things while I was here.

The room was quiet as we all ate. Brett and Lily chatted about the market that morning to fill some of the silence, but I was more than content to listen to their conversation.

"Did you see much of the town when you drove through today?"

This was it. This was the segway I needed. A clang sounded in the dining room as I set my fork on the plate. Lily went all out with the good china for the meal.

"Actually, what do you know about the house up on the hill about ten minutes from here?"

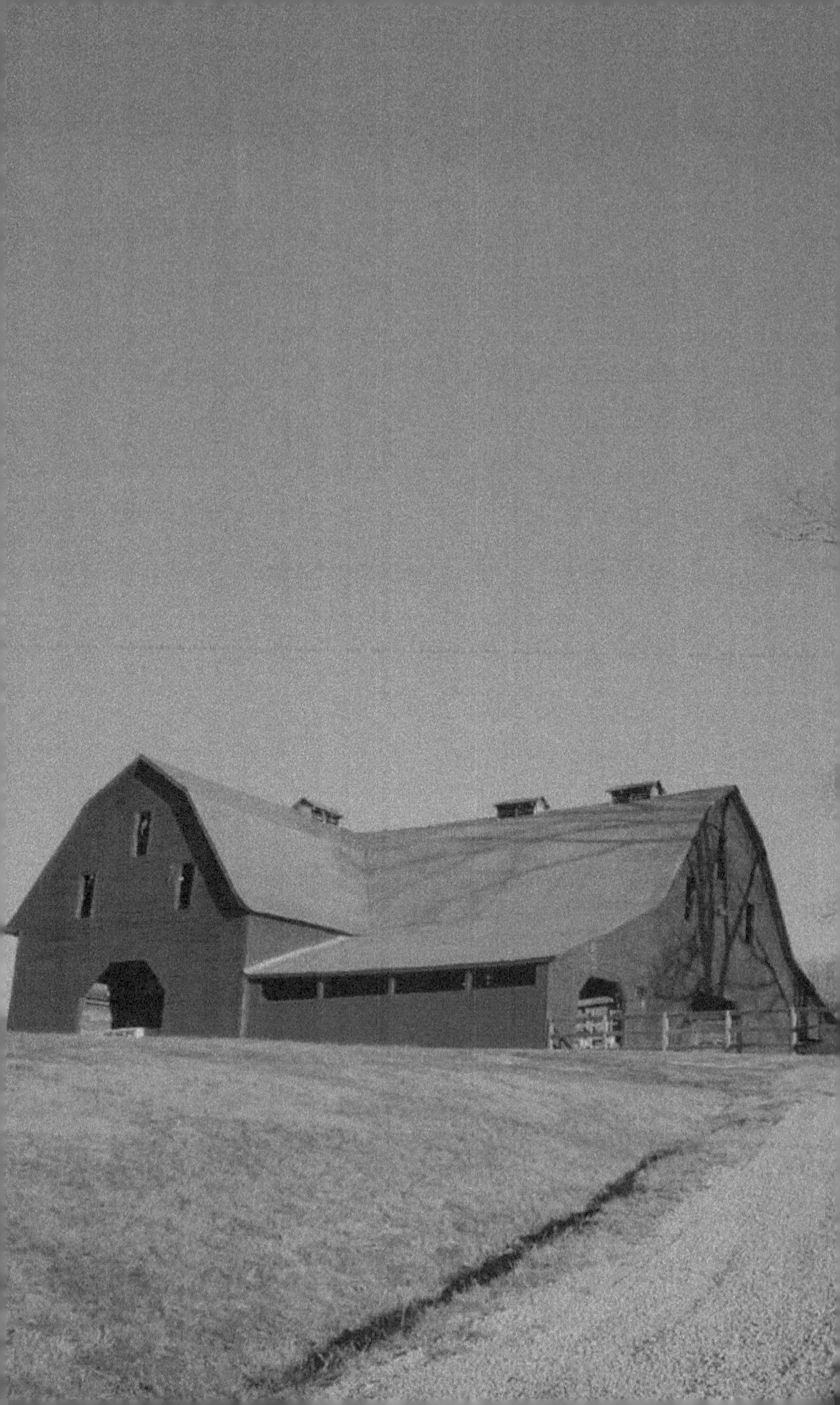

Chapter Six

Autumn

The theater was more crowded than I anticipated as I turned in my seat and watched another group of people stroll in. It took some digging, but we'd learned that the sheriff was holding the house auction in the town theater to make sure there was ample space. Our courthouse was too small for the function.

The place was something straight out of *Architectural Digest*. It opened in 1929 and was a staple in our town, supported and funded by our community.

There was even a local theater troupe that hosted two plays every year.

It was one of our town's pride and joys. I'd forgotten how beautiful it was.

But an odd place to hold an auction. What did I know, though? The sheriff seemed to think there was going to be a large turnout, and from the way strangers were filling the seats, he wasn't wrong.

"Mom, I don't think we're going to be able to bid enough. Look at all these people." I whispered the concern in my mother's ear, my heartbeat thumping erratically. My parents were willing to cash out everything in their name if I won the bid. They gave me a substantial number to work with, but I feared it wasn't going to be enough.

"What are they doing here?" Aspen snarled from my other side. I turned to look in the direction she was staring and found a few men in suits, congregating against the wall.

"Who is that?"

"They're the land developers that keep snooping around the farm. Dad's had to call the cops on them for trespassing twice in the last month. They're relentless dirtbags."

"The sheriff said the land and property couldn't be awarded to a developer. They weren't allowed to bid."

"They're probably trying to see who they can weasel it out of, I'm sure."

"What do they want it for anyway?"

"Not sure. But Betsy at the grocery store overheard them talking about an industrial park of sorts."

That was not what I expected. Our town was all for change and expansion when it did right by the people, but an industrial park wasn't something they were going to be too happy with. Back in high school, they voted to keep three other developments like that from moving in. We thought we'd proven our point, but apparently not.

"Now I really wish I had more money with me to make sure they didn't figure out a way to get their grubby hands on it."

"Everything will work out how it's supposed to, sweetie," my father said from the end of the row where he sat next to Alex. Rory was between her and Aspen. My sisters had all taken the day off work for the occasion. They wanted to support me and help get our land back.

The booming room quieted when the sheriff took the stage and began describing the property. I felt ill listening to him talk about the land and home that had once belonged to us. It felt dirty watching the eyes of all these people light up at our misfortune.

A man in a three-piece suit stepped onto the stage and moved behind the microphone stand the sheriff vacated. Mom's hands gripped our registration papers as the bidding began.

I didn't raise my hand right away, more engrossed in listening to the numbers climb as people furiously threw their hands up to place a bid.

The offers began to slow and I saw my moment.

The bids were settling around the fifty thousand mark and I raised my hand to place a bid at seventy-five thousand. The couple in front of me turned and sneered before raising their hands to counter bid.

This continued with a few other people in the auditorium until I was reaching one hundred thousand over my initial bid. My family and I knew what the house and land were worth. That was really what we were paying for, but no one else did. They didn't know the significance of that property or the impacts it had on history, being one of the first farms in the area. They were there for a pretty piece of land to make their summer home.

"Mom." My voice shook as we approached the top of our budget. My parents had offered more, even suggested a personal loan at their expense, but I refused. I could do with the money they were willing to cash in because I knew I could pay them back for it in time. That was money they already had. I couldn't ask them to take out more on such a gamble. That was how our family ended up in this mess to begin with.

"It's okay, Autumn. Go with your gut. If you're not comfortable going higher, we can deal with someone else on our land."

"But we shouldn't have to," I explained as I raised my hand as the bid hit the two hundred thousand mark.

"One million, fifty thousand, with lien payments on top."

The bid silenced the crowd. That was far more than the house or the land were worth. Someone was playing a devious game.

Collectively, the crowd looked back at the bidder only to find him tucked in the far back shadows of the theater, ball cap covering the remainder of his face in its own shadows.

"Sold?" the auctioneer questioned, as no one countered his bid. "Um, well, uh. Congratulations. You can meet with the sheriff to determine the collection of your winnings. Thank you all for coming."

Beside me, my sisters grumbled that they all needed a drink, but I was too busy focusing on the figure slinking further back into the shadows before he ducked into a stairwell altogether.

"Autumn?" Mom said from beside me and turned back in my chair quickly.

"Yeah, I could use a stiff drink. Think The Purple Goat would serve alcohol at 10 a.m.?"

My mother patted my knee in condolence. "I think Harold will make an exception today."

"I'm sorry, Mom. I'm so sorry I let everyone down."

"You didn't, sweetie," Dad said from the end of the aisle where he stood and began gathering our light jackets. "That was a crazy bid that I don't think anyone here prepared for. It's obvious the man wanted the property. We can only hope that he's not as slimy as those men that keep trespassing."

As one, we filed out of the row and made our way down the aisle and out of the main theater into the lobby. Conversation flowed around us. Everyone wondered who the shadowed man was and where he came from. He was the new town mystery and rumors were going to swirl. On the bright side, that took the heat off my reasoning for returning home. I didn't want to feel ashamed of my return.

"I'll let you girls enjoy your morning. I'm going to head back to the house."

"Aspen, are you staying or going?" At twenty, she wasn't of legal age to drink yet, but I didn't want to keep her from being with us.

"I'll stay and give everyone a ride home."

"That's a great idea," Dad said as he tugged me into his arms – my favorite place to be. "I'm sorry we lost that one. At least we know we tried. Who knows? Maybe we'll be able to work something out with the new owner."

In my head I was certain it was going to be torn down by the time we arrived back at the ranch, even though I knew my mind exaggerated that scenario. It still left me bereft.

"I know, Daddy. Thank you all for supporting me, even if it didn't turn out in our favor."

Dad said his goodbyes and the rest of us headed across the street to The Purple Goat. To this day, I was still unsure how the bar came about its name. Mom theorized it was something Harold lost a bet on.

It seemed everyone we knew liked to make a wager every now and then.

"Morning, ladies," Harold called out from behind the bar where he was wiping down the dark oak finish. It had lost its glossy luster years ago.

My favorite part about The Purple Goat was that it had some of the best food in town. Not just the typical bar food, but Harold had a retired, award-winning chef working in the kitchen. There was no menu before 9 p.m. If you wanted food, you got what the chef was making that day. We had never been disappointed.

"Harold, dear." Mom put on her most pleasant voice as she worked on the older man. "It's been a long and arduous morning for us. Do you think we can start with some mimosas? I have a feeling we're going to be spending most of the day in your lovely establishment."

The man chuckled as he tossed his rag over his shoulder with a slap. "I don't know half of the words you said, but I don't see why not. It's almost eleven and those cataracts have been messing with my eyes lately." Harold smiled at his lie as he watched us find a booth close to the bar.

"You're the best, my friend."

Not five minutes later, Harold delivered a wooden board with champagne flutes resting in their cut-out spots. He followed up with three more so each of us had four mimosas to start with. I'm not sure how he knew the severity of need for those acidic beverages, but they were welcomed with open arms.

I downed the first one before my mother could take off her jacket that my father had returned to her. I didn't even care that I still wore mine.

"Autumn," she chastised as my sisters giggled, quickly gulping their first glasses as well. Aspen stared on longingly.

"Mr. Shaw, I'll take a Diet Coke when you get a chance," Aspen told him.

"Sure. You all need some food to go with those drinks?"

"Absolutely," I replied as I lifted the stem of my second glass, prepared to send it down the depths of my throat like the previous one. Harold scurried away.

"Slow it down, missy. You don't want to spend tonight and tomorrow making friends with the toilet, do you?" Alex asked as she shrugged off her jacket and pulled her phone from her bag.

"No, but it gives me something else to think about."

Smartly, Harold returned with Aspen's drink and set another flight of mimosas in front of me.

When I cocked my brow at him, he shrugged and replied, "Just heard what happened across the street. Sorry to hear you were outbid. Would have loved to see ya do something with that home. I know your daddy's happy to have you back, though."

"How'd you hear already?" my mother asked, aghast at the notion.

"My wife told me. She was at the store and Betsy heard it from Melissa, who heard it from Bob, who was working the registration table."

"Ugh, the town gossip train," I grumbled as I slammed my head against the table. It was going to leave a nasty mark, but I didn't care. Small town chatter was the worst and it spread faster than wildfire in the heat of summer.

Rory's delicate hand rubbed between my shoulder blades. Usually, the motion would calm me instantly, but not today. I was too wired and angry and disappointed. "I'm sorry, Autumn," she whispered in my ear, close enough that no one else would hear.

I flipped my head on the table and faced her, doing my best to give her a convincing grin, but I could tell she wasn't fooled.

A hand slapped down in front of my face and I jumped up to a straight sitting position, nearly knocking heads with Rory in the process.

"Look. We know you're upset about this. We wanted it for you just as much as you did for yourself. But it's over and done with. Best case, the winner does nothing with it and the land and house stay untouched. Worst case, he tears it down and builds his dream house on the land. Either way, our family made the mistake a long time ago and we've done our best to right that wrong. We lost, and that's okay. Maybe it was meant to be that way. Maybe that land and the house were meant to be for someone else."

I heard what she was saying, but it didn't sit right with me. That house was mine. It had always been mine. It was in my dreams and I swear every time I passed the plot, I felt like the sun shone a little brighter. If the house could actually smile, I felt like it would.

"She's right, Autumn. As brash as Alexandra can be sometimes, she's right about the land. We gave it our best shot. Now we can spend this day moping about. Or we can have a few drinks and have a proper girl's day. You have years of New York City living to catch us up on."

Mom always had the best way to put a spin on things. Even when it was the most ghastly of things, she knew how to put it in a better light.

Taking a sip from the second mimosa, I asked them if I ever told them about the time I accidentally mistook the doorman for a homeless person.

By the time we had filed into Aurora's sedan, four out of the five of us were feeling a delightful buzz. Thank goodness Harold and the chef kept food on our table. They started us off with a type of egg souffle, then at lunch we each had a trio of sandwiches. A turkey club, a Cuban, and a Reuben. They were the best I'd ever had and I'd dined at some of the most acclaimed sandwich shops in New York. By lunch, we had transitioned from the mimosas to mojitos. Mom was generous enough to pick up the tab and I was glad I didn't get to see the bill. I lost count of the drinks after my third mimosa flight.

"Can y'all cover my eyes when we pass the house? I don't want to see the betrayal."

"Aw, you said y'all like a true southern girl," Rory said from my left, while to my right Alex hiccupped, then added, "The house didn't betray you, silly."

"Mom, Alex called Autumn silly. That's not nice when she's in distress," Rory whined with a nasally note that was headache inducing.

"It's depressed, not distressed. Your sister isn't in crisis, she's just upset. And stop tattling on your sister. I have two ears, you know," Mom replied in her well-known authoritative tone that had my sisters silencing themselves quickly while I was left in amazement. I could barely speak without slurring after the amount of alcohol we drank at The Purple Goat while Mom sounded as fresh as a daisy.

With the backseat quiet, Aspen pulled the car out of the spot on the street Rory snagged that morning and turned us toward home. Beside me, Rory and Alex chattered quietly about their plans for the week. The school year would start in full swing mid-week so we would see Rory less and less, especially since this was the first year she would have her own class. She'd been volunteering at the school for as long as I could remember. Alex basically ran the bar she worked at while finishing some master's degree courses online, so with the night creeping in earlier and earlier, the bar tended to fill up with patrons once dusk broke.

Gazing out the window, the fields and shaded trees were nothing more than a blur around me. I felt disconnected from it all. It looked like I was moving, but it seemed like I was stuck in place because everything else was shifting. Everyone else was on some sort of road they'd designed for their life and mine was nothing more than a patchy dirt path that hadn't been traveled on in centuries.

Maybe that's why I connected so much to the house on the hill. It had weathered a storm and needed that love and care. It needed its purpose. I thought I knew what my purpose was. What I was destined to do. I'd been so sure, so adamant, but that only got me red-faced back at my parents' place. I was blacklisted with the elite planners in New York, all because my ex didn't want me around him to remind anyone of his screw-up. I could only imagine what he was off telling our colleagues or the clients I'd once had. They probably thought the same of me as the rumor Mr. Granger had disclosed. That I'd been the homewrecker. I'd been the one to cheat. I'd been the one to use company dollars on an extravagant trip for my lover. Max had done all those things, which was why the lies came so easily off his tongue when he spoke to others. It was easy to tell the story as if I'd been the bad guy because he'd known all the details.

I still missed that apartment.

But did I miss that life?

I thought I did. It felt like I was missing something by being away from the hustle and bustle of the city. I'd never believed I was cut out for small town living. Mom used to tell me that the moment I could walk I wanted to explore my surroundings. She's caught me more than once asking our older brother to drive me to downtown Ashfield. He was sixteen and had a car, so it made sense to my three-year-old mind.

"Cover her eyes," Aspen whispered harshly from the front seat as we approached what I liked to call the Easterly curve. It was an almost ninety-degree turn in the main road and that was right where the Easterly family property and Sunny Brook Farms began.

Rory reached across and I swatted her hands away. "I'm fine," I said sullenly. I wasn't, but I lied all the same.

The house was in full view as we passed the bend in the road and I tried my damnedest not to gaze up at the farmhouse, but as if it summoned me, I glued my eyes to the statuesque property. The gasp escaped before I could cover my mouth with my shaking fingers. The auction had only ended a few hours prior, but there were already a handful of construction trucks in the yard.

"What's going on? Auction closings never happen that fast. Even when the paperwork is rushed and payment is made, they still take a minimum of a few weeks," Alex said in alarm.

"Should I slow down?" Aspen asked as the car's speed began to drop. "They're using the easement that's on our line of the property."

"Keep going, Aspen. I'll message your father and ask him to go see what's happening."

"Maybe we should send Andrew? He seemed closer to the age of the guy that bid on the property." Rory made a good point. Our brother was intimidating at first glance, but he had a heart of gold. Unless you pissed him off or messed with his sisters. He traveled a lot as a contract lawyer doing various jobs for the farm but always returned when one of us was in trouble.

Except this time, it wasn't just us. There was a chance that whatever was going on at the old house would affect our farm.

I pulled my eyes away from the home and watched Mom type away on her phone. The clicking of her nails was the distraction I needed.

"Your father said he'd head over there to see what's what. Andrew is out in California at a robotics convention." Luckily there was a straight path on our land that led to the decrepit home. Us girls used to ride our bikes that way in the summers.

"Andrew is never home anymore. Why'd he have to move to Knoxville? He only comes to the ranch once a week unless Dad is harvesting or needs to have a meeting." Aspen missed our brother more than anyone. Being the youngest, by the time she was born, he'd left the coup for college.

Mom left Aspen's earlier question lingering in the air as we approached the farm's entrance. Its stone pillars, iron gate, and white picket fencing were breathtaking even in their slightly worn-down state.

There was something regal about the entry to the ranch. It gave a very different first glance than when you traveled through the gates to find the miles of corn fields. The front fields were not of corn, but of wheatgrass that wasn't harvested. They were for display only. My parents kept it as another barrier to keep people out of their property. Dad used to call it our grassy moat before arriving at the castle. The castle of stone and wood and large pane windows overlooking the farm.

It never ceased to take my breath away whenever the vehicle careened over the hill and into the valley where the house sat. I may be in love with the newly purchased farmhouse next door, but my parents' house was – home.

Once the car came to a stop, Aspen and Rory flew out of the vehicle while Alex and Mom took their time. I sat nestled against the passenger door trying to figure out my next move. It was obvious a nap was in order after a glass of water and an aspirin, but what was I going to do after? Not just today, but moving forward. I knew I had made that promise to my father, and one month was such a short time. Before I knew it, it would be time to make a decision. Until recently, I never questioned my decisiveness, now I am worried about making the wrong choice. How would I know if it was the right one?

A knock sounded on the window where my head rested and I jumped to attention. Mom stood on the other side with a careful smile. She was treading carefully around me and that made me feel even more terrible that I lost the bid on the family home. I felt like a disappointment all over again.

"Come on, sweetie. No sense in wasting the day in the back of a car unless you have a handsome man sitting next to you," my mother said with a casual wink.

"Mom!" I said thoroughly grossed out at her innuendo as I stepped out of the car.

"What? I was a young adult once, too. I remember the days of being a little wild and crazy."

"I don't want to hear this," I mumbled with my hands over my ears, so everything sounded muffled as I stepped onto the porch.

"Hear what?" Alex said as I stepped through the door.

"Mom is being weird," I explained as I continued through the hall toward the kitchen, where I checked on my sunflower. She needed clean water and I quickly took the vase to the sink and refilled it.

Mom's phone buzzed as I made my way back to the island and set the flower in the center. I could feel the headache building along with the cotton mouth that was always a tell-tale sign for me that I'd had far too much to drink. I really hope my parents were making something carb-filled for dinner to soak up all this alcohol from earlier. Otherwise, I had a feeling I'd still be feeling this way, or worse, in the morning.

Grabbing a glass from the cabinet by the sink, I filled it with tap water as I searched the drawer next to me for some aspirin. I came up short just as Alex nudged me with her hip and handed me the bottle. Clearly, I wasn't the only one searching for some relief.

I chugged the water, then filled up the glass again before taking the medicine. I was starting to feel a bit woozy from the day. Definitely not from the numerous drinks I'd indulged in.

"I need to lie down," I whispered to Alex just as she laughed and nodded her head toward Rory who was snoozing on the couch while sitting up. Her head was tilted back against the cushions and her mouth was as open as the front door.

The front door that my father passed through minutes later.

"Hey, everyone. I have someone I want you to meet," my father called out from the front of the house, his voice echoing around the thick walls.

"Oh, no," Alex said in a disgruntled voice. I looked over to find her brows furrowed closely together and her lips pursed as if she'd eaten a sour lemon.

Confused, I whispered to her, "What's going on?"

"Girls, this is Colton Crawford. He's the man that bought the house next door."

I hadn't turned away from Alex, wanting to see her reaction first. And by the way her eyes widened in shock, I knew it wasn't going to be good. Gosh, I hope it wasn't one of those developers Aspen had been speaking of at the auction.

It was too quiet in the house. No one said anything in the seconds after my father's introduction. Reluctantly, I pulled my stare from Alex and sought the man of the hour. His shoes were new, with smudges along the side like he'd just trudged through fresh mud. His jeans were distressed, but the kind you purchased that way. Designer brand. The shirt was navy blue with a texture that reminded me of the long johns my dad wore when he worked outside in the winter. Hesitantly, I took in his face and gulped. It was the man from the store. The man that I'd felt up without meaning to, though I'd never apologize for it. The man that held my gaze like he knew me inside and out.

The man who smirked as he said, "I see you kept my flower."

"Um. . .I. . ." Viciously, my stomach began to churn and I hastily wrapped my hand over my mouth.

As I bit back the urge, I rushed toward the bathroom.

"I'm going to throw up."

Chapter Seven

Colton

"Well, I'm not sure what to say about that," Mr. Easterly said with a heavy sigh from beside me.

I wasn't quite sure what to make of it, either. I'd recognized her the moment I'd set foot in their kitchen. She wasn't facing me, so it gave me a chance to take her in. She was a bit shorter and curvier than her sisters, something I appreciated. I'd always been drawn to petite women. The long waves of her hair were pinned up on top of her head in some sort of messy ponytail-bun combination. I didn't know what to call it.

When our eyes met, I felt that same spark of awareness I'd felt at the grocery store on Saturday when she collided with me. But I'd also been struck dumb and had no idea what to say, so I said the first thing that came to mind when I noticed the flower I'd given her set in a vase on the counter.

Somehow that triggered an avalanche of conversation around me as the woman bolted off looking an uneasy shade of green.

"So, you're the guy," one of the other women in the room said as she wobbled in her attempt to sit on a barstool at the kitchen island.

"What guy?" I asked her.

From the attached living room, a sleep-filled voice called out, "The one that gave my sister a flower at the store."

"Oh. Yeah, that was me, I guess."

"Hello. I'm Mrs. Easterly. I apologize for my daughters' behavior."

I glanced at Mr. Easterly as he moved toward a dining table set between the kitchen and living space. "It's nice to meet you," I greeted as I held out my hand. She quickly shook it but held my grasp as she asked, "Are you single, dear?"

My gulp must have been audible because the three remaining sisters collectively giggled and Mr. Easterly told his wife to knock it off.

"I'm waiting." Mrs. Easterly emphasized her impatience by squeezing my hand. She was far stronger than I anticipated.

"Um. . .yes. . .at the moment. And please, call me Colton."

Releasing her grip, Mrs. Easterly returned back to the kitchen, but not before she stopped by her husband sitting at the dining table and exchanged a kiss. If I hadn't felt so out of place, I'd have thought it was sweet.

"You can call us Marisol and Nash. Are you staying for dinner?"

"I, ugh, actually have plans. But thank you for the invitation."

"Come sit down, Colton. I want to hear your plans for the house," Nash said as he waved his arm in my direction.

I chatted with him for a while as he told me stories about the farm and his family heritage. The most intriguing part was that the house I'd bought had once belonged to his family. It almost made me feel bad that

I'd outbid them this morning, but he assured me that he was happy I wasn't going to tear it down.

At least, that was my plan. I already worked it out with the sheriff to have some crews assess the damage to the roof so that it could be fixed as soon as possible. I was pushing to rush the paperwork in the hopes that I could move onto the property by the end of the week since it was vacant.

Brett and Lily were ecstatic for me, selfishly, of course, because they believed it meant that I was going to stay, but I hadn't decided any course of action past renovating the house.

"My daughter, Autumn, has some really great ideas for the place. I'm sure she'd be happy to go over them with you."

"Dad," one of the sisters mumbled in alarm. It was clear that they did not share the same sentiment.

"What?" he said naively. "Maybe Colton would like to hear about all the historical aspects of the house."

Collectively, the group turned their attention toward me and I subconsciously wiped my hands against the legs of my jeans.

"Um...yes. I haven't really thought about how I'd design the interior, but keeping it historically accurate would be nice. Are there any pictures?" I asked as I let the idea fester and grow in my mind. Maintaining the house's history would absolutely make it more appealing for renters or buyers if I decided not to stay on the property.

"I'm sure there are. Alexandra, why don't you see if Autumn is feeling more like herself and have her come chat?" Marisol gave her instructions as a command and I peeked over my shoulder to find Alex rolling her eyes at her mother's back.

This family had an interesting dynamic, that's for sure.

After ten minutes, Alex never returned with Autumn, who I pieced together was the woman from the grocery store. I'd listened to Nash go on about the property and their ranch. He even let me know he went by the farmhouse frequently and did his best to keep up whatever maintenance he could. That explained why it was in far better shape than the contractor I'd hired expected. Listening to Mr. Easterly talk about the property that had once belonged to his family was fascinating and I'd wanted to stay longer, but I wanted to run by the house one more time before heading back to the Chisolm's.

"I need to be heading back, but if it's alright with you, I'd really like if you would join me at the end of the week when I get access to the house."

"Well, that sounds nice, son. I appreciate it. I don't see why I can't get away, though it's getting close to the corn harvest."

"Is that what you all grow?" I asked, intrigued.

"Corn is our main produce, but we also have a small garden the girls keep up with for the local farmer's market."

"I've always been fascinated by agriculture. Even thought I'd be a farmer when I was younger. Then I caught the hockey bug and the rest is history."

The man's face lit up. "You play hockey?"

"I did."

From the couch, one of the daughters said, "Huh. That explains why you're so big."

I didn't know how to reply to that one, so I turned my attention back to Nash. Marisol walked over to stand behind his chair, gently placing her wrinkled hands on his shoulders.

"You must be the one staying with Coach Chisolm. He hasn't stopped talking about it for the last few weeks."

My cheeks flamed as I nodded.

"Yep. That's me. I played for Coach when I was in the minors. We've kept in contact since I went to the NHL."

"Well, I can't say that we watch a whole lot of hockey in our house, but I do like catching a game every now and then. Predator fans here, though. Sorry," Nash said with a chuckle as he rose from his chair and grasped Marisol's hand.

I could tell that there was a lot of love between the two of them. It left me wanting to know more about their history.

Nash held out his weathered hand and I shook it as I made my way to the door. I'd followed him over in my truck since I wasn't staying nearby. He'd surprised me when he showed up at the property earlier and mentioned the easement on his land. We chatted for a minute about the house and what I'd planned to do, then he invited me back to his home since all of his property surrounded mine. I hadn't even realized that the house sat on fifty acres of land, which was far more than I needed, but I already had ideas stirring in my head of what I could possibly do with the extra space.

Maybe that hockey rink wasn't such a pipe dream after all.

As I said my goodbyes to Nash's family that remained in the room, I saw myself out of the house and headed toward my truck parked next to a little red sedan. When I pulled up, I hadn't put two and two together that the girl from the store could possibly live at the house. Now she was my neighbor.

The girl intrigued me for sure, but I was in no shape mentally or emotionally for a relationship. But maybe she'd see the appeal after a few nights in my bed.

Settling in my truck, I looked up at one of the second-floor windows wondering if any of them belonged to her. The house was massive, so there was a good chance she could be anywhere in the home. As I inspected the windows, my eye landed on a curtain pushed aside as if a hand held it out of the way so the person beyond could see out. Before I could blink, a small hand shot out against the window and I could just make out the imprint of a middle finger jutting up in the air.

I couldn't be sure which sister it belonged to, but I had a feeling it was attached to the woman that captured my attention.

Chuckling, I turned the truck around and headed down their driveway and back to the main road. I'd have to get Nash to tell me who built his gate and fencing. They marveled me as I crossed the threshold. A perfect mix of modern and classical.

As I continued down the road toward the Chisolm's house, an incoming message read through the stereo.

Brett

> Change of plans. Meet at the HS.

Stopping the truck in the middle of the road, I did my best to complete a three-point turn, but it ended being six or seven due to the narrow lane, and I made my way in the opposite direction. At least it meant I could drive by my soon-to-be house one more time.

I gazed out at the Easterly's farm as I passed their entrance and found myself sighing. Those girls had no idea how lucky they were to grow up in a place like that with the parents and family that they had. I would have given anything when I was younger to have just a smidgen of that.

My soon to be house stood proudly as a few crewmen still milled about the place. The setting sun cast yellows and golds on her faded exterior, but I swear the house looked happy. It had to be nothing more than my imagination, but it seemed like she was alive. Which was both exhilarating and terrifying. A weird horror story was not something that I was cut out for.

As I continued past the house and maneuvered slowly around the bend in the road that I was determined to tackle before leaving Tennessee, I thought back to my conversation with the sheriff. The current owners had stopped paying state taxes on the house a decade ago and despite years of trying to reach out, the state decided they'd had enough. All parties involved seemed to be thrilled and surprised that I was willing to pay everything off as quickly as possible so I could move onto the property. I had the money just sitting in the bank and needed to find a good investment. My financial advisor thought I was crazy when I spoke to him early this morning and hashed out my plan to buy the estate Brett had mentioned was going up for auction today.

Everything seemed to fall into place just as it needed.

I continued on the main road until I came about a mile outside of the hub of the town and took a turn that Brett had shown me yesterday when he gave me a drive-by tour of Ashfield. I still couldn't grasp that he drove to this school every day and assisted with coaching the minors team. There were no quick trips anywhere in this town, everything was half an hour minimum. I'd been spoiled in the city where I could walk everywhere if I wanted. My apartment had its own luxuries in the building, so I rarely had to leave.

At the school, I quickly spotted Brett's truck and I parked beside it. The rest of the lot had older cars and trucks splattered throughout. I was surprised at how new everything looked, from the school to the stadium. I had been expecting a century-old building in decay and an outside rink. This looked more like a well-funded private school.

Stepping down from my truck, I grabbed my duffle out of the back seat. I'd kept my practice equipment with me, just in case. And it seemed that I'd made a smart choice because, despite my retirement, I still felt alive on the ice.

My feet crunched with each step as I approached the doors to the stadium, where I assumed Brett was holding practice. Adrenaline started pulsing through me and for the first time in what felt like forever, I was nervous. What if these kids looked at me and saw nothing more than a joke? A retired old man that couldn't hack it anymore.

Pulling the door handle, I took a deep breath. The smell of the ice immediately washed over me and I felt at home. The nerves didn't disappear, but they changed when twenty sets of eyes turned in my direction.

"Holy shit," a voice called out, abruptly followed by many of the same sentiment.

Brett's voice belted over the others. "Hey! You made it," he said as he walked over to me from the stands. "They were just running some drills."

"They seem surprised to see me."

"Well," he began, his hand rubbing against the back of his neck. "I didn't say anything just in the off chance you didn't get my message or weren't ready to come out."

What he was saying was that he didn't want to disappoint them.

"That's okay. I was headed back to your house when I got your message. I just happen to have my practice stuff in my truck."

"Clean, I hope," he joked as he led me toward the ice.

Was it? Leave it to Brett to ask the hard-hitting questions, but I'm pretty sure I washed everything before I left New York, just to be safe.

His team of teens stared at me as I got closer. None of them moved except for the goalie who was slowly joining the rest of the group. Their jaws hung loosely below their helmets as I leaned against the boards surrounding the rink.

"So, I'm assuming you all know who Colton Crawford is. He's come to watch you guys skate and offer any advice or pointers. Alright?"

The group didn't respond but continued to stare at me. I felt like I was in a fish tank and one of those kids was about to tap on the glass.

Brett repeated, "Alright? Come on guys, don't make it weird or he won't come back."

"Yes, Coach," they said collectively, then skated off to continue their drills.

"They're good kids. You can join them or just watch. I think a couple has what it takes to go pro or play in college, which is my recommendation to them."

"I agree. A degree always gives them something to fall back on. Any of them play for juniors?"

"Naw," he said as he turned to face me. "It's expensive and most of these kids work their farms with their parents. It's hard enough to get them here to play at the high school level. I've watched most of them in our rec teams since they were little, but it was never certain who would be showing up during harvest times."

What the hell was harvest time?

"You'll. . .ugh. . .have to tell me more about this harvest stuff later. I met the guy my house is next to and he was talking about the harvest."

"Oh, you met Nash Easterly?"

"Yeah," I said as I sat on the bench and tugged my skates free from the duffle bag, followed by some thicker socks. "What do you know about him and his family?" I worded the question in a way that wasn't suspect because I really wanted to know more about one particular daughter.

Brett let out a deep-bellied laugh as he tossed his head back. "Man, in small towns, you only know what people want you to know. They used to tell me that everyone knew everything, but that's not always the case. The Easterlys are as much a mystery as they are a staple in the town. But from what I know, the Easterly name has been part of that land since before the town existed. The majority of the land belonged to them at one point. Apparently, one of the relatives was a gambler and liked to toss around acreage like they were pennies.

"It's probably why they were at the auction today, or so I've heard. The house you bought used to belong to them."

"Yeah, Nash said as much."

Brett nodded as he called out one of the kids' names and told him to watch his footwork. "As for the wife and the kids, not much to say there. Marisol was married before, lost her husband in Desert Storm. Andrew, the oldest Easterly, is from her first marriage, but Nash has raised that boy like his own son. The girls came a few years later from what I remember.

"When we moved here, Nash and Marisol were some of the first people to visit and welcome us to the town. They're good people."

I stared at the man, trying to figure out a way to broach the topic of the daughters as I finished tying my skates blindly.

"And those girls are like the town treasure. So don't poke around," he said sternly.

"Poke?" I joked as I stood and towered over him. I was tall on a good day, but with the blades, I was inching toward seven feet.

"Yeah. Poke. And you're too old for them anyway. But I'm certain some of these boys' moms will be more than happy to take their place. A few are divorced if I recall."

"You and I both know that it wouldn't matter to them if they weren't."

"True."

I skated around the rink in giant circles as I watched Brett work with his team. He was always a great coach and those kids were going to learn from the best. He still never gave me any information about the Easterly sisters and there was no way I would ask him. He was right, though; the girls were young. Early twenties at best. But the one Nash called Autumn was stuck in my mind and I couldn't shake her free, even while skating. She suited her name with her dark blonde hair and tanned skin. I wasn't sure if it was residual from the summer or if her skin was olive-toned year-round. Nash had darker skin, but he worked outside regularly while her mother and sisters were more fair-skinned.

It didn't matter though, I was thirty-five. At least a decade older than I presumed Autumn to be.

My cock didn't seem to care, though. He definitely wanted to poke her.

Chapter Eight

Autumn

It had been a week since I'd embarrassed myself *again* in front of the mystery man. The man who was named Colton Crawford and he was a forward and captain of the New York Renegades. Or he was. Dad told us that he'd recently announced his retirement after his ex-girlfriend tore his reputation to shreds. That was all after sustaining an injury two years prior.

The man had been at the forefront of my mind all week. His name suited him. So did his occupation. We'd also learned that he was the one here visiting

Coach Chisolm. That explained why he was here in Ashfield but not why he'd bought fifty acres of land with a dilapidated house on the top of a hill.

Alex argued that maybe he was bored and was looking for something to invest in. I kept countering that he could invest in a school program or a charity.

Unfortunately, though, Dad seemed to like him and had spilled the beans about my desire to take the home back to its historical roots. I had a sneaking suspicion that my dad was hoping to get me to help our new neighbor. Well, he had another thing coming. My eyes were now set on the venue space and the time I needed to turn it into something.

Sitting at the dining table with my laptop in front of me, I stared over the screen into the backyard. It was peaceful outside with the leaves changing colors. Fall had always been my favorite season. I supposed the naming gods had smiled down on me at birth.

"Whatcha doing?" Aspen asked as she slid into the seat beside me, a strudel in her hand. I quickly pressed the enter key on the laptop's keyboard before slamming the screen shut.

"Sending out my resume," I told her, shame blossoming in my chest.

Aspen licked some of the gooey icing that dripped down her fingers. "Thought you promised Dad you were going to stay for a month."

"I did. And I plan to. I just want to make sure that I have some applications floating around, just in case."

Aspen's elfish features hardened as she turned her attention away from the pastry and onto me. "So, you've been here a full week, and you've already decided that you're going to up and run away again when the time is up? Have you even tried to give the town a chance?"

"I. . .I. . .Aspen it's not like that," I tried to explain, but I couldn't get the words out.

"It's exactly like that. What's so terrible about this place that you won't give it a fair shot? What did any of us do to you but beg you to stay?" Aspen stood rapidly, the feet of the chair scratching against the hardwood floors. "Instead of pretending like you care and want to be here, why don't you just leave again?"

She retreated quickly, and I stared at her disappearing back before turning my attention to the pile of crumbs she left scattered on the table. My heart felt like those crumbs after listening to what Aspen had just said. I never wanted anyone to think that I hated living here or growing up here. It was the opposite. I just thought I needed *more*.

An image of Aspen as a young girl clinging to my waist as I packed my car to head off to college popped into my mind and I couldn't shake it free. Did she feel like I had abandoned her? Did my entire family feel that way?

I scooped the crumbs she left behind into my hand and carried them over to the trash can, where I dumped them into the stainless steel can that still squeaked whenever the lid opened.

There had to be a way to make her see, to make everyone see, that I had dreams bigger than Ashfield could handle. The more I considered the barn on the west field, the more I questioned the decision to turn it into something more. The venue was large, but how much use would it actually get? Locals may inquire, possibly a few couples from surrounding counties, but there was no way it would be marketed the way it needed to be successful. Aspen had been right about one thing; I was just wasting my parents' money.

Walking down the hall, I popped my head into the small office my mother had converted into a personal library. She sat in her leather chaise reading a book I was certain she had read a dozen times already.

"Hey, Mom. I wanted to talk to you about something."

Not sparing me a glance, she turned the page of her book while saying, "Is this about the venue and your leaving?"

"What? How did you know?" I asked, perplexed. With all the confusing conversations going on today, the lines between my eyebrows were going to form permanent creases.

Finally drawing her eyes over to me, she delicately marked her spot by lying the book face-down on her lap. "Did you forget how everything echoes in this house?"

I had. It used to drive me nuts as a teenager. There was no use in trying to sneak anything past my parents or sisters. Someone always knew. The walls had eyes and ears.

"I heard your conversation with Aspen. And though her delivery left a lot to be desired, it did leave me thinking. What is your intention, Autumn? You know your father and I are always happy to have you at home. But if you're so unhappy with staying here, I'd rather loan you money to get yourself on your feet than to invest it in something you won't see through."

"I said I'd give it a month."

"You did, but if you know in your heart that you're not going to stay, then don't get our hopes up. We'd be happy just to have you home while you look for a job. We know you love the city, but we'd hoped that you'd find something here to love, too. Your sisters have missed you. We have missed you."

I wanted to tell her that people change. That our ideals and wants were always shifting. In reality, it was because I wanted to be in a place where no one knew me. No expectations. No set path designed for me. I could be anything when no one knew me.

Here, everyone had already decided my fate.

"I'm sorry, Mom. I just. . .I feel out of sorts, you know? Like I don't feel like I fit in here."

Tapping the edge of her chaise, Mom beckoned me to sit beside her. "I remember when I moved here with your father. I thought no one would welcome me and I was prepared to fight tooth and nail against small town living. I knew how crazy it could be. But this town has a way of making people feel like outcasts when instead they've opened their arms to them. You've always stuck out, Autumn, and I could see how that would make you feel like an outsider. But think about all the great things you got to experience here. I mean, how many of your friends in New York climbed a water tower with their father and had their first beer?"

My eyes widened in shock. "It wasn't a well-kept secret, sweetie. Your father did the same with all of your sisters when y'all turned eighteen."

"I'm not sure I'm following, Mom."

Chuckling, Mom patted my thigh and said, "I kind of lost my train of thought, to be honest. But just remember how much fun you had growing up. Not just here on the farm, but in the town. All the festivals, all of the people celebrating even the tiniest of things, the way everyone came together when someone was in need. You don't find that everywhere.

"I know how much your independence means to you, but that doesn't mean you have to desert the people closest to you."

"You're right. And I'm sorry about the venue thing. I do want to pursue it. I just haven't quite wrapped my head around living back here again. I think I got excited about the project, but not all the fine details it would entail, especially if I ended up involving everyone.

"I've also thought about looking around Knoxville for a place to live. Andrew seems pretty content there."

"That's a good start and I'm happy to hear it. And maybe apologize to your baby sister. She missed you the most when you left and never really came back often."

"Yeah, I will."

"And maybe go with your dad over to the Crawford house. You could possibly help."

Astonished, I crossed my arms against my chest. "The Crawford house? Is that what we're calling it now? And how would I help?"

"Well, you could offer advice on how he could maintain some of the historical elements. When he was over on Monday, he seemed very keen to the idea."

"I suppose," I said reluctantly as I stood.

"He's very cute, too."

"Mom! He's like ten years older than me."

"Eleven, but who's counting? And you're probably right. I did hear from Betsy that Travis was looking for you. Maybe you should give him a call and meet up. You two did make the cutest couple."

Travis had been my high school boyfriend and we parted ways amicably after graduation. He was staying to work at his father's accounting firm while he went to college locally. He had texted on Wednesday asking if I wanted to meet up. I hadn't given him a response yet. For some reason, seeing my old friends would solidify my return.

"Maybe," I replied. I had no social media, so I had no idea what the people I grew up with were up to. "I'll grab my things and meet up with Dad."

"He should be coming in soon." As I started to walk out of the room, Mom called out my name. "And Autumn? I think everything works out the way it's supposed to be. So don't be disappointed if it's not what you saw for yourself. Okay?"

"Yes, ma'am."

Turning the corner to head toward the back door, I smacked into my father. He asked if I wanted to join him, smiling in a way that I couldn't ever say no to. Rushing upstairs, I grabbed my notebook full of all the historical information I'd gathered about the house. I was hesitant to take it to the Crawford house at all. These were my ideas and plans, but I needed to remember the home was never going to be mine. It now belonged to Colton Crawford, and if I wanted to see it preserved in any way, I needed to hand all of this over to him.

I'd never let anyone see how many hours I poured into the giant three-ring binder. I'd spent days and nights in high school finding any information I could at the library and the town's historical records. I even found old bank statements with items purchased and used the internet to find similar pieces.

The paperwork for the historical society was nestled inside as well. Even though Dad made it seem like Colton planned on keeping the house, there was always a chance that it wasn't structurally sound or that a developer would swoop in. We needed to do what we could to keep that from happening.

I rode with Dad over to the house, staring out the window the entire journey, but never actually looking at anything. I was too lost in my own head.

When we pulled up, it surprised me to see that a brand-new roof adorned the house.

"Wow, he worked fast," Dad said as he turned off the truck. I had come to the same conclusion. It surprised me a bit since I wasn't sure the joists or foundation of the house were even solid enough to hold a new roof. But maybe it was just a quick fix to keep the inside from growing more damaged. The more I thought about it, the entire place seemed like a lost cause.

"Do you think it's safe?" I asked as my dad stepped out of the truck. I gripped the binder against my chest as I did the same.

My dad left the question hanging in the air as he approached the front porch that seemed to have some more beams added for reinforcement. I walked slowly, each step causing more and more apprehension. Why was I here again?

Dad stood at the bottom of the steps and glanced back at me. My nerves were shot and I had every intention of turning around and ducking back into the truck. I was about to face the guy I'd embarrassed myself in front of twice. Twice!

I tripped over my own feet as I stumbled my way closer to the house.

"Whoa, there." Two hands gripped my shoulders and steadied me as my face flamed. Before I could tuck my chin any closer to my chest, Colton moved around me and held his hand out to my dad.

"Nash, thanks for coming by. I see you brought someone with you," he said as they shook hands.

"Yep. This here is Autumn. She's the one I was telling you about."

Colton held his hand out to me and I blinked a few times before I extended mine. "Glad to finally get a formal introduction."

The man had rendered me speechless. Something that I was unfamiliar with. As an event planner, I was used to making conversation with just about anyone. Apparently, that did not include Colton Crawford.

Our hands were still connected and moving up and down while he stared down at me and I peered up at him from beneath my lashes. I didn't know what to say or do and he seemed to be trying to get a read on me as his eyes narrowed. Heck, I couldn't get a read on myself either.

Thankfully, Dad interrupted and asked if it was safe for a tour. Colton pulled his hand away and I felt like I could finally breathe. Whatever this man was doing to me only frustrated me more. And I hated feeling out of sorts.

"There was a crew in all week stabilizing the frame and doing some generalized cleaning. I don't even want to talk about some of the things that were living inside here," Colton explained as he turned and carefully walked up the porch steps.

"Whelp, I'll let Autumn go over the things she's found while you show her around. I suspect you can bring her home later?"

Spinning around, I felt like I'd been slapped in the face. "What? Where are you going?"

"Forgot I need to pick up some things from the feed store. Best get to seeing the place before the sun sets. Doubt the electrical is running yet," Dad said as he walked backward, then opened the door to his truck.

"Don't you want to see the place?" Colton asked from behind me.

"Who do you think kept up with the outside repairs?"

Before myself or Colton could argue with my father any further, Dad hopped inside the vehicle, turned on the ignition to the truck, and backed out of the dirt drive.

"I think we just got set up."

Spinning around, I narrowed my eyes at Colton as if he had just said the most obvious of things and it was all his doing.

"Are you telling me that you had nothing to do with this?" I said sternly, my fingers gripping the sides of my binder.

Colton's hands jutted into the air in surrender. Even from this distance I could make out the calluses on his palms. Definitely not delicate like the previous men I'd dated.

"Scout's honor. I had no idea your dad would jet off like that."

Moving past him, I gingerly took the steps up to the porch and stood at the front door to the house. "I doubt you were a boy scout."

Colton joined me and pushed the door open wide. "What makes you say that?" he questioned as he held his arm outward, gesturing for me to enter.

"No reason. You just don't seem the type." Moving past him, I held my breath as I took my first steps into the house I'd dreamed of owning one day. My eyes darted around the space wanting to take it all in.

"And what type is that?"

"Sh…" I insisted, flipping my hand wildly in the air to emphasize my need for a moment of silence.

"What are we looking for?" he whispered next to me. He was closer than I expected and I swear I could feel his breath caressing the outer rim of my ear.

I rolled my eyes and turned to stare up at him, only to be surprised to find him mere inches away. "This house is part of my family's legacy. I just need a minute to take it all in. I've never been past the outside." Colton seemed to understand and nodded as I took a step further into the space. It was dark and dingy, and had a distinct scent of death, but it surprised me at how well maintained everything seemed.

There was a decent sized foyer that gave way to a wood paneled staircase. They designed intricate woodwork on each stair spindle and wooden board. Reaching out, I let my finger slide across the swirled pattern as I traced the display.

"Wow," I murmured before lifting my now dusty finger and having to wipe it on my jeans.

"Sorry about that," Colton said as he sheepishly shrugged his shoulders and tilted his head to the side. He seemed embarrassed. "The cleaning crew mainly focused on getting the debris cleared."

I didn't want to like the guy and let him off the hook, he owned my home after all, but I did feel bad for him.

"No harm done," I said and asked him to continue showing me around.

I already knew the layout of the house having spent hours pouring over the original blueprints. I always thought they'd be a nice touch to have framed and hung on the wall.

There were three bedrooms on the lower level and six on the upper. Colton spoke about converting two of the lower rooms into something else since he had no need for that many bedrooms. It was on the tip of my tongue to tell him that the house would make a perfect bed-and-breakfast, but he did not seem like the kind of person to welcome strangers into his home. From what information Mom told us over dinner these past few nights, Colton had been chased by paparazzi since he started playing for the New York Renegades. I couldn't fault them for calling him one of the hottest men on ice. He was definitely easy on the eyes.

We carefully ascended the stairs to take in the second level. It was mainly bedrooms and baths, but there was a sitting room and really intricate alcoves down the hallways. I peeked in as many of the rooms as I could. Torn wallpaper cascaded down the walls and disgusting carpet covered the floors. I knew there was original hardwood underneath and I hoped for Colton's sake that some of it was salvageable, if not all. I may have already started noting a mental list of people he could contact to have it assessed.

Damage from the old oak tree left the east facing walls covered in plywood and builder's paper.

"The contractor says we'll need to pretty much rebuild the entire back side of the house. The water damage is too severe."

"That's a shame, but unavoidable."

"The third story is probably my favorite. It's just one giant open space." The bed and breakfast idea sprung forward in my mind again. If it was as open as he said, that would make a great master suite. Away from the guests, but still close by if needed.

"That sounds nice. Any thought on what you'd do with it?"

"I have no idea. I'm still trying to come to terms with the fact that this house is in as good of shape as it is considering everything it went through and how old it is."

Colton and I took the back hall stairs down to the kitchen area where we stepped into a butler's pantry. It was larger than my entire apartment in New York.

"Did the contractor give you any idea on what needs to be done?" I asked as we stepped into the kitchen that looked like a tornado had spun through. Delicately, I reached out and ran my finger across the old wooden countertops. There were knicks and scratches worn into the block.

"Honestly, he said he was surprised it was still standing. It needs a lot of work, pretty much from the ground up. Plumbing, electrical, all of that needs to be upgraded. We'll use what we can, but most of it will be taken down."

My heart seized. Colton sounded as if the news meant he could design something brand new, tearing down what was already here. The bones of this house were good. We were standing in the middle of it, after all.

"So, what's your plan? You going to tear it down and put some modern castle in its place? The new Crawford homestead?" I seethed in anger as I turned toward him using my trusty notebooks as my shield as I poked at his chest.

"Whoa!" he replied, clutching my finger with his hand. "What has your panties in a twist?"

Chapter Nine

Colton

When she gasped in disgruntled anger, I realized my mistake. Before I could release her finger, she used that white, plastic binder and pelted my shoulder with it. She had one hell of a swing.

"Excuse me, but you do not *ever* get to think about my panties."

Well, that was all I was going to think about now.

"I'm sorry, you just caught me off guard. I spent a million dollars on this place. We both know the property isn't worth that."

"Then why buy it?" she asked me, her blue eyes shimmering beneath long, dark lashes.

"Because something about this house reminded me of a place I grew up. I have no intention of tearing it down unless it's absolutely necessary, Autumn," I said, wishing Ms. Cathy could see this place.

She remained silent, absorbing my words and deciding if I was being truthful. There was more of the house I wanted to show her, little hidden spots the contractor and I found earlier in the day, but that was going to have to wait until another time. My phone buzzed in my pocket and I explained to Autumn that I needed to head outside.

Barreling down the drive was my old teammate, Lance, who lived in Knoxville where he grew up. Behind his pickup he towed an ancient looking trailer.

"What's that?" Autumn's confused voice said from behind me as I stepped onto the porch.

"Where I'll stay if I'm here while the crews are working."

"I thought you were staying with the Chisolms."

"Ah, so you were asking about me," I said as I smiled down at her. She seemed annoyed as she wrapped her arms around that binder and held it tightly to her chest. I wondered what it would take to have that woman let her guard down. Or smile. I bet she had a killer grin. The kind that knocked you on your ass and took names.

Everything about her held that kind of appeal, but I needed to remind myself that I wasn't here to be selfish. I needed to keep out of the press and figure out my next step in life. Especially with the letter I received at Brett's house this morning. I was trying to ignore it, but I knew it was going to fester. It was the second letter I'd received in a month. My mail was being forwarded to my agent and he was sending the important ones my way. He was the only one I trusted with my whereabouts.

"I wasn't asking about you at all. I haven't thought about you at all this week. Mother brought it up at dinner."

She was lying. Her eyes darted everywhere on the porch but me and she absentmindedly twisted the ring on her right hand. If I'd learned anything by being a public figure, it was that I could read people quickly.

Lance brought the old camper around back behind the house as I requested and I followed his truck's path, Autumn dutifully trailing after.

"Is that even safe?" she whispered and I wasn't sure if she knew she'd spoken it out loud.

"Haven't you ever heard not to judge a book by its cover?" I asked as Lance hopped down from his truck and began unhitching the trailer.

"But. . .it's all dingy."

"Have a little faith."

"Sorry," she mumbled as I introduced her to Lance. The married father of six wrapped Autumn in his arms, surprising us both. The moment he had her tucked against him, I wanted to tug her free and pummel his face.

Fortunately, Lance couldn't stay long and left just as quickly as he came. His wife was home with their newest addition, born just seven weeks ago, and her mother. I knew from my experience with ex-girlfriends that the mother scenario could go either way.

I opened the door to the camper with the keys Lance had handed me before driving off.

The interior was just as he'd showed in the video chat the day before. I was thankful he was letting me borrow the trailer while I was here.

I was already inside the camper and turned to glance down at Autumn as she stared up at me in confusion.

I waved her in as I stepped farther into the confined space. There was a dinette, a small kitchen and bathroom with a shower, and a queen-sized bed in the front. Lance had upgraded everything last summer. It looked more state of the art than run-down as the outside made it appear.

"Wow."

Glancing at her from over my shoulder, I cocked my eyebrow, waiting for her to elaborate.

"You just. . .keep surprising me."

"How so?"

"I don't know. I mean, you're like a mega sports star, here in Ashfield, living out of a trailer while you renovate a century-old farmhouse. You're just not what I expected."

Testing the waters, I took a step closer to her. I half expected Autumn to push me away as I invaded her space, soaked in her warmth, but she only casually ran her finger along the dinette tabletop. I practically covered her body like an umbrella. My frame cast a shadow over her form, but she didn't move or falter.

"What did you expect me to be?"

She turned back to face me and it was the closest we'd been since that incident at the store a week ago. An incident that I'd been playing on repeat in my head.

"Cocky. Self-absorbed. A player. Take your pick."

Her assessment didn't surprise me. It's what most thought of sports players and most of the time they weren't far off. I'd been like that when my career started, but I'd learned that it was just as tiring as being myself. Being the man that Ms. Cathy, my first foster mom, wanted me to be.

"Well, I'm not those things."

Pursing her lips, a sound rumbled out of her as she internally questioned my response.

"We'll see," she finally replied. Changing the subject, she sat her trusty binder on the table and said, "Dad mentioned you were interested in learning some of the historical things I'd found."

The hair on the back of my neck felt like needles prickling my palm as I ran my hand across the skin. I wasn't sure why, but I was nervous about asking for help. I'd always been that way. My therapist said that it stemmed from childhood trauma.

"Um. . .yeah. Maybe we could go somewhere and you could show me what you've found."

"Why can't we do it here?"

"I just figured it was dinnertime, and with Brett and Lily gone for the weekend, I kind of need to fend for myself. And cooking is not my expertise unless you want some mac and cheese from a box. And since you grew up here, I bet you know all the best places to eat."

Her eyes narrowed and I wondered what was going through her mind. I wanted to know everything about her. Autumn intrigued the hell out of me.

"Like a date?"

Shrugging my shoulders, I added on, "It's just dinner."

I could tell by the way she straightened her shoulders Autumn was trying to come up with a way to decline the offer. It would be a first for me, that's for sure. But suddenly a rumble sounded from her direction and I watched as the blush creeped up to her cheeks.

"Betrayed by your stomach," I said with a chuckle as I moved out of her personal space and retreated back to the door.

"Fine. Yes, I'm hungry. I know a great spot."

She waited for me as I closed up the camper and together we strolled over to my truck parked in front of the house. Something inside me wanted to reach out for her hand, but I suspected it would be crossing a line.

When I first met, or collided, with Autumn, she'd seemed interested in me. Her eyes had glazed over and she'd fisted my shirt, but once I mentioned the flowers were for dinner, her entire demeanor had changed.

"You know," I said to her as I opened the door to the passenger side. She was a tiny thing and without thinking I placed my hands on her waist and lifted her into the truck. My fucking palms sizzled from where I'd touched her. I wondered what it would feel like to touch her bare skin.

"Know what?" she asked as she settled in the seat, adjusting her seatbelt. I'd lost all train of thought by the mere touch of her body. It took me a moment to remember what I was going to say.

Clearing my throat, I replied, "The flowers were for Lily, if you hadn't figured that out."

It was fascinating watching her brows furrow as she connected the dots. It was clear she thought I was going out on a date or meeting up with a woman. And while I adored Brett's wife, our relationship was purely platonic.

"Does that change things?" I added as I leaned closer into the vehicle, my hands bearing my weight on the frame of the truck.

"I. . .I don't know." Autumn's tongue peeked out as she licked at her lips and turned her face forward, away from me. Her profile was just as striking as seeing her head on. "I still hate that you bought my house."

"There is that. But maybe you can see that I'm not such a bad guy."

Closing the door, I strutted around the front of the truck and hopped into the driver's side.

Autumn remained quiet on the drive, only pointing out something when I asked. It didn't bother me, though; I didn't care for a lot of noise and chatter when I drove.

I found a place to park on the street right in front of the place she called The Purple Goat. This town had the funniest names for restaurants. The Purple Goat, The Witch's Brew, and The Naan Stoppers were just a few.

Just as I was about to get out of the truck, Autumn placed her hand on my arm. I could feel the warmth of her palm beneath my light jacket and it made my stomach clench. Fuck, she was turning me on with just the simplest of touches. I wondered if she had any idea the way she was affecting me.

"Look, Colton, the second we walk in there, or anywhere, together, the rumors are going to start. Imagine the gossip rags, but on a smaller scale with people that live just next door."

"But they don't know me?" I countered. Surely, I wasn't going to be the backbone of some small town gossip. That was all just a rumor in itself. *Right?* Brett and Lily had never mentioned anything more than a little smidgen of chatter here or there.

"They don't, but they will. And they know me. My coming home was perceived as somewhat. . .scandalous. I don't want to add fuel to the fire."

Placing my hand over hers, I patted it gently. "I'm a big boy. I can handle it." Not really. I hated false claims, but I could see how it was affecting Autumn. Her eyes were wide and her mouth pinched in the corners. She looked worried and a little miffed that I wasn't being more cautious.

"Okay," she said as she removed her hand and gripped her binder for dear life. She was using it as a shield again, pressing the large white plastic against her chest.

Another yearning came over me as we walked through the entrance to The Purple Goat. I wanted to wrap my arm around her waist, hold her body against me, show everyone she was mine. Especially the dozen or so male eyes that tracked her every movement as we were seated at a booth near the bar.

Autumn fidgeted with the drink menu as I took in the place. It reminded me more of an English pub than a weird eclectic diner, which is what I had been expecting based on the name.

"How'd this place get its name?" I asked Autumn as I grabbed my own copy of the drink menu.

"No idea," she said as she placed her menu and binder aside. Her dancer-like arms came up and rested on the table as she clasped her hands together. "It's been a well-kept secret for decades. Also, there is no regular menu. You eat what the chef makes. And believe me when I tell you that everything is delicious."

"I trust you," I told her as I eyed a local brew that sounded right up my alley.

"Really?" I glanced back at to find Autumn staring at me in both awe and confusion. Her doe-like eyes were wide, making the blue irises sparkle under the dim light of the restaurant. Her plump lips parted forming the shape of a tiny O. Somehow my simple statement had rendered her shocked and speechless.

"Yeah. I knew the moment I met you that I could trust you."

"How?" she whispered, still in amazement.

"I don't know. I just get a good read on people. My coaches always said it helped with my game."

"Huh."

She was still perplexed when an older man came to the table and introduced himself as Harold. He instantly brightened when he saw Autumn sitting across from me. In the two seconds he'd been at the table, I'd already watched him crack a joke at Autumn's expense and tears glistened from the corner of her eyes as she laughed. The giggle was melodic and honest, just like her.

By the time he stepped back to the bar with our drink orders, I couldn't remember what he'd said was being served for dinner. But as I told Autumn, I trusted her judgement.

"So, want to show me your goodies?" I probed as I reached for her binder, only for immediate pain to splinter across my skin as she slapped the back of my hand.

"You could ask nicely."

"Autumn, I would be honored if you could please share with me the well-researched information you found regarding the house." I even threw in my signature smirk at the end. It was usually the way I could get Nina to end whatever argument she was having with me at the moment.

"Um...yeah. Okay."

At least I knew the smolder worked on just about everyone as Autumn opened the binder and turned it to face me. A server placed our drinks on the edge of the table and we both immediately reached for our respective glasses.

As she flipped through the pages, I took note of how much effort it must have taken to find such detailed work. There were images of furniture that would have resided in the house and the pattern of wallpaper that used to decorate the walls. She had multiple images of similar homes and colors that I could draw inspiration from and utilize. Autumn's notes were so detailed that she had ten pages of paint color and wood stains that would achieve a true historic aesthetic.

It may have been a working farmhouse, but it was extravagant nonetheless.

"I've been trying to research the town archives for pictures of the house. Interior and exterior. But I'm not having any luck. The town came after the house."

"This is fascinating," I told her as I sifted through the stacks of pages again.

"You really think so?"

My gaze collided with hers and my breath left my lungs in a whoosh. Somehow, I knew that a chink in her armor had fallen away. I'd taken down one of her walls with a simple compliment.

It left me wondering about some of the men she'd dated in the past. Were they the kind of men that cared for her, or did they look at her as a possession? I knew a lot of guys like that and their girlfriends and wives became shells of themselves.

One of the servers quickly refilled our drinks without us having to ask as I leaned back in the booth.

"So, want to tell me a little bit about yourself, Autumn?" Now that I had a chance to really take her in, I let my gaze casually travel across her body. She was the same size as her sisters, but with a bit more curves. She was a knockout.

Taking a sip of my beer, I let the cool liquid linger in my mouth before swallowing. From behind the glass, I noticed Autumn's eyes glaze as she watched the movement.

"Not much to say, really." She nervously played with the ring of condensation left by the bottom of her own beer glass. Impulsively, I reached out and twisted my finger in hers as she traced the water.

"I'm sure that's not true."

The beautiful waves of hair surrounding her oval face fluttered as she puffed out an exasperated breath of air.

"Well, if you must know. I grew up here. I have three sisters and a half-brother. He's closer to your age, actually.

"I lived in New York for the last few years and worked at Regent Events as an executive event planner. The owner and I dated the last two years until he cheated on me with one of our married clients. They are now living together in the apartment we shared. And here I am. . .homeless and jobless at the ripe age of twenty-four."

"Fucking pathetic," I mumbled and instantly regretted my words as Autumn's body stiffened. Her shoulders pressed against the booth back and she raised her body another few inches. "Excuse me?" She was hostile and pressing for a fight.

"Hey, hey, hey. I wasn't talking about you. I was talking about your ex. What a fucking pathetic asshole. Who the hell would cheat on you? You're smart as fuck and beautiful. That man must have lost his mind."

"Oh...ugh...no, he was quite brilliant, actually," she said hesitantly.

"I don't give a fuck if he was as smart as Stephen Hawking. That man was a fool to leave you. Let alone cheat. Bastard."

"Thank you," she whispered, her body now lax against the booth again. "For...uh...defending me. All of our mutual friends sided with him. Which I guess is for the best, since I find myself in the place I wanted so badly to get out of as a teen. It would be nice if he would stop calling and messaging me, though. He ended things but can't seem to let go."

"Ashfield is amazing. You have no idea what I would have given to grow up somewhere like this. Or anywhere to call a home, really."

Our server chose that moment to bring out our food. A pasta dish of some sort. It sat untouched as Autumn asked me what I meant.

"I grew up in foster care. Even as an infant, no one wanted to adopt me. So, I hopped from foster home to foster home. Hockey was the only home I had.

"Funnily enough, I spent the last few years playing for the New York Renegades."

"I know," she said with a giggle as she took another sip of her second beer and swirled the pasta around her fork. "I may have looked you up."

"Did you now?" I was intrigued. She didn't peg me as the sort to follow any gossip considering how terrified she was of the rumors swirling around the town.

"Don't be so surprised. I needed to know who was living on the land next to ours. For safety reasons, of course. I'm sure you understand."

"Of course."

The rest of the meal was made talking about some of our favorite places to eat in New York City and I argued with her for a solid ten minutes that not a single restaurant could hold a candle to The Purple Goat. I was so adamant I ordered a second plate of the pasta to take home with me.

"You know, you're making me like you," she said as the server brought her a third beer. I stopped after the second since I was driving.

"Is that a bad thing?"

"Maybe," she murmured.

"Hm… we'll have to see what we can do about that." A coquettish smile grew on her lips as she tucked her chin down and finished her meal.

The lights seemed dimmer as the crowd grew during the progressing hour. Bodies now pressed against the edge of the booth as they waited for the bar and darkness had descended upon the town. With a quick glance at my watch, I saw that three hours had passed since we arrived at The Purple Goat. And those three hours had seemed like minutes. This perplexing woman who seemed so defensive of the town and its people enraptured me, but also seemed out of place. I couldn't quite put my finger on it, but there was something about the town and Autumn that brought out a different side of me. And I wanted to learn everything I could about both.

"Ready to get out of here? I bet your dad's waiting up," I joked, but I secretly feared Nash. The man was stronger than most men my own age. And I wanted his approval. Not just as a potential neighbor, but as a friend. Maybe he could guide me into the good graces of his daughter.

"Sure."

Autumn and I stood simultaneously, her gathering her binder and a few extra pages that had untucked themselves from the built in folders, while I tossed a hundred-dollar bill onto the table.

"Mind if I stop by the restroom?"

"Sure." Autumn nodded as she leaned against the wall in the dim hallway connecting to the entrance.

I did my business quickly, noting that there were a lot more people lingering about as I exited. Autumn didn't stand out at first, but thankfully my height allowed me to pick her out. A group of boys that looked about her age surrounded her. Nothing more than teens with a few extra years tacked on.

Fury and possession bubbled up inside me. I didn't know what it was, but I'd claimed Autumn and I wanted everyone to know. It was impractical and cavemanlike, but I couldn't control myself. A roar burst from somewhere inside me and it threatened to break free.

My feet stomped through the wall of men, the group parting without me having to lift a finger. I didn't care if any of them recognized me. All I cared about was the woman with the binder clutched against her body and the asshole with his arm pinned against the wall at her head. There was a familiarity between them, that I was certain, but she carried a look of alarm.

Whomever this person was, she didn't want them that close.

Autumn and I locked eyes, and as I strutted closer to her, I watched her timidness evaporate into temptation. I silently asked for permission. The tiniest bite of her plump bottom lip was all the encouragement I needed. The guy leaning into her had no idea I was staking my claim.

My body slid up against Autumn's, suitor be damned. I towered over the woman and that played in my favor. Reaching out, I placed my large hand just above her breast, sliding up the exposed skin from her v-cut shirt until I cradled her neck and jaw in my palm. With the slightest of pressure, I pulled upward, tilting her face toward mine.

Our eyes locked as I descended my lips in the direction of hers as I forced hers closer. I felt Autumn's body shift onto her toes and I smirked down at her just before our mouths collided.

The kiss started forcefully, but as our eyes closed, I felt Autumn's lips give way to mine. She wanted it as badly as I did. Her body couldn't lie to mine. I always thought hockey had been the only thing of real passion in my life, but now that I'd tasted

Autumn's lips, felt her tongue against mine, I knew differently.

My fingers gripped her jaw a little harder as I slanted her head to get a better angle. I wanted nothing more than to escape into this kiss. She may have given off a cold exterior, but Autumn was all warmth and heat.

"Oh," she said with a jerk, grasping at the binder that was falling from her fingers. Our lips may have parted, but I couldn't quite let her go yet.

"Couldn't help myself," I told her, as if the crowd wasn't still surrounding us.

Sheepishly, she tried to use her hair to cover her face as I reluctantly released her.

"I understand."

She peered up at me from those long lashes and I thought that maybe she did, actually, understand.

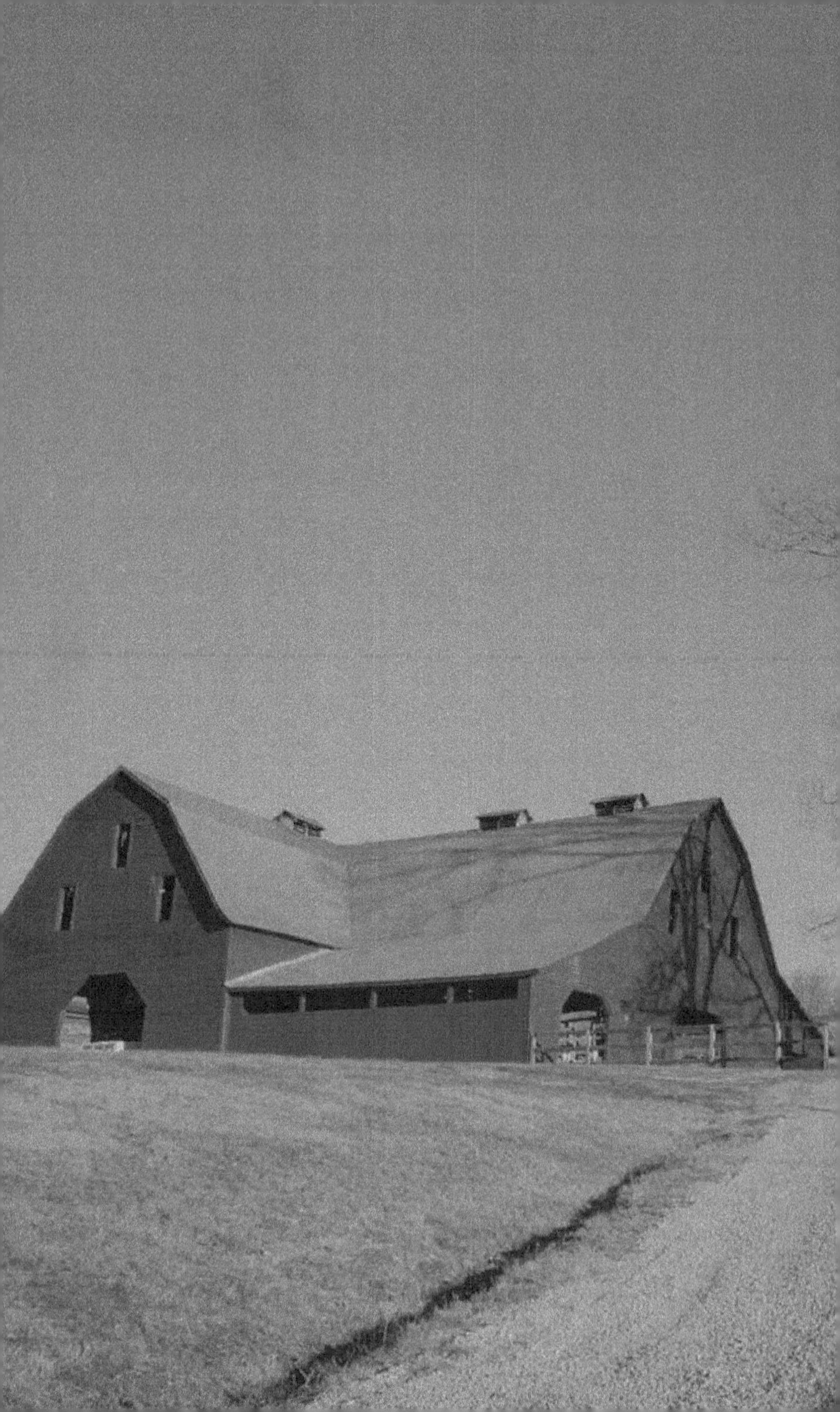

Chapter Ten

Autumn

I'd ignored everyone Saturday after the unexpected, but not unwelcomed, kiss from Colton. It left me confused and out of sorts, like I was trapped in my own skin.

He'd surprised me for sure. And the moment his lips crashed against mine, I was a goner.

"Hello, earth to Autumn." Alex waved her hand in front of my face in an attempt to bring me back to reality. I hadn't been acting like myself since Colton dropped me off at my parents' house the night before.

I'd secretly been hoping that he was going to take me back to his camper, but Colton had been a gentleman and kept his word to my father that he'd see me back home safely. Damn chivalry.

The feel of his hand on my neck and the scorcher of a kiss ran through my mind on repeat all through the night. The sheets felt rough against my skin and the room was two degrees hotter than it needed to be. By the time five in the morning rolled around, I'd been wide awake and exhausted.

That man's mouth had sent me spinning in a whirlwind.

"Sorry," I replied to Alex as I helped unload another batch of vegetables from the back of her truck onto our stand.

I'd been mum about yesterday's events when Alex picked me up this morning, but I knew she could tell something was up. The problem was, I wasn't sure what to tell her. The kiss had been nothing more than a ruse to get me away from the crowd of guys I'd grown up with. Colton must have noticed how uncomfortable I'd looked in the situation.

Right?

It's not like I'd ever ask him. The sexy Adonis had been voted on the Sexiest Man Alive list about a dozen times and he'd dated actual supermodels and A-list actresses. I wasn't unattractive, but I definitely wasn't of their caliber.

"If you don't stop scowling, you're going to scare away all of our customers."

I grumbled under my breath, realizing that I was frowning at the thought of Colton being with another woman.

Somehow this man had festered under my skin and I couldn't shake him free. And I really needed to keep my mind on the target. I was only going to be here three more weeks before I needed to make a decision. I couldn't have him swaying that choice.

"Stupid man," I murmured as I unloaded the last stack of vegetables.

"What was that?" Alex questioned, just as Rory joined our group. Aspen was helping our father and brother with the corn harvest today. The ranch hands and helpers throughout the town had been going at it since the break of dawn this morning.

"Nothing."

"Didn't sound like nothing. Rory, Autumn here is talking to herself. I think it has to do with the tall good-looking hockey player that she was spotted with at The Purple Goat last night."

My heart stopped as shock registered. Even if I wanted to deny anything, I waited for her to continue.

"Hm. . .there is a picture of quite the lip lock on the town's social media page."

"What?" I said in alarm. Fear pecked away at my skin. Fear not just for me, but for Colton. He didn't want to draw any attention to himself. "There's no way. Show me," I demanded as I tried to reach for the phone in Rory's grasp.

"What are you doing?" she shouted as she held the device out of my reach. I really hated being the shorter sister in moments like this.

"Let me see, Rory. This is not good."

"Ah, so there was a kiss." Alex snickered behind me as I continued to jump up and down to grab the phone from Rory.

"Yes, but it wasn't what you're thinking, okay? He did it to get everyone to leave me alone. I need to see the picture. This could be awful for him."

Finally, I was able to grab the device, but only because Rory's arm lowered.

"Hey," she said calmly as I started furiously swiping through the town's social media page that was already on the screen. "Autumn, calm down. There's no picture. I was just joking."

"Rory," I seethed as I gripped my fist around her phone, prepared to haul it across the gravel lot.

"There is a rumor, however, about a mysterious man capturing the attention of one of the Easterly girls. It happened too quickly for anyone to capture the moment for validity."

Too quickly? The kiss had felt like it lasted for at least ten minutes. I could still feel the way his tongue had brushed against mine.

"Why the worry?" Alex asked as she sidled up beside me, draping her arm around my waist. "Was it a bad kiss?"

"No. . .um. . . I mean, it was amazing, guys, but neither of us wants that kind of attention right now. He's here to stay hidden from the reporters. Something to do with his ex and his retirement from the New York Renegades. And, well, I don't need the drama. It was just a kiss to get me out of an awkward situation. Don't read too much into it."

"I didn't know, Autumn. I'm sorry." Both of my sisters apologized, but that didn't help my mood much. I was still bewildered about the entire scenario and why I wanted more.

I never wanted more.

Even with my ex, he had been the one to approach me and push for a relationship. And in high school I dated Travis because he asked and I assumed that was what I should be doing.

"So. . .it was good?" Alex pushed as she leaned against the corner of the stand.

"What was?"

"The kiss, silly. I can't imagine a man like that is bad at anything."

"Alex, I don't want to talk about this here," I said as I side-eyed the growing crowd.

"Too bad. I haven't kissed anyone in what feels like ages."

"And why is that? What happened to that delivery guy?"

"Autumn. I broke up with Brandon a year and a half ago."

I really needed to pay better attention to everyone.

"Sorry." I winced.

"Anyway," she said as she wrapped up a bag of carrots for a customer. "Yes, he was the last one I'd kissed," Alex said, but her cheeks flushed and I knew she was hiding something there. But unlike my sisters, I wasn't going to press her to tell me more. "As you know, it's slim pickings here in Ashfield. And I'm too busy to head to Knoxville every weekend."

"Mom said a bunch of new people have moved to town. Any prospects there?"

Alex narrowed her eyes at me as if I was asking her to climb Mount Everest on a dare.

Rory chose that moment to chime in and asked if I'd met up with any of my friends from my school. They both rolled their eyes when I replied no.

"Autumn, have you done anything since you've been home? It's been an entire week."

I'd always hated being chastised as a child and my sisters weren't making me feel any better. I lived to exceed people's expectations of me. It was the perfectionist in me. Their disappointment was palpable.

"I'm trying, okay? I spent most of last week lamenting over the sale of the house and looking for potential jobs in Knoxville."

"Knoxville?" Rory asked, as Mrs. Hensen approached our stand. The older woman's eyes darted across the vegetable display.

"Yeah. I talked to mom, and if this small town living isn't for me, I thought about living in Knoxville. The city is big enough and Andrew commutes pretty frequently."

"So, you don't think you'll move back to New York City?"

Shaking my head, my sisters wrapped me in their arms, squeezing me tightly against them.

"That's really good news," Rory said, just as Mrs. Hensen asked if this was everything we had. The woman walked away with only a small supply of red bell peppers, disappointment etched on her wrinkled face.

"I really don't want to know what she needs such large produce for," Alex said, her face puckered in disgust.

I was trying my hardest not to think about it either.

The rest of the morning progressed, customers grabbing some vegetables while Rory shopped for some things for herself. Alex and I manned the booth.

We were packing up just as the crowd milling around the lot parted like the Red Sea. I glanced up as I hefted one of the wooden containers off the stand. My gaze traveled up and down his large frame, taking in the way his jeans fit snuggly against his thick thighs, barely containing the muscles. His chest flexed beneath his tight shirt as his arms swung slightly with each step he took. I was mesmerized. So much so I smashed my hip against the corner of the stand while I adjusted the crate in my arms.

"Fuck," I cried out as I nearly dropped the container.

"Autumn, are you okay?" Alex asked as the weight of the heavy crate was lifted out of my grasp.

Rubbing the spot that I knew would turn purple and blue by morning, I nodded that I was fine through a fake, forced smile. I was anything but fine. The sore spot reminded me of the time one of our horses nipped at my arm because I was hiding the sugar cube.

My palm caressed the rough denim that encased my hip and I pressed harder as I watched Colton's slow approach. The eyes of every woman followed his path. I wasn't even sure he knew the attention he garnered. He towered over everyone else in the lot.

"Shit." Furiously I shook my head from side to side, trying to find a way to escape. This man I'd sworn to hate had somehow rewired my circuits and now he was all I could think about. What kind of magic did that man possess? Instead of the hatred I felt yesterday morning, I now felt some sort of excitement when I thought about fixing up the house.

Not with him, of course.

I still wasn't thrilled that my father had manipulated both me and Colton. Sneaky old man.

"What are you doing? You look like a cartoon whose head is going to explode."

"What?" I asked, brushing past her and ducking down behind the truck. The smoky smell of exhaust immediately caused my throat to close up and I forced out a few coughs.

"Autumn, you're being ridiculous," she added, but I was too busy trying to peek around the tire to see how close Colton was. He was stopped by a few townspeople and he chatted with them. Just as I tried to plan my escape, he quickly glanced in the direction of our family farm stand. A gasp escaped my lips as I turned around and slammed my back against the tire.

"Lover boy is coming," Alex tittered.

"Stop. He is not my lover."

"He's also not just a boy. Colton Crawford is definitely all man."

Something unfamiliar bubbled up in my stomach and I anxiously tamped it down. "If you're so interested in the man, why don't you go after him?" I suggested, trying my hardest not to picture my gorgeous sister with the town's newest resident.

She glanced down at me and we exchanged narrowed eyes at each other, egging the other on to make another comment. Any further remarks were halted when Colton stopped in front of our stand where Alex greeted him.

I slapped my hand over my mouth to stifle my gasp, trying not to get caught. Did I believe Colton hadn't noticed me earlier? Not at all. But I held out hope that he would simply believe I had wandered off somewhere else in the market.

Just as quickly as I built up my hope, it was quickly squashed as a large shadow loomed over me.

"Hiding out?" the deep voice said with a chuckle. I peered up at him, the sun shone behind his oversized frame, making it hard to see his face. But those deep brown eyes of his still called out to me. I hated it.

With a huff, I replied, "No."

"Taking a break?"

Instead of a response, I narrowed my eyes at Colton expecting him to take the hint.

"Hiding out from a sexy hockey player that bought your house?"

Mumbling under my breath, I adjusted from my crouched position, taking Colton's offered hand to assist me in standing up.

My palms felt like they'd been submerged in water as I wiped them off on my jeans, and I could only hope that Colton hadn't noticed. "You're not a hockey player any longer. You retired."

I expected the dig to cause him to wince, but I was quickly learning that Colton was full of surprises. Instead, he took a step closer to me and leaned against the side of Alex's truck, folding his arms against his chest. Of course, that move showcased his biceps that threatened to tear his shirt into shreds.

"But you agree, I'm sexy."

There was no point in denying it. The man was damn sexy. The entire country knew that.

"And you bought the house that I wanted," I reminded him, not going into more details about how that house had been my dream. Somehow, the night before I was able to skirt around that topic and focus on the plans to have it approved by the historical society.

"I did," he said sheepishly as he uncrossed his arms and ran one of his large hands across the back of his neck. "But in my defense, I didn't know at the time of the auction."

"Then why did you drop a million dollars on it? It's not worth that amount, you know." That was the part I still hadn't figured out. He had talked about his previous foster mom, but that was it. Either he knew something none of us did regarding the property or he was working with someone else on it. It would devastate my family if he restored the house, only to sell it to a developer.

Colton reached out and swirled a piece of hair that had escaped my ponytail around his finger before tucking it behind my ear. "I don't know. Seems pretty worth it to me."

If I wasn't so angry at the man for the house problem and the kiss at The Purple Goat, I'd probably have melted into a puddle at his feet. Incidentally, my pulse may have picked up when his finger had caressed the side of my cheek.

"We, uh, probably need to talk about the kiss yesterday." I hadn't planned on discussing it at all, but the way Colton was staring at me made me think the kiss hadn't been such a poor decision after all.

"Yeah?" he said with a cocky grin that released a slew of butterflies in my stomach. This man needed to keep his arsenal of sexiness in check. "What about it?"

"There is already talk swirling around here and it won't take long for people to realize it is more than a rumor."

"Really?" he said nonchalantly, as if this was a miniscule problem.

"Yes, really. It won't take long for someone to post something about you and me on social media. And there is probably a picture out there somewhere. Ashfield being a small town, but we're not disconnected from the world."

His broad shoulders moved upward in a shrug and I gasped in shock. The man was here to hide from paparazzi and salvage his reputation. Small town gossip was the last thing that he needed.

"How can you be so flippant about this, Colton?"

"Because it's no big deal."

My breath caught in my lungs. He thought the kiss was no big deal while I'd been lamenting over it for the last twelve hours.

"I want to do it again," Colton added.

"Do what?" I asked, confused.

"Kiss you."

Licking my lips, my confusion grew. "Why?"

He leaned closer to me as he whispered, "Because I like you, Autumn. And I think beneath that grumpy exterior, you like me, too."

Colton was like the sun, drawing me closer to his light, and I couldn't pull myself away. I wanted to be closer to him, but self-preservation kept me tethered in place.

"People will see," I murmured as Colton's lips gently glided along my cheek.

"Everyone left, Autumn. There is no one around," he pointed out and pressed the slightest of kisses at the corner of my mouth. I squeezed my eyes shut and shivered when his hand landed on my hip, brushing his fingertip under the hem of my shirt. The rough pad of his thumb rubbed a circle on my skin.

It took only a split second to turn my head and brush my lips against his. I wasn't sure if Colton was right and I did secretly like him. What I did know was that I liked his kiss. I liked the way his lips felt against mine. And when his tongue swirled around mine, I swore that there was nothing better.

I could chalk it up to his years of experience and that was why the kiss was so memorable, but I knew it was because it was just Colton. He knew he was affecting me in a way that left me wanting more.

And I did.

It seemed like hours had passed when he finally pulled away, but in reality, it had been just seconds. Colton had this way of causing me to lose all sense of time when I was around him.

"Are you two done?" Alex's voice called out from behind me. Shock and embarrassment threatened to overwhelm me as I took a step away from Colton. His hand dropped from my hip and I immediately missed its warmth. Something I was going to have to force myself to forget.

Those walls I'd taken down quickly resurfaced as I realized what my sister had witnessed.

My eyes narrowed into slits as I focused them on Colton, who shook his head.

"I thought you said no one was around," I said angrily. If I knew it wouldn't make me appear like a petulant child, I would have stomped my foot simultaneously.

He may not care about being front page news in the local newspaper, The Ashfield Times, but I sure as hell did.

"She just came back, Autumn. No one saw anything. You don't have anything to be embarrassed about."

Behind his carefree smile, I saw the hint of something else. Something that looked like I'd hurt his feelings.

"Colton. . .I. . ." I began as I reached for his hand, but the words were stuck in the back of my throat. I didn't know what to say to make any of it better.

Thank goodness for Alex's interruption when she jingled her keys and said that she was leaving.

Together, Colton and I both stepped away from the truck. I did my best not to swoon when he placed his hand on my lower back as we waved goodbye to my sister.

The large gravel lot was now empty save for the glorious mountains across the way. Neither of us spoke for a moment, but I relished in the feel of Colton's hand remaining on my back.

A minute passed before he slid his hand around to rest on the dip at my waist as he stepped around to face me, blocking my view of the peaks.

"In actuality, I came to let you know that you left your binder in my truck last night. Your dad had mentioned that you and your sisters had a stand here at the market, so I took a chance that I'd find you here."

"Well, you found me," I said, sounding breathless to my own ears. I didn't run often, but I imagined that was what I'd sound like after a marathon.

"I can grab it and bring it to you if you can tell me where you parked."

"So, you didn't come here just to kiss me again?" I asked, puzzled by the complete change in topic.

"That was just a nice hope. One that I hadn't stopped thinking about since I kissed you yesterday." My gaze dipped downward at the realization that I had affected him the same way that he had affected me. I'd never imagined a kiss could hold that kind of power.

"So, the binder?" he prompted with a gentle squeeze at my waist.

I shook my head slightly and brought my attention back to Colton. A thought launched in my head, one that I was probably going to regret, but I found myself asking anyway.

"We have family dinner on Saturday nights. I know you mentioned you don't cook and I thought, maybe, if you wanted, you could. . .I don't know-"

"Are you asking me to come to dinner tonight?"

"Yes. I mean, no. I mean. . .you could bring the binder to the house. And I know my dad would love to hear-" The man silenced me with another kiss. This one was quick but no less heated.

"Stop talking," he commanded as he pulled back. "I would love to join your family for dinner tonight."

I had a secret suspicion he had chosen those words carefully.

Abruptly, Colton requested to walk me to my car and he followed dutifully until we reached the spot I snagged on the street.

"Dinner is at six," I added as I opened the driver's side door and turned to face him.

Colton's eyes darted around the street, probably taking in the number of people milling about. We weren't secluded as we had been before.

Reaching out, he gently squeezed the hand that hung loosely at my hip, then gestured for me to get in the car with a small tilt of his head. "I'll see you then."

In the car, my hand shook as I pressed the ignition button to start the car and it took all my strength not to turn my head to watch Colton as I pulled out of the parking spot. But I snuck a few glances in my rearview mirror, wondering what kind of mistake I had just made.

From my purse I heard my phone buzz and then the Bluetooth in the car prompted to read aloud the message. Taking a deep breath, I pressed the okay button.

"From Alex. Lucy, you got some explaining to do."

Yeah, I was definitely going to regret asking him to join us for dinner. I just wasn't sure if that was on my behalf or his.

Quickly I darted into the parking lot for Chuck's Grocery and dialed my mom, who picked up immediately.

"Autumn, is everything okay?"

"Yeah. . .um. . .do we need anything from the store?"

"I don't think so. Why?"

"Well, um. . ." I began, knowing I was about to be on the receiving end of my mother's high-pitched squeal. "I invited our new neighbor to join us for dinner."

"Eeep!" And there it was. I had to yank the phone back from my ear until she settled down.

"Mom. Mom. Mom!" I finally shouted to get her attention. She'd started rambling on incoherently about weddings and grandchildren. "Do we need anything else from the store?"

"No, dear. We're having steak kabobs. We have plenty. Oh, I am just so excited. Now hurry home. I can't wait to hear everything." Mom quickly ended the call and I debated on turning around and heading back to the ranch. Instead, I made my way into Chuck's in search of a bottle of wine, knowing that I was going to be subjected to my mother and sisters for the next few hours.

I searched the shelves and snagged a bottle of red that I adored but quickly grabbed a second bottle as well. There was a good chance I was going to need it.

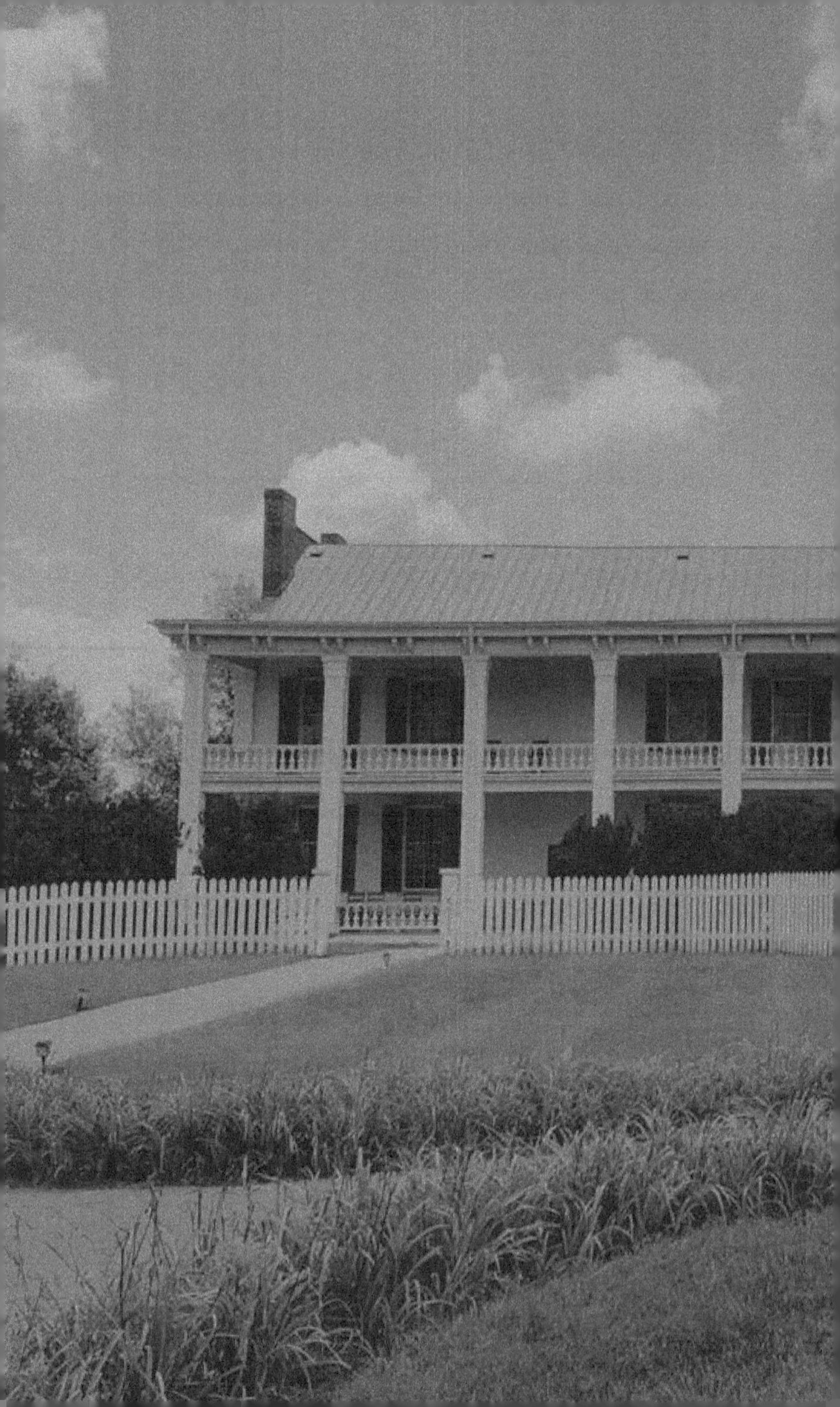

Chapter Eleven

Colton

The sun set just beyond a valley between the mountain ranges. It projected oranges and reds throughout the clouds on the darkening evening, and I couldn't help but relish in its glory. My reasons for ending up in Ashfield were mine and mine alone. I'd left the world believing that it was a way to escape the storm that was brewing in New York related to my ex-girlfriend and retirement, but that wasn't all. Only my agent knew of the last straw that led me to Eastern Tennessee and that alone was a fluke.

I'd considered disclosing the secret to Brett, but the surprise was still something I was trying to wrap my head around. But it was eating me up inside. I needed advice or just someone I could talk to. Someone that wouldn't have an ulterior motive.

Glancing up at the large farmhouse as I crested the dirt path between our two properties, I thought, *I need someone like Autumn.*

It was obvious that the woman hated the fact that I bought the home her family had once owned. Of course, I had no way of knowing that at the time. Her father had been understanding and was happy that it was going to be lived in again, even if it wasn't by his family. But convincing Autumn of that was something I'd have to save for another day, maybe when we were on better footing.

While I knew she didn't want to like me, she was fighting against wanting me. When I stole the kiss from her at The Purple Goat, I was taking a chance that she wouldn't push me away and it surprised me when her lips had parted and welcomed me in return.

There was chemistry between us. One I hoped to examine if we had the chance, but first I needed her to warm up to me. The entire town did from what I could gather.

It didn't take long in Ashfield to learn that everyone was surprised by Autumn's return and the reason for it. Heck, just a trip to the hardware store gave me more than I wanted to know. But no one was convinced that she was going to stay. There was a betting pool on how long before she hightailed it out of dodge.

Which left an ache in the pit of my stomach.

Autumn had warned me about small town gossip and the rumor mill, but witnessing it firsthand was something else. Now I knew why she was so hesitant to let anyone in.

The house grew larger as the distance between me and the property shrank. A few combines sat vacant in the fields while one continued to work just beyond my point of view.

Nash had mentioned that the harvest would last about a week. I secretly hoped he'd let me try one of the combines. It was an oversized tractor that made me think back to being a three-year-old obsessed with monster trucks.

My truck crossed the dirt path onto the solid gravel drive that led to the front entrance of the Easterly estate. Immediately, I noticed Autumn's red sedan parked in front of one of the garage bays. I wondered if they parked vehicles inside or used it as storage as many of my foster parents had.

Just as I put the truck in park, the front door was flung open and the youngest daughter shouted something before stepping out onto the porch.

Slowly I approached, taking in the way the girl eyed me. Not in one of interest, but of preservation. It didn't take a rocket scientist to know that she was looking out for her family, which was interesting since she was the baby of the clan.

"Hi," I said as I took the first step. "I didn't get to introduce myself the other day. I'm Colton Crawford." Warmly, I held out my hand.

She blatantly ignored my greeting as she crossed her arms against her chest. "You're early."

I didn't need to glance at my wristwatch to know that she was right, but I'd planned it that way, hoping to get some alone time with Autumn before dinner.

Dropping my hand back to my side, I switched my hold of the wine bottle I'd brought over, but left the binder tucked under my arm.

"I am," I said.

"She won't like it."

Shrugging, I added, "She doesn't like me much, anyway."

"That's true, though I suspect otherwise." I suspected the girl kept tabs on everyone in the family and used it to her advantage when needed.

"What makes you say that?"

Pushing off from the porch railing, she moved toward the door. "No reason." Once she stepped over the threshold, her voice took on a volume that left me cringing. "Mom, our neighbor is here."

"Thanks," I murmured, standing in the same spot on the porch.

She turned around and held the door open for me with a single arm, the slide of her eyes gesturing me to come inside. I followed obediently. "Aspen, by the way."

The door slammed behind me as I stepped inside the house for the second time. "Nice to meet you, Aspen."

Marisol came around the corner and greeted me with a warm hug, her small arms wrapping around mine, pinning them to my body. "So glad to have you, Colton. Let me take that bottle and you can join Nash in the living room. Dinner will be ready soon."

"Thanks, Mrs. Easterly."

"It's Marisol. Autumn will be down shortly."

As if she heard her name, Autumn descended the stairs, surprise in her eyes as she registered my appearance in the foyer.

"Oh, hey," she said, sounding almost nervous.

"Hey," I returned. We stared at each other until the awkwardness became too much and I remembered what was under my arm at the moment. "I, ugh, brought back your binder," I said, holding it out to her.

"Thanks," she replied as she took it from me and placed it on a small table in the foyer.

"I hope you don't mind, but I skimmed through it before I came over. What's the stuff in there about a barn?"

I noticed the small packet at the back of the binder, tucked between two folders containing information about the historical submission for my house. It was as if she had hidden it there for something else and it left me curious since I didn't have a barn like that on my newly acquired land.

"Oh...that...it's um," she started, then tucked some of the loose waves of her hair behind her ear. "It's just something I thought about tackling while I was home."

From what I had gathered, it was a barn that was in decent shape but needed some cosmetic work in the hopes of turning it into a wedding venue. The idea had merit and I could immediately see Autumn tackling a project like that with her family if it gave her a reason to stay in town. I knew it thrilled Nash to have her home. I secretly suspected that was why he pushed us to work together on the house. The Easterly parents were trying their hand at matchmaking.

"Tell me more," I replied as I reached out for her hand. My body craved her touch knowing she was so close. My skin practically itched for the feel of hers.

Autumn glanced down as my fingers brushed against hers and I was afraid she was going to snatch her hand away, but in typical Autumn fashion she surprised the hell out of me as she allowed my hand to intertwine with hers.

"Maybe later," she whispered, her eyes still glued to our joined hands.

"I'll make the time," I told her and her head jerked back to face me. Confusion was written all over her expression and it left me wondering if anyone had ever made the time for her. I assumed with her ex that his priority was himself and it was clear that with four siblings, her parents' time was minimal, not that it was their fault.

"I'll make the time, Autumn," I repeated confidently.

"I. . .er-"

"Dinner is ready!" Marisol shouted from the kitchen and both Autumn and I released a sigh. Autumn's probably in relief, mine from being interrupted.

I wasn't surprised when Autumn released my hand as if it had electrocuted her. She gestured for me to follow her, and I couldn't help but lock my eyes on the gentle sway of her hips. She wore dark jeans that looked as if they'd been painted on her skin. I was hypnotized as she took each gentle step. I wasn't even sure that she was aware that I was under her spell.

I was so entranced by her I almost missed the collective group sitting at the table. Her three sisters sat at the table along with their father. Five other men sat in the chairs that surrounded the oversized wooden table. One slightly resembled Marisol and I wondered if that was Autumn's half-brother. He'd only been mentioned in passing, but I was curious of how that came to be. It was clear that he was closer to my age than his sister's.

"Oh, good. Everyone is here," Marisol said, as she began setting out platters of food onto the table. "Autumn, you and Colton can take the two chairs next to Andrew."

"Yes, ma'am," Autumn said as she headed toward two empty chairs seated at the middle of the table, next to the man I suspected to be the half-brother. I wasn't surprised that she headed toward the chair that would seat her next to her mother, leaving me next to the sibling.

Before she could do it herself, I tugged out her chair and motioned for her to sit, earning me a scowl in the process.

Taking my own seat, I introduced myself to Andrew, returning the squeeze in his handshake.

Marisol finally took her seat and the group began passing around the platters of vegetables and meat. Patiently, I waited my turn and took in the surrounding conversations. The farmhands were discussing the loads of harvested corn they'd collected the last couple of days and how much longer they'd need to be out on the field.

Beside me, Autumn ignored her sisters trying to make conversation, instead focusing on adding mashed potatoes to her plate.

"So, you play hockey?" Andrew said, drawing my attention away from Autumn as she handed me the bowl she finished using.

Helping myself to the starchy goodness, I replied, "I did. I officially retired at the end of the last winning season two years ago."

"Oh, what team did you play for?"

Just as I was about to answer, Autumn chimed in with a stern tone. "Andrew, you know what team he played for. I can guarantee when Mom mentioned he was coming to dinner you ran some sort of background check on him, amongst other things."

Autumn moved her gaze from her brother over to me as she added, "He's trying to be the big protective older brother and failing at it. Not that it's needed."

"Why isn't it needed?" I asked as I passed Andrew the potatoes and took the green beans from Autumn's grasp.

"Because I was being nice to our new neighbor."

It stung to hear her say that she invited me just to be nice.

Thankfully, no one had to see the way her words affected me when Alex piped in across the table. "Oh, were you just being nice when you let Colton kiss you twice?"

"Alex," Autumn gasped at the same time Marisol scolded, "Alexandra! That was unnecessary. I'm sorry, Colton. My daughters seemed to have lost their manners along the way."

Both women tucked their chins as they continued loading their plates.

"That's okay, Mrs. Easterly. I never had siblings of my own, but I imagine that it's like this in most families."

"Were you an only child, dear?"

"I was in foster care most of my life."

"Oh, Colton. I'm so sorry. I didn't mean-"

"That's okay," I said, reaching for a hearty steak kabob. "It's common knowledge at this point. I'm envious of your family. It seems like there is a lot of love here."

Noticeably, the table grew quiet, but no one seemed to touch their food.

"God, man," Andrew whispered beside me and I felt embarrassed for whatever had settled over the family. I wasn't sure what I had said that left them all out of sorts. Not even Nash would make eye contact.

The scratching of chair legs across the hardwood floors drew everyone's attention to Autumn. "Wine. Does anyone else want wine?"

Hands shot up from around the table and I eagerly agreed to help Autumn in the kitchen. Together we poured the wine, chuckling when we realized we had both bought the same brand at the store. It definitely made it an easier process to divvy out.

Once the wine was served and the alcohol flowed through our veins, the chatter around the room filled the open space. The sisters and farmhands joked around while Andrew asked me about being a sports celebrity.

It felt. . .like home. There was a time where all I wanted as a child was to feel like I was accepted and wanted. Ms. Cathy had done her best to include all of us kids, but it was a strain on her and her family. I could easily imagine the large gathering of the Easterly family around a plump, juicy turkey at Thanksgiving. Or the girls excitedly bouncing around a Christmas tree. It was something I was determined to give myself in the future. A future I hadn't really thought much about.

Not until the letters began arriving.

And now, it seemed, the text messages if the buzzing of my phone was any indication.

As Marisol began passing out pieces of an apple pie, I reached into my pocket to check the message from an unknown number.

"Do you need to get that?" Autumn asked from beside me, leaning over in her chair to whisper.

Quickly, I shoved the phone back into my pocket, knowing that I was going to have to deal with it later and dismissed Autumn's concern.

The pie was one of the best things I'd ever eaten, and I made sure to let Marisol know. I left out the part where I wanted to smear the pie filling over Autumn's body and lick up each morsel from her skin.

Nash and Andrew began cleaning the table, and I offered to assist, but the matriarch brushed away my invitation.

"Next week I'll have to have you all stop by the house," I said as Marisol poured herself another glass of wine.

"How is it coming along? I imagine it will take months just to get it to living condition, especially with the storm system moving this way this week."

"Well, it helps that I'm paying for twenty-four-hour construction. The contractor estimated he'd have the place habitable in three weeks at that rate. Though I suppose we'll lose a couple days if the storm is as bad as they're calling for. But the exterior will be solid by Wednesday. The plumbing and electrical are getting tackled the following week."

"That's fascinating. Hopefully, Autumn can help you along the way."

Pulling my gaze from Marisol and toward her daughter, I replied, "She already has been."

"Dad," Autumn interrupted as she stood from the table. "I'm going to take Colton to the barn. Can we take the Polaris?"

"Sure, honey. The keys are hanging in the mudroom," Nash called out from the sink where he was loading the dishwasher.

"Come with me," the temptress said and I eagerly followed. Hell, I was so infatuated with Autumn, I'd follow her just about anywhere.

She hopped in the driver's seat of an off-road vehicle that I definitely planned on ordering for myself when I got back to my trailer and I took the passenger seat. Together we rode in silence, our bodies rocking back and forth across the uneven terrain, until ten minutes later we came upon a clearing where I recognized the barn from the pictures.

Autumn parked the UTV in front of a barrel of hay and turned off the vehicle. A brisk wind picked up as we exited the vehicle and it swirled Autumn's hair in its midst. She looked like a warrior princess at that moment and I was entranced.

"I always knew that I wanted to be an event planner. When I was in high school, I'd set my heart on NYU, because if you could make it in New York, you could make it anywhere, right?" she said dryly.

"But I knew my chances were slim and I would need a backup. I could go to school locally and make something of this barn. I could see it so clearly, the weddings, the retirement parties, the birthdays. It was the perfect space for Ashfield. Until recently, we didn't even have a social hall for the town; that was added onto the church a couple of years back.

"I saw it all and I had a plan on how to make it happen. When I was wait-listed for NYU, I started putting all the pieces together to make this plan work. I was determined. But then I got the notification that I was accepted to my dream school and that's all it took before I set my sights on my original plan. Plan B was great, but Plan A was what was going to help me make a name for myself."

"And then your ex screwed you over."

"Bingo. Despite what people think, I'm not here licking my wounds. I was the first couple of days, but I saw that he did me a favor. Max took every idea that I had and sold it as his own. Every client I reined in, he took on. I felt more like a salesperson than an event planner."

"So, now's your chance to do something great for yourself."

"Maybe," she said, turning to face me. "I promised my dad I'd give it a month in town to see if I could make roots here, to feel settled here before I took a step like this. It would cost a lot to overhaul the place, advertise, get staff, all of that."

"Your dad's a smart man."

"He's the best. And he's right. I've been here a week and I'm still not certain I could make a go of living here again."

"What's your plan C?"

"Plan C?"

"Yeah. It's clear you have something else up your sleeve."

She huffed out a deep breath and I wondered what gave her such worry. "I've been applying for jobs."

"That's not so bad. You could still be close."

"Yeah, but not all of them are local. I've put in applications all over."

"What for? What are you running from?"

"That's the thing. I have no idea. I don't know why I have this burning desire to prove myself. My family loves me just the way I am."

Her conflict pained her, I could see it clear as day. Her body was tense as she spoke about the choices she was making and the agony in her voice was pure.

"Do you want my opinion?" I asked her, surprised when she sullenly responded yes.

"I think the notion of living in a big city gives you the opportunity to hide away from everybody. You're young and still figuring out who you are, and the thought of failing at that probably terrifies you. Here, you can't hide. Everyone knows everything. If you fail at this venture, it doesn't just reflect on you, it reflects on your entire family."

Autumn rung her hands together as she absorbed my words.

"Here's the thing though, Autumn," I added, taking a step closer to her and placing my rough hands on the soft skin of her cheeks. "I see you."

"You do? What do you see?" she whispered.

"I see a woman that works tirelessly to make those she loves proud. And I think if the perfect job comes along, then you should take it. Your family won't be upset so long as you're happy. But I also think you need to let go."

"Let what go?"

"Everything."

The urge to bend down and kiss her was strong, and by the way Autumn's eyes glazed over, I could tell that she was expecting it as well. It took every ounce of energy to pull back and drop my hands back to my sides.

"Want to show me around?" I asked, hoping that I didn't just cause any forward motion I was making with Autumn to fall back.

"Um...yeah."

The barn was much larger than I expected, with a second-story loft space used for storage and a non-working kitchen from when the ranchhands used to stay on property. Overall, I could see the appeal of Autumn's vision.

"You know," I said. "If you decide to continue with this venture, I'd be happy to help. I can even loan some of my crew for any serious work that needs to be done."

I wasn't sure what made me offer my services, but as the idea settled in my mind, I was happy with the choice.

"You'd do that?"

"Sure." I shrugged as we headed back to the UTV. The sun had set and darkness blanketed the sky.

"What's in it for you?"

Just as she tried to step toward the driver's side of the vehicle, I reached out and tugged her against me, wrapping my arm around her slight body.

"Time with you."

It had been torture walking around the barn for the last thirty minutes without being able to touch her. My body ached to taste her again. And now here in the darkness, I took that opportunity.

My mouth crashed against hers and as my tongue begged for entrance, it surprised me how willingly she opened up for me. My sweet obsession wanted me just as much as I wanted her.

Autumn's hands clawed at my back over the thin cotton shirt I wore. I almost wished I hadn't been wearing it so I could wear the scratches from her with pride.

My hands roamed around her hips until they rested on the globes of her bottom, my palms squeezing the round flesh in my palms. Fuck, her ass felt better than I imagined it would.

Our tongues danced against each other as we savored the kiss. Like a vampire in the night, I craved the soft skin of her neck. I wanted to feel her pulse beating against my lips. I wanted to smell the sweet scent of her perfume. I wanted to mark her.

Begrudgingly, I broke the kiss and placed the softest of pecks across her jaw as I made a path toward the sensitive spot just below her ear. I took delight in her soft moan as I nipped at the skin and then ran my tongue over the assault.

"I want you, Autumn," I told her as I continued to nibble at her neck between kisses. Her body grew languid in my arms as she moaned. Her hips moved in the tiniest of circles against my rock-hard erection and my fingers flexed against their hold on her backside.

"Colton," she groaned and I found myself falling into an abyss at the sound of my name from her lips. She was so responsive and all I'd done was given some attention to her neck. I couldn't imagine how she would react if I gave that attention to every other part of her body.

"Hold on, baby."

Lifting Autumn, she wrapped her legs around my waist and my cock threatened to explode like I was a teenager when I felt the warmth of her center against my jeans. In a few steps, I placed her on the edge of the Polaris, balancing her body in my arms as my lips never left their assault on her neck.

Autumn's hand dove into my hair as I moved to the opposite side of her neck, exploring the spots that made her body tremble in response.

I knew I should stop, but I was so lost in her I barely heard her calling my name again. This time with urgency.

"Colton, stop. Someone's coming."

"What?" I asked in a lusty haze, my body aching as I pulled back from her, allowing her to jump down from the vehicle.

"I can hear another UTV coming."

The lights of another vehicle crested the hill and illuminated the space around us. Thankfully, my erection had quickly subsided at Autumn's words.

"Yeah," I murmured as I took my seat.

"Colton, I. . ." she started as she took her own seat and turned on the ignition.

"Look, Autumn. You know I like you and I want to spend more time with you. Maybe outside of helping me with the house, you can show me some things around town? It could be a way to remember the things you like here."

"You want to spend time with me?"

"I thought I had been very clear about it."

Autumn had the decency to wince just as Nash pulled up beside us.

Her father back looked between the two of us and clearly put the pieces together.

"I don't know if I should beat you or thank you," he said directed to me and then turned his vehicle around.

The rest of our conversation came to an end as we followed her father back to the house.

Nash never mentioned anything more when we returned to the house. I thanked her parents for dinner and said goodbye to her siblings as I made my way from the house back to my truck. I was surprised when Autumn followed me out.

"About earlier," she began, but I cut her off with a press of my lips against her cheek.

"The ball's in your court, Autumn. I'm working on sanding down some of the original woodwork this week if you're interested. Just stop by the house. You know where to find me."

It took all my strength to leave her standing there beside my truck with a look on her face of confusion and hurt.

I was too old for games and knew what I wanted. I didn't need a relationship, but I wasn't opposed to having her warm my bed at night. And I did enjoy her company. When she spoke of the things she was passionate about, her entire body lit up and it was hard not to want to be surrounded by that desire.

I could only hope that Autumn's body craved mine the same way I yearned for hers because I wasn't sure I could be around her and not want to put my hands on her. Autumn left me with an unquenchable appetite and I worried she was the only woman that could feed that hunger.

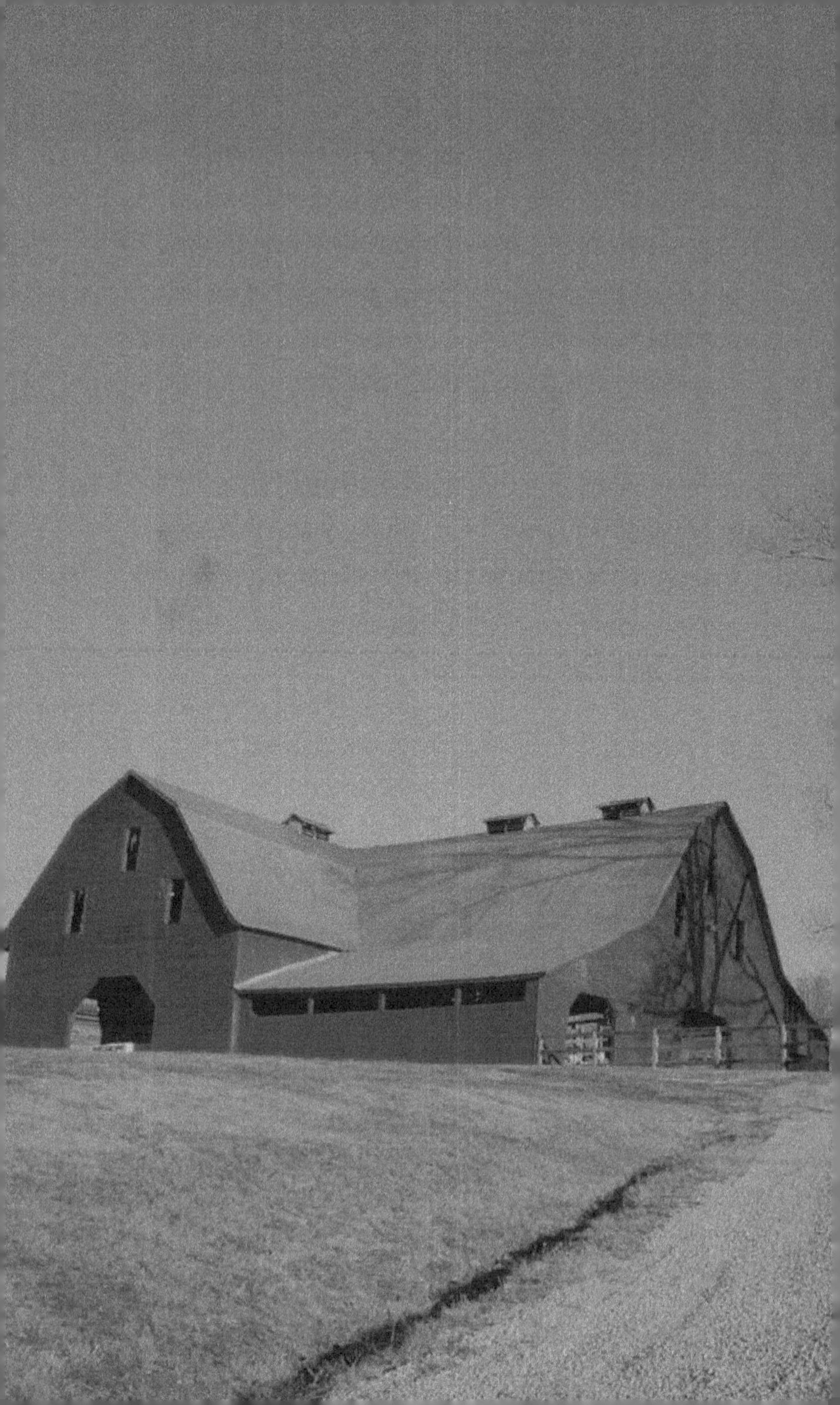

Chapter Twelve

Autumn

I wasn't sure how I had managed to go three days without seeing Colton, but I knew it had taken every ounce of willpower I possessed to not drive to his house.

To keep my mind off of him, I'd spent Sunday with Alex at the bar and helped her run inventory. She gave me hell for running Colton off. Monday, I volunteered to help in Rory's classroom, admiring the way she interacted with the first graders. I was so proud of my sister for the way she knew exactly what to do and say with the kids. And Tuesday Aspen caught me sulking in the living room and asked if I wanted to help her get supplies for the farm at the store. It hadn't taken long, but it was nice to take my mind off the intrusive thoughts swirling in my mind.

What if I stayed and failed? What if I left and something happened to someone in the family? What if Colton met someone?

The latter plagued my mind for hours before dawn had risen.

But here I was now, standing beside my car, watching as fifteen or so men worked around the house I'd once imagined myself raising a family in. I hadn't been back over since Friday when Dad had tricked me into staying and it surprised me to see how far along it had come.

They cleaned the bricks and put fresh mortar in the spots that had begun to crumble. New windows were in the process of being installed, and the foundation looked as if it had been re-leveled.

Things that I was sure took weeks or months to accomplish only took days when you had millions of dollars to throw around.

I gave myself a mental pep talk as the sound of a jackhammer echoed across the land.

"Can I help you?" a voice with a hint of a drawl said from behind me.

"Hi, I'm looking for Colton Crawford?"

The man looked at me skeptically, and I wondered if he was worried that I was a fan or reporter. Leave it to Colton to have security on site.

"I'm his neighbor. Autumn Easterly. And I brought him a pie."

After a moment, the man chuckled and advised me that Colton was in the house in the library.

"Thanks."

Grabbing the small duffle bag from the back seat, I made my way toward the house, inhaling the scent of fresh wood as I went.

Plaster had been removed in many of the rooms revealing the framing behind the walls. I had thought I'd be upset to witness the changes like the taking down of walls or ripping up the floors, but instead I felt a sense of delight. Colton wasn't doing any of those things to destroy the home's bones. It was to better her. New electrical wiring was being installed and better fixtures for the plumbing. It was all for a reason.

"Colton?" I called out when there was a break in the construction noise. When there was no response, I made my way back toward the wing of the house where he had pointed out the library on Friday.

"Colton?" I said again as I stepped into the room, only to find the space filled with dirty sheets and tools.

"Shoot," I murmured as I adjusted my hold of the duffle bag in my hand and rested the glass baking dish against my hip.

Inspecting the space, I could imagine the wood with a glorious walnut hue filled to the brim with books and knickknacks, a desk in the center, and lush reading chairs beneath the window. The room screamed dark academia and the need to get my hands on the room was powerful.

"Autumn?"

Abruptly, I spun on my heel to face Colton, nearly losing my balance in the midst. He reached out and gripped my arm to steady me.

"Colton, hi."

"Hi," he said with a hesitant smile.

He was busy wiping his hands on a rag, but my focus was solely on the fact that the man wore no shirt. I'd imagined all the ways his chest and abdomen would look uncovered. I'd even seen a few pictures online from magazine shoots Colton had taken part in. But none of that did justice to the absolute Greek god standing before me. My tongue itched to taste the skin and I wanted to trace the ridges and valleys of his eight-pack.

"Can I help you, Autumn?" he said as he moved around me, heading toward the tools in the center of the room.

"Oh. The um. . .man outside said I could find you in here."

"Well, you found me," he said flippantly as he tossed the rag over his shoulder.

"I, er, wanted to apologize for how I acted the other night."

"Really?" he said, peering at me from over his shoulder.

"I baked you an apple pie. My mother's recipe."

"You bake?" he said in surprise.

Wordlessly, I held out my peace offering, then added, "I also came to help."

"Well, I won't turn down either. I'll run the pie over to the trailer and then you can help me sand these shelves down."

"Sure."

As Colton sauntered away with the pie, I grabbed a few things from the makeshift tool bag I had put together this morning. I'd done a few projects around my parents' home, but nothing of this magnitude.

The sound of a screen door slamming alerted me to Colton's approach.

"The wind is really starting to pick up out there. That storm they're calling for is going to be brutal."

"Yeah, they've issued some hail and tornado watches," I added as I turned to face Colton.

"What is that?" He pointed at the canvas toolbelt I was wearing as I finished tying the straps around my waist.

"A toolbelt?"

"That is not a toolbelt." Walking over to a massive leather and suede contraption draped on a sawhorse, Colton said, "This is a toolbelt. It will actually hold tools."

"Well, this is what I had, so it will have to do," I said stubbornly.

It was clear that Colton didn't want to argue. He shrugged and then went to work showing me how to use the small orbital sander and how to work on the smaller details of the moldings.

My legs and back ached after the first shelf, but I felt like I'd accomplished something. It felt good. And as I glanced over to watch Colton working on a shelf at the other end of the room, it felt even better to be working beside him.

"How many more of these do we have?" I asked. When I arrived, I'd noticed that a few had already been worked on.

"Four and then we can go test some of the stains to see what color you think will work best."

The contractor came by not shortly after and announced that his crew was packing up all of their items in the storm's wake and would return the next day. Colton thanked the man graciously for staying onsite as long as they had.

I'd lost track of the hour as I moved onto the next shelf.

"Hey, want to go check out the stains while there is still some good natural lighting?" Colton asked and I eagerly jumped up from my crouched position only to groan in pain. I was definitely going to be sore the next day.

"Yeah. Let me go grab my binder from the car and we can look at some pictures I found of woodwork from the same time period."

We went in opposite directions when we exited the house, and I took a moment to look off in the distance toward the looming clouds in the sky. The storm was still a way off, but it was going to be brutal. Some fluke of nature that had dumped snow in the southern half of the western United States like Arizona and had unleashed countless tornados in her war path.

I quickly grabbed the binder filled to the brim with new goodies I had researched online before heading over.

The mud and grass sloshed underneath my feet as I forged a path around the house toward the area Colton had set up with some pieces of the molding we were going to use to test the colors of stain. I could see he had five different shades set up.

"Hey," I said as I approached. I greedily ate up the view of Colton's back. "So, let's see what you've got?"

"Enough to keep you busy, but let's talk about the stain."

It took a second before Colton's words registered and I felt my cheeks flame under his watchful eye.

"I do love when your cheeks turn that color."

"Really?" I asked as he started prying the tops off the multiple stain colors he had chosen. "Why is that?"

Grabbing a brush, he dipped it into the first stain, the darkest of the colors as he said, "Because I imagine what color your other cheeks would turn under my palm."

The man didn't even raise his head as he stroked the brush back and forth on the wood, spreading the stain.

"You shouldn't say those things," I whispered, hating the way my husky voice betrayed me. I absolutely wanted to feel his hands on me, but I knew nothing could come of it. There was a good chance that neither Colton nor I were staying in this town. I had potential jobs, or at least the desire to live in a bigger city like Knoxville, and Colton had bigger and better things as a sports star.

"Doesn't mean I can't imagine it. Now, what do you think of that one?" he asked as he moved to the next color, one with a redder undertone.

"No. It's too modern and the one you're doing now is too red. Let me show you a picture of what I was thinking."

Opening the binder, I came to the page I'd added that morning and moved to Colton's side to show him.

"You see this stair wainscotting? That color is the closest I could find to the natural color we should be going for." When Colton remained quiet, I began slowly flipping the pages, showing him the other examples that I found using the same stain color. "What do you think?"

Instead of answering, Colton placed the brush gently on the top of the can and turned to face me. "You really enjoy this, don't you?"

"Enjoy what?"

"Bringing things to life. It's why you enjoy event planning. Taking an idea and watching it come alive. I can see why you were so excited about buying this place."

"Well...um..."

"Sorry, I didn't mean anything by it. You should just know that I appreciate all the work you've put into this."

"Thank you," I whispered, safely securing the pictures back into the binder. "So, do you think you have something like that color?"

"Maybe not exact, but something close. But let's look at all of them. You never know if inspiration will strike."

Agreeing, I watched as he laid down the four other stain colors. Two struck me right away and I let Colton know the ones I favored. Thankfully, he agreed and we closed up the rejects.

As we cleaned up the mess, I suggested we take the stained pieces inside before we made a final decision to see how they would look in the space. Colton was hesitant since there was no electrical yet, but there was enough sun from the day where we could get an idea of what it would look like.

We gathered everything outside because of the impending storm that was approaching faster than I had expected. Driving back home was going to be hell. I'd never enjoyed driving in the rain, let alone a storm of this magnitude. Even though my parents were literally next door, I was already growing anxious, but I tried not to let Colton know.

"Let me start the generator really quick, just in case we want to see what it looks like under lights."

"That's a good idea," I said as I followed him inside with the molding tucked under my arms and two stain cans stacked in my other hand.

Soon the house filled with the sound of buzzing from the generator as it kicked in as I made my way back to the library. The sound of my shoes pattering on the floor meshed with the buzz, reminding me of the clatter of a gentle rain. Glancing out one of the large paned windows, the angry clouds closing in reminded me that the storm was going to be anything but gentle.

I could hear Colton's heavy footsteps advancing as I set the items in the library.

I should probably text my parents and let them know where I am, I thought to myself.

Colton didn't say anything as he moved the molding toward the window to see how they looked in the natural light.

"What do you think?" he asked, taking a step back and almost barreling into me as I came to examine our choices.

I set the binder on one of the open shelves of the bookshelf and narrowed my gaze at the two pieces. One of the colors spoke to me like a siren's call and I could only hope that Colton felt the same. The other reminded me of spilled red wine that had dried on an oak floor.

It wasn't my choice to make, so as I glanced up at Colton, I waited to hear his response. Though I was willing to fight tooth and nail for him to consider my choice.

His eyes darted back and forth between the two. Those powerful hands and rough, callused fingers rubbed against the scruff of his chin as he considered his options.

"It's got to be the one on the left, right?"

My eyes grew double their size at his suggestion. "What?"

"Yeah. Clearly, the redder stain is the obvious choice. Look how lively it is in the space." Colton's hand splayed out as if his choice needed no explanation.

"I'm sorry, but are you serious right now?" I asked, fists balled on my hips as I stared him down. "You cannot tell me that you think the stain on the left is a better choice than the one on the right?"

"What? You're joking, right? The left is so much livelier."

"Colton. That stain looks like dried blood on the floor. You cannot stain your entire library that color."

"You're right, I can't stain my entire library that color."

"Colton, we need to have a serious discus. . .wait, what?"

"I'm just messing with you, Autumn. The left looks awful in here. The one on the right is the best one," he said with a chuckle, the joy from his joke illuminating his face. I loved his smile and I wanted nothing more to see it every day.

Shoving his bicep with all the strength I could muster; I frowned when the man barely budged. "That was mean. I thought you were going nuts, Colton. That color is awful."

"It really is. I immediately knew it was wrong for this space, but I couldn't help but play a joke on you a little bit."

"Well, at least I know you don't need your eyes checked. Let's turn on a light to see how it looks."

Colton quickly moved the molding we chose away from the window and under one of the lamps he'd brought into the space. It was a floor lamp that looked like it had spent some time in a bachelor pad or two.

Even under the gross white light, the color looked amazing.

"Nice job, partner. I think we have successfully chosen a stain for the entire house."

Gleefully, I bounced in place while I clapped. "This is so exciting! I can't believe we made such a big decision already."

"I like that, you know," Colton said as he set down the wood against the pile of sheets and turned to face me.

Calming down, I asked, "What's that?"

"That you said we," he replied as he stepped closer until our bodies were inches apart. His deft fingers reached out and quickly untied the straps of the toolbelt wrapped around my waist while never taking his eyes off mine. He was going to kiss me again. I could see it in the lusty haze in his eyes. I was certain it mirrored my own. We were alone in the house I'd dreamed of living in with no one to interrupt us.

Except for Mother Nature.

Lightning and thunder cracked outside the house, startling both of us.

"Shit, that was close. I need to cut off the generator and gather any loose items from outside."

"Let me help."

Quickly, we dashed from the house and I grabbed any loose buckets or tools I found sitting outside and tucked them into the house for safety. Just as I did my last pass around the house, the sky opened up. Within seconds my clothes were soaked through and I was certain my blonde hair was nothing more than a gross rat's nest. My waves had a way of betraying me whenever they got wet.

"Autumn!"

I heard my name from behind the house and I scurried from around the front as I called out Colton's name. I wasn't sure he could hear me over the sound of the thunder clapping in the sky.

Twice I tripped in the mud, my clothes now covered in muck as I found Colton anxiously looking around as he hollered my name.

"Autumn!"

"Colton! I'm here!" I yelled back. The relief on his face when he saw me would be something I would never forget, but as lightning lit up the sky, I was going to have to think about that at another time.

Doing my best to run on the damp, sloshy ground that reminded me of the quicksand I'd been so terrified of as a child I headed toward the house, only for Colton to grab my arm and tug me toward his trailer on the opposite side of the backyard.

"We need to go to the trailer!"

"What? Why?"

"I'll explain when we get inside," he said as we ran through the buckets of rain. Each drop stung as it collided with my skin, and I knew that I'd have welts in the morning.

Colton grabbed my hand as the wind whipped up around us, pushing my smaller body around like nothing more than a rag doll. I stumbled a few times and Colton did his best to help me along. When the trailer came into view, I released a sigh of relief. It wasn't even but two hundred yards or so from the house, but it felt like miles with the wind and rain. Not to mention the lightning and thunder that cost me a life with every crack and boom.

Colton reached for the door and it swung back shut twice before we were able to duck inside out of the storm.

"Oh, my God," I sighed as I leaned against the white wall to catch my breath, then quickly remembered I was completely soaked through and covered in mud. "Oh, Colton, I'm so sorry."

"Hey, don't worry about it," he said as he leaned over, bracing his hands on his knees as he worked to catch his breath. For a hockey player he seemed pretty out of shape if that run left him breathless, but I didn't care to let him know that.

"I swear I lost ten lives when the storm opened up and I couldn't find you," he said between heaving breaths.

Well, maybe he wasn't so out of shape after all. He simply. . .cared.

"I'm okay, Colton."

"Yeah?" he asked, turning his eyes toward me.

"Yeah. Just a bit. . .wet."

Chuckling, he seemed to come back to himself as he moved around the trailer. "Let's get some dry clothes on. I'm sure I have something you could wear."

"Do you have your phone? Mine is still in the house in my bag and I want to let my mom know that I'm okay."

"Sure, it's on the counter. Call whoever you need."

"Thanks."

I did my best to keep from leaving a muddy mess as I took giant steps toward the kitchen island where his silver phone rested. It surprised me that the phone was unlocked and required no code to open up. With the celebrity status that Colton had, I would have thought he'd need at least three ways to unlock his devices.

Quickly I sent a text to my mom's number and let her know I was at Colton's waiting out the storm. She replied swiftly that she was glad I reached out and was about to send Dad looking for me.

I didn't linger on Colton's phone and made sure to ignore the incoming text from a number with the letter S as the contact name that asked if he could chat soon as I placed it back on the counter. His personal life wasn't my business, but the jealousy that bubbled up couldn't be helped.

"So, why is the trailer safer than the house?" I asked, as another clap of thunder sounded after a flash of lightning. I'd never been afraid of storms as a child, but there was a first time for everything.

"Because the house has open electrical wires. We could be electrocuted if lightning struck. The trailer runs on conserved solar power. It's safer in here and I took the precaution of having the trailer staked down so the wind won't rock her too bad. Here we go," he added as he held out an oversized hockey jersey with his name across the back.

"Is this some devious way to have me wear your jersey?"

"Absolutely." He chuckled. "If you want to go change in the bathroom, I'll stay out here."

With relief, I thanked him as I made my way toward the back corner of the trailer that housed a small shower and tiny toilet. I wasn't sure how Colton hadn't broken the darn thing given his massive size.

I imagined him like a bull in a china shop inside the camper, barely able to move around without crashing into anything. It was much more spacious than it appeared on the outside, though.

I whipped off my soaked shirt and bra, then did my best to tug down the waist of my jeans. Damp denim was never fun and I struggled as I tried to pull them off. My elbow slammed into the wall and I cursed under my breath.

"You okay in there?"

"Yeah. I'll be out in just a minute," I told him.

Finally, my legs broke free from the encasement of the jeans and I sighed, knowing that my wet underwear was going to have to stay in place unless I could convince Colton to spare a pair of boxers.

Collecting every ounce of strength I had, I called out to him. "Colton? I could use some help."

Chapter Thirteen

Colton

I'd just jiggled my pants down my legs, the wet material landing with a slap on the vinyl plank floors when she called my name and asked for help. I was already having the hardest time standing in this small space with her scent, not diminished in the slightest by the coating of moisture on her skin, and keeping it together, but hearing her call my name made my cock jump to attention.

"Yeah?" I replied. "Everything okay, Autumn?"

Peeking her head around the door of the bathroom, her big blue eyes blinked as she took me in, standing before her clad in a pair of black boxer briefs. I wasn't someone too concerned with my looks, but I'd never had a hard time finding a date or having someone warm my bed. With the way Autumn's eyes drank me in, I was damn proud that I kept up with my workout routine. With Brett's permission, I'd even used the high school ice rink to get in a few laps during the week.

"Um. Do you have a pair of shorts or boxers I could borrow? Everything of mine is soaked through."

Embarrassingly, it took a minute for her words to register. She was standing in one of my practice jerseys, not wearing any panties. My fists clenched at my hips as I bit back the urge to grab her and toss her onto the bed.

"Colton?" she prompted again and I began rifling through the few drawers I'd filled with some of my clothes. I still stayed at Brett's house for the most part, but on the nights I stayed on my property into the late-night hours I stayed in the trailer. It just made it easier for everyone.

I found a pair of black boxer briefs I knew would be huge on her tiny body, but it was all I had.

She quickly thanked me and slipped back into the bathroom while I grabbed my wet pants off the floor and tossed them into the sink for the time being.

The squeak of the door's hinges announced Autumn's exit from the bathroom.

"I hung my clothes in the shower. I hope that's okay."

"That's great. I was going to do the same."

I left her standing awkwardly in the middle of the small space eyeing the bed since it was the only place to sit at the moment while my clothes joined hers. By the time I came back out into the room, she hadn't moved a muscle.

Her eyes narrowed as she took in my semi-undressed state and my laugh harmonized with the clap of thunder outside. "I'm covering the good stuff, sweetheart," I said as I started reaching into the cabinets for some of the easy-to-prepare meals I had on hand. My eyes landed on some containers of microwavable cheesy macaroni, and I smirked as I showed my findings to Autumn.

Following the directions, I placed the containers into the microwave just as the trailer rocked from an overzealous gust of wind. Autumn's hand reached out to grab the counter. I noticed her white knuckles and felt like a bastard. I'd been so focused on her state of undress and less about the horrific weather just outside the walls.

"Hey, we'll be fine."

"I sure hope so."

"Why is that?" I asked as the microwave chimed, alerting me that our meal was complete. I stirred the contents and handed one of the bowls over.

"Because I plan on killing you when this is all over."

Together we sat on the bed, scooching our way to the head with our legs out in front of us. Her feet barely made it past my knees.

"Well," I said around a mouthful of the pasta. "I'll look forward to it."

We ate in silence and it didn't go unnoticed that Autumn flinched with every flash of light and crack of thunder. The storm was getting closer and stronger. I began to second-guess my plan to stay in the camper, but Lance and the contractor who secured everything said that the stakes and straps were what they used on construction sites. It just felt far less secure when you were inside.

After she finished, I grabbed her bowl and spoon and tossed them in the trash, then made my way back to the bed.

"What time is it?"

Glancing over at the microwave, I looked at the time. It was just after eight at night, too early for bed.

"Mind if I shut off the lights? I want to conserve what I have just in case the storm knocks out full power."

"Sure," she replied, but the wobble in her voice wasn't overlooked.

After cutting the lights and turning off the power to the trailer, I settled back into the same spot on the bed. Luckily, the lightning illuminated the inside through the windows.

"It's getting really dark out there."

"Yeah," I said as I grabbed my phone from where I'd tossed it on the bed when we sat down to eat and checked the weather app. The storm looked more like a hurricane and was still miles away. This one was going to be a doozy. Thank goodness we had replaced the roof and windows of the old house.

In the darkness of the storm, we laid on the trailer's bed in silence. The thunder, wind, and rain were doing enough to fill the space. My body was in agony having her so close. All it wanted was to touch her, to taste her. There was something about Autumn Easterly that felt like she was a piece of me that I didn't know I was missing.

"You know, I feel like you know a bit about me, but tell me something about you, Colton. Something I can't read on the internet," she said in a whisper. The bed bounced and jostled me as she turned on her side. I mimicked her movement.

There wasn't much about me that my ex had disclosed to the press, some of it true, most of it just shit she said to stir things up. My agent said reporters were still calling daily to get an article from my side of the story. As far as my childhood, there wasn't much to that either. When I signed with the New York Renegades, they'd released a well-choreographed press release with the information about my upbringing. It was easier than having reporters snooping around my business.

"There isn't much," I told her, just as a deafening boom of thunder sounded above us.

Both of us startled at the sound and I instinctively reached out to Autumn, only to find her shaking.

"Come here." Wrapping my arm around her, I slid her body closer until we were pressed up against each other. I knew it wouldn't take long for my body to realize that her breasts were pushed against my chest.

"Please tell me something. I swear I'm an adult and I'm not scared of storms, but I really need you to take my mind off of everything happening right now because I'm freaking out a bit," Autumn said on a single breath. The wind chose that moment to rock the camper again and her small hand reached out and gripped my bicep that rested across her body.

The breath whooshed from my lungs as I told her about the mysterious letters addressed to me through my agent that had turned into text messages. There was a twenty-year-old girl that thought she may be my half-sibling. We were all suspicious, but none more so than my agent who thought she was after a bit of my fortune.

"What made her reach out?" Autumn asked as she adjusted her body, sliding her leg between mine.

"Her mom recently died from cancer, and she said she came across some letters and paperwork when she was sorting through her things."

"Do you believe her?"

I'd thought about that for the last couple of months since I received the first letter, but until Autumn had asked, I hadn't given it more thought.

"I want to believe her. I want to think that I have a family out there somewhere. But I also know how conniving people can be, all in the hopes for a quick handout."

Another rumble erupted around us and Autumn tucked her head against my chest. When the thunder subsided, she murmured something incoherently against my chest.

"What was that?" I was curious about her thoughts on all of this. I trusted Autumn in a way I hadn't trusted anyone before, at least not in such a short amount of time. I wasn't sure why that was.

"I think it's real. Something in my gut tells me she isn't in it for anything more."

Hearing her confirmation of my own suspicions eased something cold and dark in my chest. I wasn't being conned or used like I had with my ex. Maybe it was simply nothing more than someone wanting to connect with family – the thing I'd been searching for my entire life.

"My God, that wind is terrifying. I hope it's not damaging all the work you have put into the house."

I hadn't been paying any attention to the wind whirling outside. Instead, I was focused inwardly. But now that Autumn brought me back to the present, all I could focus on was the warmth of her body against mine.

Taking a chance, I hitched my lower leg a tad higher so that my thigh was inches away from her center. Autumn immediately pulled her face away from my chest and looked up at me, her innocent blue eyes shimmering up at me.

"Colton?" she questioned. Her pink tongue slipped past her lips to coat them. I'd tasted that tongue and I only wanted more.

"You know what else is real, Autumn?"

"No. What's that?" My palm trailed down from her waist to rest on her ass, that was becoming one of my favorite body parts.

"That I want so much more than to just kiss you."

In surprise, she replied, "You do?"

"Fuck yes, I do. I want to spread those gorgeous legs of yours and eat your pussy like it's my last fucking meal. And it would be so damn delicious."

Risking rejection, I rolled her onto her back and settled my thigh between her legs right at that sweet spot I wanted to taste. Her answering moan was like music to my ears and I rocked my erection against her hip.

"I want to kiss and lick every inch of your skin. I want to feel your tight cunt squeezing my cock. I want your body to crave me just like I've been craving yours."

Leaning down until my lips barely brushed the outside of her ear, I added, "Would you like that? Would you like me to fuck you, sweetheart?"

My name was nothing more than a whispered cry from her lips as she groaned when I subtly rocked my hips.

"Tell me you want this, Autumn. I need to hear you say you want me as badly as I want you. Show me the side of you no one else has seen or heard."

Patiently, I trailed my lips down her neck as I waited. It was all an act. My cock was already on the verge of bursting and whatever patience I maintained had blown away with the wind.

Her hands moved in small circles around my shoulders as she squirmed beneath me. Every kiss I pressed against the pulse of her neck, her lithe body jerked. And hell if that wasn't a turn on.

"Autumn. What do you want?"

"You, Colton. I want you."

"Yeah?" I asked, unable to hold back any longer and pressed my lips against hers. I was addicted to

Autumn's taste and I knew anything that happened tonight was only going to intensify that craving. "What do you want from me?"

As lightning cracked across the sky outside the windows, the words I'd been dying for spilled from Autumn's next breath. "I want you to fuck me. Please."

A growl shuddered through my body as she begged and rolled her hips against my thigh. I wanted to make this good for her. I wanted her to feel like no one else compared. I wanted to make her mine for the night.

Shifting so that I rested back on my heels, I blindly reached out for her ankles. I wasn't sure if it was the weather outside or the chemistry between the two of us, but my palms tingled as I trailed them up her calves toward her thighs.

The soft pants of her breathing grew as my thumbs rubbed soft circles on the inside of her thighs as they forged their path on the way to the hot center between her legs.

"Take off the shirt," I demanded as my fingertips brushed along the edge of my boxers she was wearing that kept me from reaching the place I wanted most.

I felt the whoosh of the air as she quickly ripped off my jersey and tossed it aside. Seemed she was as eager as I was. Who was I to keep her waiting?

Gripping the edge of the cotton material, I yanked as I told her to lift her ass so I could remove the boxers.

"I don't even need the light to know how perfect this pussy is," I told Autumn, as I ran my thumb across the exposed lips. Her slit was soaked and grew wetter as I ran my digit up and down across it.

"That feels so good," she whispered, her legs bending on either side of my hips as she squirmed against my hand, searching for more.

"How do you like it, Autumn? Show me. Show me how you touch yourself."

Even in the darkness, I could see her eyes flare in my direction. But my girl didn't hesitate as she slithered her hand down her chest, bypassing those amazing breasts I couldn't wait to get my hands and mouth on, and joined mine between her legs.

"I like it like this," she said, her raspy voice swirling around me. Shifting so that I sat to her side, I gently placed my hand over hers and combined our movements. The base of her palm rubbed against her clit while she slid her fingers in and out of her sex.

I was entranced by her movements. There was something both erotic and trusting as she brought herself pleasure. But I couldn't wait much longer and I needed to have my mouth on her.

Autumn's grunt of irritation when I removed my hand made me chuckle and I pressed a kiss to the top of her bent knee as I made my way back between her legs.

"My turn again, Princess," I said as I slowly moved her hand away and replaced it with mine. Leaning forward, I placed gentle kisses from her knee all the way to the apex of her thigh until the scent of her arousal assaulted all my senses. My cock hung heavy and ached between my legs as I inhaled her aroma.

"Colton," she moaned. I replied by pressing my mouth against the two drenched lips between her legs.

"Oh, my. . ." Her words trailed off as I licked at her slit, swirling the muscle around her entrance.

As her hips rocked, my tongue licked its way up to her swollen clit and flicked back and forth as my fingers slipped inside her channel.

She was tight and for a moment I worried I'd hurt her with my cock, but the vixen was so wet I knew I'd have no trouble sliding inside.

"I want more," Autumn whimpered as I continued working her body with my fingers.

"I need one, Autumn. Give it to me," I demanded.

Her fingers tangled in my hair as Autumn's legs began to shake on either side of my head. She was taking what she wanted and it was everything that I wanted to give her.

"Oh, God," she cried out as her fingers clenched a fistful of hair, but I felt no pain. Instead, it was like a switch straight to my cock as he grew even harder between my legs.

Her body rocked against my face as she rode out her release and slackened her grasp of my hair.

"That was. . ."

"Just the beginning," I finished her sentence.

I disposed of my boxers and repositioned myself over Autumn's trembling body. The tip of my cock grazed across her mound as I hovered above her. My mouth sought out hers in the darkness, the sounds of our heavy breathing overpowered by the howling wind outside.

Swaying my hips, my shaft glided across her pussy, coating itself in her wetness. Our tongues tangled as we kissed with urgency. The anticipation was palpable.

"Are you on birth control?" I asked her, praying she was, but knowing that I was in arm's length of a box of condoms I'd stashed away.

"Yes, and I'm clean," she added. "I got tested after Max cheated."

"Fucking bastard had no idea how good he had it," I growled in her ear as I continued to rock my hips back and forth. "I'm clean too, baby. I want you with nothing between us."

"Take me, Colton."

That was all the encouragement I needed as I reached down and aligned my cock at her soaked entrance.

Inch by agonizing inch, I inserted my cock into her channel. She was hot, and wet, and so fucking tight I was sure I was going to lose my load before I had the chance to make her come again.

With my dick halfway into her pussy, I paused and released a shaky breath. "Fuck, Autumn. You're so goddamned tight."

The little minx reached out and gripped my ass in her hand, pulling me closer.

"I've got to go slow, baby. I don't want to hurt you," I tried to explain as she moved her body to try to get closer.

"More, Colton. Please, more," she begged and that was my undoing.

Blindly, I ran my hand across her hip until I found her clit and started swirling my thumb over the nub as I thrust my cock to the hilt.

"Fuck," I groaned as she cried out, "I'm going to come again."

I loved how incredibly sensitive she was. I continued to rub her clit as I slowly thrust in and out of her body. It wasn't long before her body began pulsing around my shaft and her cries overpowered the thunder.

I knew I wasn't going to last much longer as her walls clamped around me.

My thrusts became less rhythmic and more aggressive as my hips rocked against her. The sound of our sweaty skin slapping was our own melody. I pounded into Autumn, not knowing if the trailer rocked from the wind or from our fucking. But I didn't care.

"I need another, Autumn. Give me one more," I commanded as I felt my balls tighten.

She thrashed beneath me as her fists gripped at the sheets on the bed. I was turning delirious as I waited for her to come again. I needed to feel her sheath grip my cock and milk it dry.

Her back arched off the bed and she clawed at my arm as another orgasm tore through her body. I knew there was no chance of holding back any longer. With one more powerful thrust, I emptied myself inside her body, and then dropped my head onto her shoulder, careful not to crush her body.

Seconds passed and I wondered if Autumn had fallen asleep. Turning my head, I kissed the side of her neck just as she flung an arm over my back and trailed her fingers across the skin.

"Wow," she whispered and my only response was to kiss her neck again. "That was. . .wow."

I laughed at her inability to form a sentence, not that I was any better. There was no way to describe how intense that had been. How nothing had quite felt like that before.

Wiggling beneath me, Autumn said, "I should probably get cleaned up."

Begrudgingly, I slipped my cock free and moved off the beauty laying on my bed. "You stay put.

I'll take care of you," I told her as I made my way off the bed and shuffled toward the bathroom.

I returned moments later with a wet washcloth and carefully cleaned the spot between her legs where I wanted to take up permanent residence.

"Thanks," she giggled as she sat up. "I'll be right back." I watched as she snatched my jersey off the bed and sashayed back to the bathroom.

As I waited, I reclined against the back of the bed, not surprised in the slightest that my cock was still hard and aching for Autumn. He was going to become greedy after this. *I* was going to become greedy after this.

Thunder and lightning continued to duel outside the trailer and I watched as Autumn jumped when she exited the bathroom as another loud roar sounded.

"Come here, baby," I said, holding my arms out for her.

Shuffling her way toward the bed, I gripped her around the waist and settled her on my thighs, facing me. Autumn leaned her head on my shoulder as I wrapped my arms around her waist. The scent of her shampoo, something floral and sex filled my senses as I leaned my head against hers.

"How long do you think this storm will last?" she asked me, trailing her finger haphazardly through the dusting of hair on my chest.

"I don't know. By the looks of the radar earlier, probably a couple more hours." She mumbled incoherently against my shoulder, then I felt the lightest of pecks against my collarbone. My cock jumped to attention between our bodies.

At first, I thought Autumn was going to ignore it because the tiny thing had to be sore, but her fingers trailed from my chest down to my dick. Her small fingers wrapped around the base, none of the tips able to touch, and worked their way upward toward the tip.

Closing my eyes, I groaned her name into the night air.

"What are you doing, baby?" I asked, prying my eyes open to find Autumn watching herself work me over in fascination.

"Making you feel good."

"Are you sore?"

"A little, but there are other things I can do," she said, amazing me as she shimmied back on my legs to align her mouth with the tip of my cock.

I wasn't sure I could take much of that torture. My dick was dead set on being inside her pussy again.

My hips jerked and I fisted the bed sheets as her plump lips settled over the mushroom tip, sucking gently on the skin. "Fucking hell."

Autumn worked me over with her mouth and hands until I was begging her to quit.

"I need you to stop, sweetheart. I don't want to come in your mouth yet."

"What do you want?" she asked coyly, tugging the jersey off her body, then placing her hands on those breasts I wanted to become better acquainted with.

"I want you to get your perfect pussy over here and sit yourself on my dick."

Crawling her way back up my body, Autumn replied, "Really?"

"Yes. Now fucking ride my cock."

Flashes of light lit up the inside of the camper and I didn't miss the sexy as hell smirk that grew on Autumn's lips as she gripped my dick and directed it to her sex.

"Yes, sir."

Chapter Fourteen

Autumn

I was hiding. It had been two days since I snuck away from a sleeping Colton in the early morning light after our tryst. Something about being in that confined space with him and the crazy weather that Mother Nature had brewed up had snapped something inside of me. I'd acted and done things I'd never considered before with my exes, but with Colton, it all felt perfect. He had been both gentle and animalistic as he took me over three times that night. One of which I had initiated myself.

Embarrassment flooded through me as I thought about how needy I had been that night and how much my body craved a repeat performance.

And I was mad as hell over it.

I should have known that Colton would have that effect on me. Somehow, the man had wormed his way over the walls I'd constructed the day I left New York. Those were the same walls Max had barely been able to sneak through when I had given him a chance.

"Ma'am? Can I take your order?" the barista repeated, breaking me free from my musings.

"Chai latte," I said with a grunt, scaring both the server and the woman standing behind me in line.

"Wow. If you continue to growl, no one is going to want you to move back home." Ready to give the observer my two cents, I turned to find Lily Chisolm sitting at a bistro table alone.

Stepping over to her table, the sounds of the coffee shop drowning out my groan, I asked her how she knew I hadn't made a decision yet.

"Betsy," we said at the same time and then giggled in unison. That woman knew everything about everyone.

"Yeah, the town is growing on me a bit, but I just want to make sure I make the right choice." I didn't want to tell her that the man staying at her house had a bit of something to do with my inability to decide.

"I understand, but remember, make the decision for you, not for anyone else. Anyway, I have a class to teach in a few minutes, so I hate to run off."

That was when I noticed she was dressed in spandex athletic wear from head to toe.

"I teach yoga at the small gym down the street. You should come sometime."

She couldn't have known that I'd never stepped foot inside a gym, but I wasn't about to tell her that. But she looked at least twenty years younger than she was, closer to my age for sure. Maybe that could be something new that I did for myself.

"You should also think about coming to the book club meeting on Wednesday. Your sisters are usually there and sometimes your mom joins them."

"Oh, what book are you reading? I have plenty of time to catch up."

My eyes widened as Lily freed a boisterous laugh, tilting her head back as she let it out.

"Oh, sweet girl. We don't actually read any books. It's more like a chance to get together, drink some wine, and gossip."

"Oh."

"Oh my. I haven't laughed that hard in years," she claimed as she swiped her fingertips under her eyes.

Normally being the butt of a joke would have me hightailing it out of the shop, but I knew Lily wasn't laughing at me to be malicious. The woman didn't have a mean bone in her body.

As she stood from the table, I agreed that I'd try to make it to the book club and then waved her goodbye just as my drink was ready.

I had plans to meet up with Alex this morning, so I took my order to go and stepped out onto the sidewalk. The sun was shining, as if we hadn't experienced a deadly storm just days before. People milled about without a care in the world, smiling at each other as they passed. But years of walking the New York streets had hardened me. There was no quick grin or warm greeting. I strutted with my head down toward my destination, ignoring everyone in my path.

"Autumn?" a voice called out from behind me and I cringed. "Hey, Autumn. Wait up."

My body straightened as I inhaled a deep breath as I came face to face with the man I'd snuck away from.

"Hey," he said in a surprisingly chipper mood considering the last time we were together. "I thought that was you. I was in the hardware store picking out some fixtures for the house when I saw you pass by the window."

"Oh, well, here I am," I said petulantly. I wasn't sure where my attitude was emerging from, but there was nothing I could do to push it aside.

Colton was quiet, and when I peered up at him from beneath my lashes, I found his head tilted to the side as if he was trying to figure me out. He wasn't alone. I was trying to figure myself out as well.

"Did I do something to upset you?" he asked and I shook my head in reply.

"Are you mad at me?"

"No, Colton. I am just on my way to meet my sister."

"You know," he began, crossing his arms across his chest and the image of my hand gripping his bicep popped into my head. God, I loved his arms. "I thought we had a good time that night."

Sighing, I ran a hand through my hair, pushing it away from my face. "We did, Colton. I did. I'm just. . ." Chuckling, I dramatically dropped my hand from my hair and let it fall back to my hips, my palm slapping against the denim. "I don't know what I am."

Taking a step toward me, Colton grabbed my free hand and held it in his. I should care that people passing by could see it. I should care that in this small town, Colton was making a huge statement. And I should care that anyone walking around us could snap a picture and cause issues for both of us. But I didn't. All I could focus on was how good my hand felt in his. How my body immediately lit up when he was close. How my heart raced as he smiled down at me.

I was an explosive field of emotions that I had no way of handling at the moment.

"Well, I know that you're a beautiful woman that bewitched me the first moment I laid eyes on you. And I know that you completely rocked my world the other night. And I know that you have me under your spell."

Were hockey players supposed to be poetic? Because that man just spoke to me like a freaking Hallmark card and the words have never been sweeter or more seductive. My heart was a pile of gooey mush at the moment while my brain and girly bits wanted him to take me against the brick wall of the building we stood beside.

"You think I'm beautiful?" I asked him because clearly, my brain decided to mimic my heart and turn into mush as well.

"That's all you got from that?" I nodded, unable to think coherently as he smirked. "I've missed you. I was hoping you'd come back to the house to see what the crew has started working on. They found some neat stuff in a crawlspace in the attic."

That got my attention.

"Yeah? Do you think any of it is from my family?"

"I'm not sure. Some of it's just newspaper clippings and things like that, but there is probably more in the walls."

"Wow."

"Are you ignoring the part where I said I've missed you?"

"No. I just don't know what to say to that."

Sliding his hand up my arm, he snaked it around to cup the side of my neck and face in his palm. "Can I tell you something else?" he said, changing the subject.

"Okay," I responded, trying not to gasp as his fingers tightened their grip. Colton leaned closer to me as if he was about to disclose his deepest and darkest secret.

"I want to fuck you again. All I've been able to think about is the way your pussy clenched around my cock. I need more of you."

"Colton," I moaned just as he released me.

How the man looked so composed was anyone's guess because I was barely able to stand at the moment.

"I'm going to pick you up tonight to take you somewhere."

Blinking up at him, I asked, surprised, "Like a date?"

"Something like that. So be a good girl and be ready."

"Ready for what?" I questioned as he walked past me, heading back toward the hardware store.

"Anything," he called out from over his shoulder.

I wasn't sure how long I stood staring in the direction he departed, but it wasn't until my phone buzzed in my purse that I realized I'd been in the same spot for a while. Gratefully, Alex's message shook me out of my stupor.

"Hey, sorry that I'm late," I called out as I stepped through the back door of the bar where Alex was getting ready for the day. When there was no response, I called out her name.

"Back here," I heard her shout from the kitchen area.

"Hey," I said as I set my stuff on the desk in the corner.

Alex turned to face me while holding a notebook and pen. "Wow. You look like you just had sex."

"What?" I said in alarm, my body jerking to attention at her observation. Frantically, I looked around the kitchen until I found something that resembled a mirror and took in my appearance.

My hair was a bit messy, but no more than normal, and my cheeks were red. It was the eyes that gave any inclination of the lustful moment I'd just experienced with Colton.

"Oh, do tell," Alex egged on as she continued her inventory.

"I didn't have sex, Alex. . . today."

The sound of her notebook clattering to the floor had me spinning on my heel to face my sister.

"Today? Are you saying you had sex recently?"

"Maybe."

She stepped up to me, holding my shoulders in a grip that was sure to leave bruises as she looked me over from top to bottom.

"I'm sorry, you had sex with Colton Crawford and you're just now telling me?"

Shrugging off her hands, I made my way back over to the desk in the corner near the kitchen's entrance.

"Who said it was with Colton?" I responded casually.

"Well, if it had been anyone else, the news would have spread like wildfire. You were always the girl the guys in school had bets on banging. Was it good? I bet he's amazing in bed."

Turning to face her with my lukewarm tea in hand, I replied, "Wait, let's back up a sec. There were bets on taking my virginity?"

"I don't know if that was the full extent of it, but yeah. The guys in school were determined to land you."

"And everyone wonders why I never wanted to move back."

"Hey, no one succeeded because you're tough as nails. I'm assuming douchebag in New York had the pleasure of popping your cherry. Probably a good thing too, because Colton looks like he knows *exactly* what he's doing between the sheets."

"He really does," I murmured and then smacked a hand over my mouth. "Shit."

"Oh, man. I knew it. That man has had eyes for you since the moment he stepped onto the farm."

"It's just sex, Alex. He's still a huge sports star and probably has jobs lined up back in New York or Los Angeles. This is probably a temporary stay for him." I remembered him mentioning the possibility of a sister and that made it even more clear he was probably not staying in Ashfield. Colton seemed like the kind of guy to move close to his family.

"Plus, I haven't made any decisions about what I'm doing yet."

Alex grunted at the last comment, as I knew she would. I didn't want to tell her that a little part of me wanted to stay so I could get as much time with Colton as I could. I knew it was irrational that my chest tightened when I thought about him leaving, but it was a fact nonetheless.

Walking over to my sister, I wrapped my arms around her waist and rested my head between her shoulder blades. "Would it make you feel better if I told you that Colton is taking me out tonight?"

"Mildly."

"Knoxville isn't that far away, Alex. Even if I don't stay in Ashfield, I won't be any farther away than Andrew is now."

"Yeah, but it's not the same. I've missed you these last few years. And you're my sister."

"I know," I said, releasing my hold of her.

"Plus, I can't talk to Andrew about the guy that stopped in last night and stayed in my apartment."

"Oh! Is he new to town?"

"No. He said he was just passing through. You know I don't do commitment anyway."

Alex had a tough exterior, but the biggest heart of anyone I knew. But she was terrified of relationships and ducked out before she could ever get hurt.

"Any idea what he was here for? Aspen said some developers were sniffing around the property again."

"Fucking leeches," she mumbled to herself. "The topic of his occupation didn't come up while his face was buried between my legs."

"Alex!"

"What? That man had a hell of a tongue. He does have twin girls, though."

"Oh, my God. He's married?" I shouted as I felt my eyebrows shoot up on my forehead in surprise. Alex had always been extremely cautious when it came to the men she took home from the bar, especially since she lived above it. Don't sleep where you work was her motto.

"He's not. He's newly divorced and his kids are little."

"Thought you said you two didn't spend a lot of time talking?"

"We didn't. I overheard him telling the guy seated beside him at the bar."

"Could he be lying?"

"Nope. And it's fine, Autumn. You don't have to worry about me."

"I've spent my entire life worrying about you all."

"We know," she said as she turned to reach for the notebook on the floor. "Maybe it's time you let someone worry about you for a change."

Thinking of the way Colton took care of me the other night, I couldn't fight off the idea that maybe I should.

The rest of the morning passed quickly as I helped Alex at the bar and then we went to my favorite

Indian restaurant for lunch. They had a killer buffet that I absolutely overindulged in. I opted not to tell her that Max had continued to message me non-stop. I never read the texts, but it was becoming a nuisance.

Back at the ranch, I stood in my childhood room sifting through the closet trying to find something to wear. Colton hadn't said what time he was picking me up, so I started getting ready around four. I didn't even have the man's number to call and ask if he could give me an idea of a more specific time.

The clock was inching toward six and there was still no sign of Colton, which worked in my favor because I had no idea what I was going to wear. Mainly because I had no clue what he had planned for the night.

"Autumn!" my mother's voice rang clearly through the house. It was clear she was calling from the front door at the bottom of the stairs solely by the way her voice carried. "You have a guest."

A guest?

It was weird how she worded Colton's arrival, but I brushed it off as I blindly grabbed a lilac-colored buttoned dress shirt from my closet. I already donned a pair of dark denim bootcut jeans that I favored.

"Coming, Mom." My voice sounded strange to my own ears, my nervousness raising the pitch a little too high for my liking.

As I secured the last button, I gave myself a pep talk. "Calm down, Autumn. He's already seen you naked. There is no need to be nervous."

When I came down the steps, I was surprised to see Aspen standing at the bottom of the stairs wringing her hands.

"Where are they?" I asked curiously. I'd expected them to still be standing by the door.

"Um, they went into the living room," she explained and I swung my body around the end of the banister as I reached the last step and headed for that direction. "Autumn, it's not-" but her words trailed off as I found my mother sitting in the single chair by the fireplace across from my guest. My very unwanted guest.

"Max? What are you doing here?"

"Autumn, my love," he said as he stood and extended his arms out to me as if he hadn't just crushed my soul and spirit three weeks ago.

Immediately I took a step back out of his reach, only to collide with Aspen, who had just stepped into the room.

"Don't 'Autumn, my love,' me. What the hell are you doing here, Max?"

Max eyed my mother sitting in the chair. He was never one for an audience, but I wasn't about to tell her to leave. If he thought he could show up at my parents' home and *not* have spectators, well, he had another think coming. I heard Aspen's retreating footsteps, but I didn't turn around to ask her to come back.

"I came all the way here to ask you to give me another chance. I miss you and I know I made a big mistake. You have to know it won't happen again."

The man's chin barely reached the top of my head as he tried to hug me, but I quickly ducked out of his way.

"I'm not interested in your apology, Max. I'm over it. Over you. And I don't hear a smidge of sincerity in your voice. So, try again. Why are you actually here? Is it because all of your biggest clients left? Is it because you ran out of all my design ideas that you stole from me? Or is it because what's her face moved on from you already and you want to save face? Tell me which one it is, Max."

Max chose that moment to glance over his shoulder once again, eyeing the seat my mother so quietly vacated during my tirade. Now that we were alone, he figuratively pulled off the mask he'd so cleverly worn and the Max I remembered from my last day in New York returned.

He reached out, gripping my arm in his hand and squeezing. It was going to leave a bruise, but I wasn't about to tell him that.

"Look here, Autumn. You're coming back with me to New York and that's that. You can't possibly be happy in this Podunk little town. You're probably going to get knocked up by some redneck prick and spend the rest of your days washing dishes and doing laundry. That doesn't seem like the kind of life you wanted."

Jerking my arm, I winced as his hold only tightened further. "Max, you couldn't possibly know what I want in life."

"I'll give you half ownership of the business," the snake teased.

Despite his inability to do his job, Regent Events had been in his family for decades. They were the go-to team if you wanted something extravagant. And he knew how lucrative his offer was.

"I'd let her go if I were you," a voice boomed from behind me. Max immediately released my arm, holding his hands up in surrender as I spun to face

Colton. Max was smart enough to know that he was no match for him. Not only in size, but in morals too.

The fury emanated off Colton in waves and I was astonished smoke wasn't billowing from his ears as he stared down my ex.

"Max, you need to leave. Don't come back here," I said, never taking my eyes off Colton, who was watching Max like a hawk.

"Think about what I said." It was almost laughable the way Max tried to stand his ground, only to scurry around Colton, making sure he wasn't in arm's reach as he exited my parents' house.

I bit my bottom lip and shuffled my foot as I sheepishly turned my attention back to the new arrival. "Sorry about that. He ugh. . .took me by surprise."

"Mmhmm," Colton replied, his hands twitching at his side as he took a steady breath.

"Are you okay?" Something inside me wanted to wrap my arms around this man and take on whatever it was he was feeling at the moment.

What felt like an hour later, Colton ran a hand through his dark, wavy locks and grinned down at me.

"Yeah."

I didn't believe him for a second, but I couldn't blame him at all. Colton had a protective instinct about him. I was sure that was what made him such a great team captain when he played hockey. And to see a man with his hand on me, or any woman, probably didn't sit right with someone like Colton.

But I was going to let his fib slide. Taking in his attire, I noticed that my date was dressed far more casually than me. He wore a snug gray shirt under his jacket and a pair of well-worn jeans with his sneakers.

My heeled boots and dress shirt were far less casual.

Grabbing his hand, I tugged him in the direction of the stairs and up toward my room.

"Give me just a second," I said as we stepped inside my childhood bedroom. Colton's height was almost laughable as he casually laid across the full-sized bed in the middle of the room and a good portion of his legs and feet dangled off the end.

I toed off my heels and opted for a pair of Chelsea boots instead, then began unbuttoning my shirt.

"Let me." Colton's gravelly voice immediately made my fingers pause. As if in a trance, I walked over to him. He was the green orb and I was Sleeping Beauty, spellbound.

My breath hitched as his knuckles brushed against the tops of my breasts while he reached for the first button. It amazed me how swiftly his fingers could push the button through the opening. When he reached the final one, he slowly tugged the material to either side.

"Beautiful," he said, as his eyes darkened. Large hands skirted up my waist and settled on my breasts, where even as large as his hands were, there was more than his fill. Colton tugged down the pale pink lace that barely contained the masses and I gasped when his thumb caressed the sensitive nipples.

"Oh, shit," I whimpered, tossing my hair back the moment his mouth descended on one of my breasts. His tongue swirled around the peak and any consideration of my family being downstairs was immediately thrown out the window.

My hands had a mind of their own as one dove into Colton's hair, gripping the waves as he moved to give his attention to the other breast, and then began to toy with the breast he had just released from his mouth with a pop.

I'd never known that my body could be this responsive, this electrified, but with Colton, he seemed to switch something inside me and it made me feel alive. Alive in a way that I didn't know was possible.

His name reverberated in the room as it fell from my lips.

This wasn't the time or place, but my aching body didn't care.

His heavy eyes gazed up at me and I thought I was going to explode only for a crashing sound to echo from downstairs.

"Shit," a faraway voice shrieked.

Our heavy breaths sounded like a freight train to my ears as we both pulled away. Silently, I readjusted the cups of my bra and slid the dress shirt down my arms, tossing it on the bed beside Colton.

I casually walked over to the dresser on shaky legs and sifted through some of the long-sleeve shirts I had before landing on a plain maroon colored shirt that reminded me of a pinot noir.

"Cute room," Colton said with a chuckle as he took in everything that had remained in place since my childhood. There were trophies and awards lining the shelves. Boy band and movie posters covering the walls and flowers on every other available space.

"Thanks," I said, as I spritzed some perfume over my new attire and gestured for Colton to follow me.

We snuck out of the house without a backward glance, though I was certain Aspen and my mom were peering through the windows of the front room watching our escape.

"So, where are we going?" I asked enthusiastically as he helped me into the truck.

"Well, we have a bit of a change of plans."

Chapter Fifteen

Colton

Turning my attention from the road, I watched as a lazy smile grew on Autumn's face. That was probably one of my favorites of her smiles. The one where she was truly relaxed and in the moment.

It was far better than the anger and shock in her eyes when I walked into her parents' house earlier. Finding another man with his hands on Autumn set off something inside me. She was mine, even if she didn't realize it yet.

"Well, since I never knew the original plans, these changes won't really have that big of an effect."

A chuckle bubbled up at her observation.

"We just won't be eating until later, that's all."

"I'm okay with that. I stole some of Mom's homemade cookies earlier. But just between us, my parents eat far too early. In New York, I was used to having dinner closer to midnight."

"Do you miss it? I mean, still?" It was the question that bugged me the most. Whenever she spoke about her previous job, there was a wistfulness there, a longing. But any mention of the city that ironically we'd both lived in, and she seemed more closed off. More distant.

There was something I just couldn't put my finger on.

I'd spoken with my agent this afternoon and I was going to need to fly out to New York next week and then LA to work on a few projects. He wasn't sure how long I'd be gone, but I made it crystal clear that I'd found a new home base. I felt more like myself in Ashfield than I had anywhere else. Partly due to the fact that Brett was like the father I'd never had, but also because of the woman sitting beside me.

"I don't know if I miss it, to be honest. There is a pull to New York for anyone that visits. I think, at least. It's a place that is captivating, you know. It has a way of pulling you in. But the longer I've been back here, I realize that a lot of its draw was that it was an escape for me. Except I didn't have any idea about what I was escaping from. That probably doesn't make any sense at all," she said mildly, on the edge of a chortle.

Little did she know it made complete sense to me. New York may have been where I'd made my living, but Ashfield was the place where I wanted to place my roots. Hopefully. Though my agent was bucking against that idea. He wanted me back in the game, at least on the televised side of it. But I'd been around long enough to know that he needed me to make money. My name was still a draw to the crowds and press despite the wringer my ex had taken me through.

I wasn't quite comfortable enough with the winding roads to reach out and grab her hand for reassurance, but I told her I understood.

Soon the road straightened out and we were headed to a place where I'd been spending my nights when I wasn't at the house. I was glad Autumn had opted to wear jeans, but I knew her light jacket wasn't going to cut it as the high school came into view. Thankfully, I had a hoodie in the back of the truck that she could borrow. The thought of her wearing my clothes again left me with more enjoyment than I anticipated.

I parked the truck beside the slew of other vehicles, grabbed my bag from the back, and then hurried over to the other side to escort Autumn to the rink.

"Here's my sweatshirt if you get cold," I said awkwardly as I opened the door, the cold air immediately causing her cheeks to redden.

"What are we doing here?" she asked, glancing around the space. There weren't any other spectators, just a few men on the ice.

"Well, I originally planned on bringing you here to ice skate, but Brett asked if I wanted to join their rec team, informally, the other day." I rubbed my hand against the back of my neck, feeling the hair beneath my palm that needed a trim. "Today is their first practice."

"Really?" Her eyes lit up as she looked up at me. Her joy was unmistakable. "I get to see the great Colton Crawford on the ice?"

"I mean, I wouldn't say great, but yeah."

"This is awesome. I'm going to go sit in the stands," she added, clapping enthusiastically as she moved past me.

"Hey," I called out, jogging over to her. That tiny woman sure could move fast. Searching inside my bag, I found my clean sweatshirt and handed it to her. Luckily, Brett brought all my hockey equipment with him when I started helping with the high school team.

"What position do you play again?" she asked as she took a seat right behind the bench.

"Center, but they may move me around. Brett's the coach, but he plays sometimes too if they're short on people."

Rubbing her palms together in glee, her eyes shimmered when she asked if there were going to be any fights.

"It's just practice, so I doubt there will be any fights. Why? Want to see me all bloodied and bruised?"

"Maybe I want to play nurse," she said, winking at me before turning her attention back to the ice.

"Little minx." Reaching down, I forcefully cupped her jaw in my hand and sealed my lips over hers. If I was going to be away from her for the next hour or so, then I was going to leave her wanting me just as much as I wanted her.

"Don't go anywhere," I told her as I made my way back to the locker room to change.

I changed quickly so that I could make my way onto the ice. Something I'd been looking forward to since Brett called me that afternoon. He'd mentioned the team when I first arrived, but knew I'd probably be hesitant to get back on the ice.

But this was the closest thing to home I'd ever had.

He quickly introduced me to the rest of the team, who all varied in age. None of them seemed starstruck or put out by my joining them, even when I mentioned I wasn't sure that I'd be able to devote time for each game with my potential traveling schedule. Not a single one of them cared, they just wanted to play the game.

I learned some of the guys traveled from surrounding towns and a couple all the way from Knoxville. They'd settled there when they'd played for the minor league team Brett had coached.

After the introductions, Brett put us through our paces, running drills and skating laps. The man was tough and didn't care that we were professional.

It felt amazing to feel the stick in my hand and pass the puck back and forth as we lined up shots. I may have lost the love of the competition when I played for the Renegades, but not for the game of hockey overall.

At the end of practice, Brett had us run a fifteen-minute scrimmage. The small team I played against didn't hold back and it felt good that they treated me as they did the others. Especially when I stole the puck and landed a goal within the first five minutes.

Hearing Autumn's cheers from the sidelines wasn't something I'd ever forget. I wondered how good it would have felt to have had her in the stands rooting for me instead of my ex who was too busy schmoozing with the celebrities that were in attendance.

"I see you brought a guest," Brett said, as I snuck in a quick shower after practice.

"I did. Mind if I steal the rink for a little while?"

"Sure. So, Autumn Easterly, huh? She's a nice girl. I know Lily adores her."

"She is. I'm enjoying my time with her."

"And how long will that be? I know the house isn't your end all. You'll get antsy. You were the kid that always had to be moving."

"I'm not sure how long, for either of us. We're just enjoying our time together right now."

"Just don't hurt her. You'll have an entire town coming after you."

Turning off the water, I grabbed a towel and draped it around my waist. "What makes you think she won't be the one hurting me?"

He shrugged off his response and clapped me on the shoulder as I sat on the bench with my clothes from earlier.

"Lily wants to come see the house over the weekend."

"Yeah? I may be out of town, but you're welcome to go check it out. I'll leave you the keys. Man, it's coming along really nicely. We worried about the damage after the storm, but the crew cleaned up everything and got to work."

"Pay for progress."

"Something like that."

"Well, I'll let you get back to your girl. Maintenance will close up the rink in about an hour."

"Thanks, man."

Bag and skates in hand, I stopped by the rental stand and grabbed the pair I'd set aside for Autumn. Thankfully, her sister had provided her shoe size ahead of time.

"Oh, my gosh." She bounced over to me, wrapping her arms around my neck enthusiastically. "That was so exciting to watch. When is the first game? I definitely want to come."

"Really?" I asked, surprised, adjusting the skates in my grasp.

"Yeah, of course. I mean, I've seen some clips on television before, but it was so different in person, and that was just practice."

"Well, now I wish you could have seen me play professionally. It would have been nice to have someone cheering for me in the stands." Nodding to the bench, I handed her the skates while I dumped my bag on the seat beside me and followed suit.

"Your girlfriends never came to the games?" Melancholy rang through her words.

"I don't want to talk about them," I said as I relaced my skates. "Have you ever ice skated before?"

"Not since I was little and I don't recall it going well at that time."

Standing, I gestured for her to follow me through the rink's opening, taking her hand when she wobbled on the blades. Autumn hesitated as I glided on the ice.

"Come on."

Her knuckles were white from where she gripped the ledge and took a step onto the ice. "I don't think this is the best idea."

"I think it's a great idea," I told her as I pried her hands free and took them in my own. In slow steady movements, I pulled her along with me across the hard surface. When her body started to rock as she tried to push off on her blades, I said, "Don't look down. Look at me."

"Huh?"

"Don't focus on your feet. Focus on me. You're less likely to lose your balance that way."

Autumn adjusted her grip on my hands and I worried she was going to break my fingers with her surprising strength.

"There you go," I said as she began to glide across the ice on her own. I tried to slip my hands free of her grasp, but she wouldn't relinquish her hold.

"Don't you dare."

Laughing, I continued to skate backward as I pulled her along.

"You really love hockey, don't you?" she asked as we made our first loop.

"I do. I may not play the way I used to, but I'll always be a hockey player."

"And one of the greats if the articles I've read are anything to go on."

I had the decency to blush at her statement. I was ranked alongside some of the most well-known players in history and the notion was surreal.

"Sorry. I didn't mean to make you uncomfortable," she added as she slipped a bit on the ice. I grabbed her arm as she righted herself.

"Think you can do this on your own?"

"No freaking way. If you let me go, I'll kill you."

"But you'd have to get off the ice first," I joked in return.

"Who knew Colton Crawford was a comedian? I think you've found your next journey in life."

"Actually, you're not too far off," I said as I pushed off with my skates, moving us faster around the rink. The wind forced her hair away from her face and her cheeks turned a soft shade of pink that reminded me of the impatiens that lined the Chisolm's flower bed.

"What do you mean?"

"My agent called and he has a few projects he wants me to work on. I'll be in New York and maybe LA this weekend."

"Oh."

"It's just for the weekend. I have a house to finish, after all." I tried to reassure her, but the look of shock and weariness in her eyes didn't go unnoticed by me. She may be able to put on a tough exterior for everyone else, but those beautiful irises gave her away.

"How far along is it now?"

"Well, they've finished staining the first floor and have moved onto the second. Most of the woodwork around the stairs has been stained too."

"Wow, they sure moved fast."

"Money is a great motivator. And what good was it doing just sitting in my bank account? My financial advisor said property was a good investment."

"Have you decided what you plan on doing with the house when it's done?"

I let her question linger in the air because I still hadn't a clue what I wanted to do yet. It would be hard to give it up, but I hadn't thrown out the idea of using it as a vacation spot.

In the back of my mind, I wondered what Autumn would say if she knew that a lot of my decision was resting on her.

"Don't forget, I still need you to look at the things the workers found in the attic."

"Oh yeah. I'd forgotten about that."

Finally, I was able to slip my hands free of her grasp and skate away.

"Colton!" she shrieked, her high-pitched squeal echoing in the empty arena.

"You can do it. I believe in you."

She wobbled at first as she moved her feet in slow steps. I encouraged her as I skated figure eights across the ice.

"I'm doing it! Colton, I'm doing it!" she declared enthusiastically, which only caused her feet to slip out from underneath her.

"Shit," I whispered as I jetted over to her, catching her body on top of mine as we fell on the cold surface. "Got you." It had been a long time since I fell on the ice, but it was worth it to hold Autumn against my body.

When she slipped away Friday evening, I tried not to let it get to me because it was the same thing I'd done in the past. I blamed it on her nerves and did my best to let it go and move on.

"I think I made the right choice in deciding not to become a figure skater." She giggled as I sat us up on the ice.

"I think you're right on that one. You hungry?" I asked as I yanked her up into my arms and carried her to the exit of the rink.

"Don't drop me," she exclaimed as she wound her arms tightly around my neck.

"I won't. Trust me."

Once we were safely off the ice, I kneeled on the floor and began unlacing her skates.

"I was thinking pizza."

"Angelo's? Man, I haven't been there in ages. They seriously have the best pizza around. My friends and I used to go there three or four times a week."

It was strange how she mentioned friends, but I'd yet to see her with anyone in town, not that I got out much either. From what Lily had told me, most of the townspeople were steering clear of Autumn because she'd been walking around with a scowl since she arrived. I was hopeful that I could help change that. I'd noticed she smiled more when I was around and even more so with her sisters.

"Well, let's see if it's as legendary as you say."

I finished hauling off my skates and tossed them into my duffle bag with my practice clothes and then hurried Autumn's skates back to the rental booth.

The drive to the restaurant was quick and we found a spot to park across the street. The sign for Angelo's blinked a few times before illuminating. I could see through the windows that the place was packed, even though it was late, just around eight in the evening.

When we stepped inside the place conversations continued to flow, but I noticed the watchful eyes taking us in. Autumn didn't seem to as she stepped up to the counter to place our order. In the car, we'd already decided on a large pepperoni pizza and two beers. The eyes of the teen working behind the counter widened as I handed him my black American Express card.

"I'll have your order right out, Colton. . .er. . . Mr. Crawford. . .er," the boy squeaked.

"Thanks." I chuckled as I guided Autumn to the only available table in the middle of the restaurant. I'd really hoped for a bit of privacy so the chance of being interrupted would be minimal.

"To our first official date," I explained as I held out my beer.

Autumn repeated my statement and we clinked our bottles together before taking a pull of the cold liquid.

As the people around us chattered away, Autumn asked me questions about hockey and then if I'd heard anything more about my potential sister.

I finally confessed to Autumn that I learned the twenty-year-old lived in Knoxville and after she sent me a picture of herself with our mother from her childhood, I was pretty convinced it was the real thing. The girl, Nina, had the woman's nose and pale skin color, but I had the woman's eyes. It was like looking in the mirror.

But I still wasn't sure if I wanted to meet the girl or what she was after in the long run. Thankfully, before Autumn could dissect my hesitation any further, the pizza arrived.

It was covered in cheese that dripped off the edges of the slices and grease that made the first bite even more delicious than I imagined.

"Good, right?" Autumn asked around a mouthful of saucy goodness.

"So good. I can see why you raved about it."

"This place hasn't changed in years. Even the pictures on the walls are the same." She laughed, looking over her shoulder with a wide grin.

"It's nice, you know."

"What is?" she pondered as she turned to face me.

"Seeing you smile."

In response, Autumn shoved another piece of pizza in her mouth and I went ahead and grabbed the last slice.

The bus-boy hurried over to collect our dishes and clean the table as we stood. There was a line out the door, even on a weekday, so I wasn't surprised they wanted the table.

Just as we were about to exit, a little boy tugged on Autumn's jacket. She bent down until she was eye level with a kid that could be no more than five or six, then glanced up at me.

"He wants to know if he can get an autograph. You're his favorite player." She was hesitant in her question and I knew that was because she didn't know how I would respond. If I start signing for one, I'd have to sign for whomever else asked while we were here.

But I couldn't deny the hopeful look in the child's eyes. I'd regret it for eternity.

"Sure, kid. What's your name?" I asked him as he handed me the restaurant's paper children's menu. The back was blank and I carefully wrote out the name Jackson and thanked him for being my biggest fan.

With practiced ease, I scribbled my name and handed the sheet back to the kid's parents, who were standing behind him.

With Autumn's help, we posed for a picture with the family and then one with me and Jackson.

"Thank you," the mother said before they went back to their table.

A few other people gathered and I quickly signed autographs and took pictures with them, all while keeping an eye on Autumn as she stood to the side. I didn't miss her content smile as she chatted with a few of the people seated close by.

Once I finished with the small group, I was pleasantly shocked that no one else had come up. Not that I wasn't appreciative of every single person who supported me, but I wanted time with Autumn.

"You're really good with your fans," she said as I held the door open for her to exit. She barely had to tuck her head as she passed under my extended arm.

"I am eternally grateful for them all. But I'm glad the entire restaurant didn't line up."

"I could see how that would be a bit overwhelming when you just want to grab something to eat."

"Par for the course, I'm afraid. So far that was the first time anyone has approached me in Ashfield, which is surprising."

"They may be gossipers, but they'll respect your privacy at the same time. It's a weird oxymoron, I know."

"Nah, I get it."

We settled into my truck and I headed toward both of our homes, eager to find out if I could convince her to stay the night.

But my worry subsided when Autumn's voice filled the cab.

"Colton, do you think you could show me the things that were found in the house. . .tonight?"

I know it wasn't her intention, but my cock jerked from behind the confines of my jeans.

"Absolutely."

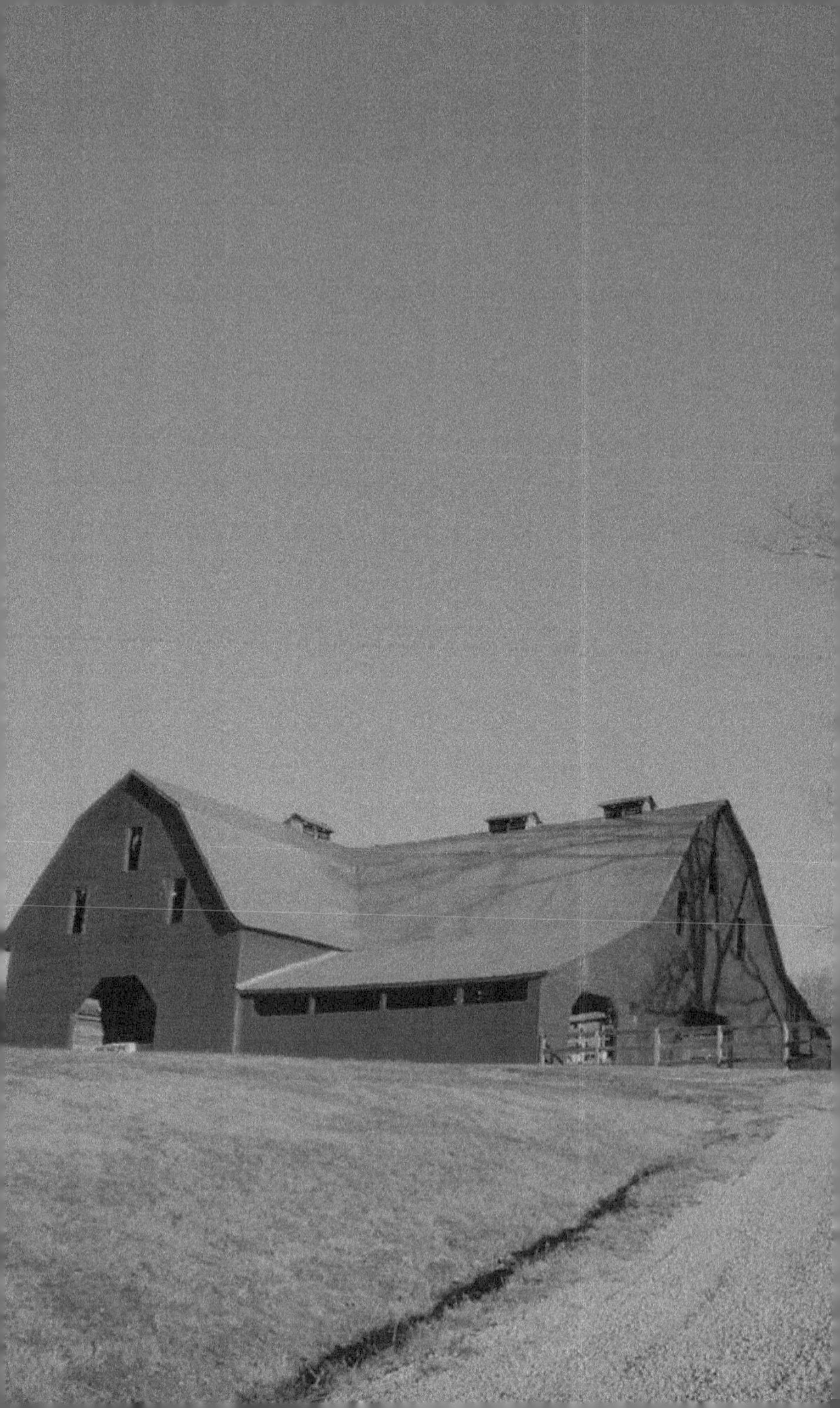

Chapter Sixteen

Autumn

In the car, I'd texted my parents and let them know Colton had found some things in the house that I wanted to look at and not to stay up for me. Even though I was twenty-four, I knew that I needed to check in with my parents. It was their home after all.

Of course, not long after the group chat with my sister's lit up with a message from Aspen. I quickly realized Mom had informed her about where I was headed. I ignored their teasing as Colton pulled up to his house. I was certain they were going to make me pay for it later.

It was still strange to think of the house belonging to anyone but me. I'd called it mine for as long as I could remember. But I was slowly learning to accept it despite the ache it left in my chest.

"Everything all right?" Colton asked me as he parked the truck. That was when I noticed there was no one around.

"Yeah. Didn't you say that the crew works around the clock?" I asked as I jumped down from the truck and strolled up to the front door behind him.

"When I asked you out earlier, I gave the night crew the day off."

Stepping inside the house that smelled of freshly sanded wood and sawdust, I joked, "I guess I was a sure thing, huh."

"Not at all. I was just hopeful."

"Mmhmm," I mumbled as I headed toward the back of the house, noting how all of the details around the stairs stood out with the freshly painted stain.

"Oh, wow. The kitchen is laid out."

"Yeah. They were working on installing the new cabinets when I came to get you. They're in the butler's pantry too."

The kitchen layout was fascinating to me. It was so small compared to modern day kitchens with a large porcelain sink beneath the window, but the butler's pantry was twice the size. That was where one of the original fireplaces still resided.

There were swatches of color on an extra cabinet door, and I loved the choices I'd helped Colton select at our first meeting. The dark blue stood out to me the most and I let Colton know as he joined me.

Across the way, the sunroom was serving more like a storage space, but I could see its potential with the new windows installed. They climbed all the way to the ceiling and gave a majestic view of the land surrounding the farm.

"This place is really coming along. I'm amazed at how quickly they were able to gut and then renovate."

I knew that most projects took months and one of this magnitude should have taken years, but Colton seemed to have luck on his side. And my father, it seemed. He had spent time and money when the house was vacant, making sure that it didn't wither away into a pile of rubble.

"Want to check out what we found?" I spun around at Colton's question and faced him.

"Yes, please," I replied eagerly, immediately moving toward the front staircase.

I noticed my makeshift tool bag sitting against the wall on one of the steps along with my cheap canvas toolbelt folded on top. Beside that was a small chest no larger than a shoe box that was covered in dirt and grim. The kind you couldn't wash away with soap and water and it spoke of years of neglect.

"Is that it?" I asked, my knees shaking in anticipation and I gripped the railing to steady myself.

"It is."

Without hesitation, I dove for the box and settled it on my lap as I sat on the stairs. I quickly forgot the hard wood as I lifted the lid and came face to face with my family's treasures.

"There really isn't much in there," Colton said beside me and I'd already forgotten that he was in the foyer with me.

Folded on top was a hand drawn blueprint of the house. It was more simplistic than layouts today with dimensions and such. This was just a generic layout of the house broken out into three levels.

"Wow. You see here, on the second story, there used to be a dumb waiter. That's so neat," I exclaimed, pointing out the small opening that would feed into the butler's pantry. I knew just from the walk throughs that the service had been torn out at some point. "Maybe you could look at having it installed again, or something similar, before the walls are closed in."

"That's a really great idea." Whipping out his phone, Colton typed something while I set the piece aside.

Beneath the blueprint were some letters from my great-great-grandfather to the woman he would build this house for and pictures of their family. My great-great-grandmother had been a transplant from Carson, North Carolina, another small town built before the population flourished. My parents would go nuts for these images. I'd wondered if they'd ever seen them before.

More pictures filled the box, along with costume jewelry. I wistfully held a ring that contained a pink stone to the light, admiring the way it shimmered.

"This is really great, Colton."

"Sorry it isn't more. So far, we haven't found much more in the walls other than scraps of newspaper."

"That's okay. This is more than enough. Are you okay if I take this to my parents? I think they'd really enjoy having these."

"Of course. That was the plan, sweetheart."

I quietly filled the box back the way I found it, sighing as I restored each item into the containers.

"Sorry it wasn't as exciting as you probably imagined it being," Colton said and I immediately apologized. "Colton, this was great. Thank you. I'm only sighing because the night is over."

That smirk that creased the corner of his eye appeared and I felt my stomach flutter with the telltale sign of butterflies.

Leaning over, Colton snatched the box from my hands and set it back on the step. "It doesn't have to be."

"What?" I asked in confusion, my eyes searching his as he loomed over me.

"The night. It doesn't have to be over," he replied, reaching up to tuck a piece of hair behind my ear. "Unless, you know, you have somewhere else to be."

My voice caught in my throat as I watched those dark spots in his irises grow. They took me in, all of me, and never faltered.

"I don't." The whisper sounded foreign to my ears. It was rough and raspy. Colton had that effect on me. Since the first moment we met he brought out something in me I'd never experienced.

"Good. Because I wasn't done with you yet." His velvety whisper caressed my ear as the scruff of his day-old beard brushed my cheek.

"What did you have in mind?" My question rolled off my tongue effortlessly as I rested back on my elbows against a step above me, giving Colton better access to my neck. The feel of his lips on my skin eliminated any pain I felt from the hard wood against my back. He was my sole focus and I kept imagining all of the things I wanted to do to him.

Slyly, I ran one of my hands across his denim-clad thigh, then across his hip in search of his zipper until I stroked my hand across the erection tenting in his jeans. God, he was huge, not that I had any doubts because of how large he was everywhere else, but in the darkness of the other night I never got a good look.

"Take it out, Autumn."

I'd always been good at following directions, and this moment was no different. Colton was my teacher and I was eagerly ready to learn.

With the flick of my finger, I unhooked the button on his jeans with a level of skill I didn't know that I possessed. Deftly, I pushed down the elastic waist of his boxers until his cock sprung free and landed in my palm.

Hesitantly, I wrapped my hand around the shaft and trailed my hand up the velvety skin until I reached the tip. The weight of his cock felt warm and heavy against my palm.

"That's it," he said as I stroked him up and down so slowly that I was driving myself insane in anticipation. I focused my eyes on the deep red mushroom tip as Colton leaned over me. His large hand reached under my shirt and cupped my breasts, my nipples immediately perking up at the attention. I squirmed underneath him as he whispered, "Give me your hands, Princess. I want to fuck your mouth."

Wetness immediately pooled in my panties as I held up my hands and he gathered them in his single fist, raising them above my head. The wood from the stair ledge dug into my back and I was sure I'd have a bruise in the morning, but I was long past caring. All I cared about at that moment was tasting him.

"Fuck," he growled as he traced my mouth with the tip of his cock, the small bead of moisture coating my lips. "Open up."

Colton was gentle as he sunk his dick between my lips, only allowing the head of his shaft to pass through until he pulled back out. He repeated the movement, my saliva building as every release ended with a pop.

An unintelligible sound came from Colton's chest as he fell forward, catching himself on the step as he increased his thrusts.

"Suck it, baby. Yeah, like that. Such a good girl letting me fuck your mouth."

"Mmm," I moaned with his erection edging to the back of my throat.

Colton's knees buckled as he cursed.

"Do that again," he commanded, releasing my hands as he wrapped his hand around my jaw, holding my head in place.

I repeated the sound, my eyes rolling back as his cock grew thicker against my tongue.

"I'm going to come, Autumn. I want you to swallow it."

"Yes," I sighed as he pulled his cock free and then slipped it back in just as his hot stream filled my mouth. I readily swallowed each drop as Colton's body jerked above me.

"Wow," I mumbled as he released my hands, his head tilted down to rest on my shoulder. "That was fun," I added with a chuckle, then sighed as my thighs pressed together. There was an ache between my legs and I needed some relief soon.

I wiggled beneath Colton hoping he would catch the hint that I had some things to take care of back at home, only he wrapped his arm around my waist and hefted my body against his as he pushed off from the stairs.

"You didn't think we were finished, did you?" he asked. "Oh, Princess. We're just getting started."

Colton lifted me in his arms as if I weighed no more than a feather and carried us around the bottom of the stairs, only for him to pause at the corner of the L-shaped staircase.

He gently placed me back on my feet and pulled at the edge of my shirt until he was able to pull it over my head, tossing it blindly behind him. Colton did the same with my shoes, socks, and pants, until I stood before him clad in my simple cotton panties and bra.

I instantly regretted my decision to wear the pale-yellow undergarments, but as my eyes met Colton's all of that lamenting flew out the window like the wind from Friday's storm.

His eyes were heavy and filled with lust as they looked me over. Consuming all of me in one glance.

His approach was predatory; cunning with each step closer to me. The temperature of the room increased and I suddenly felt like I was in a sauna, but I knew it was nothing more than my desire for him heating my skin.

"You're beautiful, Autumn," he praised as the back side of one of his fingers trailed across the top of my breast pushed high in the bra. "So fucking beautiful. I want to stand here for hours and take you in." Colton's finger dipped between my breasts, while he slyly unlatched the bra's hooks across my back.

I felt like his body shrouded me like a mist that touched my skin all over, but he'd only barely laid a finger on me.

"Colton." His name was a whispered moan from my lips as I ached for more, ached for him.

Shimmying my shoulders, the straps slid down my arms until the material fell to the floor. My breasts hung like oversized teardrops against my chest, the nipples stiff and tender as they longed for more of his touch.

"Look at you begging for more," he whispered as he walked around me. Colton's body was mere inches from mine. I could feel the heat his body was putting out, but it felt like miles. "Is it more of my cock in your mouth that you want? Or do you want it in your greedy, tight pussy?"

My body shook with each question, my panties growing wetter with each word. I was so lost in desire that I thought I'd come before he even placed a full hand on me.

Colton's body stood to my right, between the staircase and my arm, as he bent his head toward my ear. His still exposed cock brushed against my arm and I longed to wrap my hand around it again.

"I think you want to feel my mouth and tongue between your legs. Tell me, Autumn. If I shoved my hand beneath your panties right now, would I find you wet?"

Colton held his hand out and hovered the digits centimeters away from my mound. If I clenched my toes, I could cause the collision that I craved. But I held back. I wanted to be at Colton's command and as greedy as he knew my body was for him, I was also patient. He would make it worth it.

"Would I?" he repeated and I hissed out an affirmation.

"Just a little?"

"No, soaked," I countered, closing my eyes as I fought against the desire to rub my thighs together.

His voice deepened as his lips scraped the rim of my ear. "Really?"

What seemed like centuries later, his taunting ceased and Colton placed his hand between my legs over the top of my panties. My body nearly crumbled at the contact.

"Ah, yes. You *are* drenched," he declared as his free hand wrapped around the other side of my neck to twist my head to face him. Colton slowly rubbed back and forth against my underwear. The friction against my sex caused my clit to swell.

Uncontrollably, I swayed my body against his hand, but he immediately halted his movements.

"Stay still, greedy girl," Colton muttered before he pressed his mouth against mine. As his tongue slipped between my lips, he pushed aside the cotton and mimicked the movement with his fingers. His digits slowly dove in and out of my pussy until I felt the signals of my release.

"Colton," I cried out against his lips as the waves came on slowly. He increased the thrusts, adding another finger to the intrusion, until I exploded in his arms.

"That's my girl," he said as I fell limp in his arms. His large hands brushed up and down my spine as he pressed the softest of kisses against my shoulders, all while I leaned against him catching my breath.

Without warning, my feet left the ground, and just as quickly I felt the floor beneath my feet and the cold wood from the decorative casing around the stairs nudge my back.

"Hold up your hands."

Forcing my eyelids open, I watched in fascination as Colton ripped off his shirt and threw it over toward my pile of clothes and then produced a folded up cloth from his back pocket. It wasn't just any cloth though. As he shook the material loose, I recognized the canvas toolbelt that earlier had been folded on the stairs.

"Seems like this little belt isn't so useless after all." Grasping the hands I held loosely above my head, Colton raised them higher and then asked me to grip the spindle.

"Let me know if it's too tight," he remarked as he wrapped the canvas straps around my wrists, attaching my arms to the wooden supports.

When he finished, Colton gazed down at me, his eyes filled with sincerity as he asked if I was alright. After I responded with a nod, his mask fell back in place and the dominating man from moments ago came back to play.

"Fuck, I love your body," he stated as he drew invisible lines down my body with his hands. He palmed my breasts, adjusting their weight in his grasp as he brushed his fingers across the rosy buds of my nipples.

He didn't linger on my heavy chest but settled his hands on my waist.

"I love the way your body dips in here. Makes me want to run my tongue across the valley."

"Yes, please," I spoke, clutching the hard wood in my hand.

"Mmm. I could," he began, as he slid his hands farther down, taking the waistband of my panties with him as he kneeled on the floor. My panties were thrown over his shoulder, but I had no idea where they landed. I glued my gaze to the man focused on the apex between my thighs. "But I think your hungry pussy has something else in mind. And, honestly, I've been quite starved myself."

He pounced on my sex and I truly believe he was as ravenous as he claimed. He started off slow, sweeping his tongue around my clit. His groans of need fed my own hunger.

I howled out his name as he lifted my leg onto his shoulder, shifting the angle of my center to his mouth.

With his masterful fingers and tongue, I soon found myself chasing a second orgasm by riding his face. I had no inhibitions as I bore down on his mouth, the tip of his nose doing amazing things as it pressed against my clit.

Colton's hands squeezed the globes of my backside and as my legs began to shake, he subtly ran his thumb around the rim of my ass.

That was my undoing, and I uncontrollably clenched my thighs together, locking his head in place. The release was so overwhelming that I didn't have the chance to worry if he could breathe. Colton was so strong that I did not need to worry. He easily eased my thighs apart and settled my leg back on the ground, all while my body jerked from the release.

"Let go of the post," he growled. It was almost incoherent in my disembodied state, but I managed to do what he asked.

He spun me swiftly around until I faced the staircase and pressed my cheek against the cool wood as I worked hard to catch my breath.

"Lean forward," he said as he pressed the spot between my shoulder blades. With the way my hands were tied, I wasn't left much room to move my body, but Colton seemed satisfied as I arched my back and pushed out my ass.

"Perfection." I smiled inwardly, the corners of my lips just barely curving up until I yelped when his palm slapped across my backside. But as he rubbed the angry skin, there was nothing I could do to hold back the moan that sounded from my lips.

"There she is. There's my greedy girl. Want to feel my cock in you?" he questioned, smacking the tip of his cock against my plump, sensitive lips.

"Yes," I whimpered. "Put it in me, Colton."

His groan seemed as desperate as mine as he slipped his dick into my sex to the hilt and then pulled it back out.

"God, you're so fucking tight," he claimed through clenched teeth as he repeated the motion over and over again. "I love the way your walls squeeze me. Greedy, just like my girl."

I squeezed my eyes shut as I stood on my tiptoes just so I could rock back against his thrust.

"Has your pussy been hungry for me?"

"Yes," I exclaimed, silently praying that he would take me harder, faster, more desperately. The teasing and taunting were driving me wilder with each thrust.

As if he heard my wish, Colton pushed inside me, gripping my hips as he drove into my sex.

My hips ached from where his fingers dug into the flesh, and I knew without hesitation that my shoulders were going to protest for days, but none of that mattered as Colton pounded into me.

"I can feel you, baby. You're getting close. How bad do you want to come, Autumn? Tell me how bad you want to come on my cock."

I whimpered in reply. There were no words to describe my desperation to reach my pinnacle.

"Tell me," he repeated, smacking his hand across my ass again.

"So bad. Oh, God," I whined as I went off the cliff, the shudders wracking my body.

"There it is," Colton said as he twisted my body to face him, pressing his lips against mine in a chaste kiss. I could taste myself on him and it wasn't the unpleasant flavor I had expected. Mixed with the taste of Colton still on my tongue, I was mesmerized.

Before I had time to recover, he grabbed the back of my thighs and lifted me up. My back pressed against the stairs as he aligned his cock with my slit and eased inside.

His plunges became frenzied and it was all I could do to grip the post still wrapped between my hands to hold myself steady.

"Fuck, come with me," Colton demanded as he held my weight in one hand and used the other to stroke my clit.

"I can't," I told him, my body too sensitive for another orgasm. But I could see the determination in Colton's eyes.

"You can. Your selfish pussy wants another. She's begging for it, dripping all over my cock."

My head thrashed as I whimpered.

"There it is," he said a minute later. "I can feel your body clamping around my cock, aching for it. Come with me, greedy girl. I need to feel you come on me."

"Ah!" I cried out as the orgasm tore through me. My body felt like it was breaking in half as Colton pounded into me over and over while he sought his own release his body thirsted for.

"Yes," Colton and I roared in unison as my body shook uncontrollably.

Even with his body arched over mine, Colton's deft fingers untied the knot on the straps that held my arms up. My arms were still wrapped up and fell over his head as my shoulders protested. I didn't care, though. That was the sexiest thing I'd ever experienced and when my body was up for it, I wanted a repeat.

"You okay to stand?" Colton whispered in my ear as his breathing evened out.

"Yeah." Slowly, I released my arms from around his neck, holding my hands out. He slipped the canvas toolbelt free from my wrists and rubbed the angry red markings it left in its wake.

My eyelids were drooping as Colton sorted through the pile of clothing, then tugged on his own.

"Lift your leg," he said softly, carefully holding my ankle as I steadied myself on the stairs at my back. "Now the other," he repeated, then yanked the pants the rest of the way. "Hope you're okay going commando."

I giggled shyly as I told him it was fine. There was no reason to be embarrassed after everything we had just done together, but I couldn't help myself.

"I'll let you put this on," he added as he held out my bra with the straps between his fingers.

Unfortunately, he had returned all of his clothes back to his body as he helped me with my shirt.

"Autumn, stay with me."

"For the night? I mean-" I started, but Colton silenced me with his lips.

"Until I leave. Stay with me until I leave on Friday." With a single finger, Colton tipped my chin up so that my eyes were on his instead of the hem of my shirt. "Please."

"Okay," I replied, then I immediately went weightless as Colton lifted me into his arms and headed out the back door toward the trailer.

My eyelids grew heavy with every soft patter of his feet on the crunchy grass. I was barely coherent when my body jostled with each step into the camper. There was a metallic clank from the door closing that startled me. I looked around frantically, only for Colton to murmur that we were going to bed.

He slipped my clothes off of my body with the gentlest of movements and then draped the covers over me. His warm frame nestled up behind my body and I drifted off into the most pleasant dream where Colton and I had nothing standing in our way. Where time stood still.

    Colton brushed my hair away from my face but I was too shattered to smile.

    "I wish you could stay forever."

Chapter Seventeen

Autumn

There were moments when all I wanted was for time to speed up. Moments like high school because I yearned to go to college and spread my wings. Moments like losing my job because I was determined to get out of Ashfield again. Moments like standing in Chuck's Grocery looking at the magazine rack and finding my face staring back at me.

Colton had left earlier that morning, the sheets beside me cold to the touch when the sound of the construction equipment woke me up. I should have known my Friday was going to fall into a black hole when my phone started buzzing with notifications from my sisters. I hadn't believed them at first when they claimed my name was being tossed around the internet. It took me grabbing a few items for Mom and seeing myself on a tabloid for it to really hit home.

The news had moved on from Colton's ex, but not in the way he had hoped. They focused on me instead. Not exactly something I'd had in mind.

"Mr. Granger, do you think we can take these off the shelf?" I asked my old employer. My nails dug into the plump skin, leaving crescent marks and my teeth hurt from my clenched jaw.

"I'm sorry, Autumn."

"Yeah, me too." My chest ached from holding my breath while I skimmed the glossy pages. The pictures were from the Italian restaurant where Colton and I had dined earlier in the week. Most were taken through the glass, so it meant the person hadn't been inside. I was certain no one in the town had been the one to leak the images, but it was confirmed when my phone buzzed and there was a message from Max.

Max

> Photography has become a hobby of mine.

He didn't deserve the dignity of a response. Blocking his number, I put my phone in my purse and grabbed the stacks of magazines that had my face plastered on the front. I knew there would be more, but this was the least I could do for my sanity.

Mr. Granger's eyebrows furrowed as he scanned each magazine. I'd think he was angry at me if I didn't know any better. He was angry *for* me. The man was just as protective of me now as he was when I worked for him.

"Your day will get better, Autumn. I know it."

"Well, there is only one way it can go."

I waved goodbye as I headed toward my car. Colton and I had finally exchanged numbers, and I considered messaging him about the tabloids, but he beat me to it.

Colton

Are you okay?

Yes. Just angry.

I'm sorry. I never wanted this to happen. It's part of why I picked Ashfield.

> To lie low. I get it. Neither of us planned for Max to do this.

It was your ex?

> Yes. He messaged and said he had picked up photography as a hobby.

Fucking asshole. I'm going to destroy him.

> He's not worth it. What are you going to do?

What do you mean?

> I understand if you have to deny everything.

I would never deny being with you, Autumn.

I knew he couldn't see me, but my body flushed and my toes curled against the soft insert of my shoes at his compliment.

> **What do you have going on today?**

I'm co-hosting tonight on the Hockey Network and I have a test hosting gig for a cooking show.

> **😝 How is someone that can't cook hosting a cooking show?**

Your guess is as good as mine. They just want my pretty face.

> **You're probably right.**

What are you getting into today?

> **Emergency book club meeting and a massive bonfire.**

> Bonfire?

> I have a lot of magazines to burn.

Our conversation paused and I chose that moment to drive back home. I planned to work on framing the images Colton had found in the house and surprising him with a few others that I'd blown up.

It still amazed me at how far along the house had come. Inspectors were dropping in on a daily basis because it was progressing so quickly. The knowledge left my emotions in a tailspin. When the house was done it would be as closely restored to its original state as it could safely be. And the chance for it to be accepted by the National Historic Society would be available. But it also meant that Colton had no reason to stay. What was he going to do with an eight-bedroom house anyway?

By the time I returned to my parents' home, I hadn't heard back from Colton, but I had a dozen messages from the women in the local book club. They were all in agreement with the last-minute bonfire.

"Hey, Mom," I said as I dumped the bags of tabloids on the counter. When she didn't reply, I repeated her name.

"Hey, sweetie." My father's name called out from the office and I turned the corner, remembering how almost a month ago I had spent time in the same room with my mother, lamenting the idea of returning to Ashfield permanently. Now, things had changed. The town had grown on me again, or at least, Colton made me appreciate it more.

Even with my name and face plastered on every magazine stand across the country, the townspeople weren't down-casting their gazes. Instead, they smiled. They asked if I was okay. They made sure I knew they were going to be on the lookout for any reporters in town. All to protect me and Colton. They had welcomed him into this place with open arms, despite the way he had come to town so flamboyantly.

"Hi, Dad," I replied. The soft scruff of his beard tickled my cheek as I leaned in for a hug. "Not working the field today?"

"Nah. Your mother and Andrew forced me into this box today." His hand flung about as he waved in the space.

Taking the seat across from him, my body sinking into the plush leather, I asked, "What made them do that?"

"Andrew has someone coming to town to speak to me about operations. He thinks hiring a chief operating officer will help me take a step back from farming and move toward retirement. Andrew isn't interested in taking over the ranch. He's so focused on his career."

"You don't seem too thrilled about that."

"This farm has been in my family for over a century. It's hard to step away from something that I've been doing since I could walk. And the unknown of how to keep it in the family weighs on me."

"I understand, but just because you step back doesn't mean you won't be hands on. Heck, we could use some help with our garden," I said. My dad's chuckle was like music to my ears. It reminded me of the nights he spent camping with me and my sisters out in the pasture. He'd tell us ghost stories until Aspen couldn't handle it and then he turned them into fairytales.

"I may take you up on that. Now, your mother is outside brushing down one of the horses, but she mentioned we were hosting a bonfire tonight?

Something about her precious baby being taken advantage of."

"Yeah," I mumbled, my lip stinging as my teeth clamped down on the soft skin.

"Is there a neighbor I need to have a word with?" His tone didn't change, but I could hear the seriousness in it all the same.

"No. No. Colton hasn't done anything. He's been great, really. Better than I would have thought."

"What makes you say that?"

"Well, my love life is kind of a mess, that's all."

"You just haven't met the right person. I suspect Mr. Crawford is going to surprise us all."

There was more I wanted to say to my dad, but the alarm on his phone blared loudly. My limbs squeaked against the leather as they jerked.

"Sorry, sweetheart, but the man I'm meeting today will be arriving soon."

"Oh, it's no problem. I'll see you at dinner?"

"Of course," he said, peering out the window. The sound of gravel crunching outside the window alerted us of the stranger's arrival.

I bypassed the pile of magazines on the island and snagged a bottle of water from the fridge in my haste to my bedroom. There were about four hours to kill before the girls in the book club would arrive. Mostly it was my sisters, Lily, and a few people I had known growing up.

In my room, I tossed my purse on my compact desk and threw my body backward onto the bed. It whined in protest.

I needed a distraction from Colton. He'd occupied most of my time in the last week and he was all I thought about. I knew there was a good chance one of these jobs his agent had set up was going to be his next path in life. How could it not be? Colton Crawford was one of the most charismatic men I'd ever met. And I knew from the internet that the camera loved him.

My phone pinged across the room and I closed my eyes, hoping to ignore it. Only it pinged a second time. Groaning, I shuffled over to my discarded bag and toed off my shoes as I dug around for the phone.

Colton
I miss you.

I didn't want him to know how excited I was that he missed me already, but the inner teen girl inside me was jumping around like a banshee.

> **Send me a picture.**

> **It's been like eight hours.**

> **Don't care.**

Turning the phone around, I snapped a quick selfie and sent it as a message to Colton as I laid back on the bed.

> **My God, you're beautiful.**

> **I'm surprised you didn't want a different kind of picture.**

> **Naw, I'll save that for tonight. I have to go in for an interview now.**

> **Good luck.**

My phone landed with a flop on the bed as I stared at my ceiling. It had once been covered in those sticky, glow in the dark stars, but I'd removed those when I left for college. I'd always loved them, though. They reminded me of nights camping with my father.

"Hey, girl. Get up." My body was flung in the air as Alex plopped her body on the edge of my bed.

"I am up."

"I see that," she replied as we sat up on the bed simultaneously.

"What are you doing here, anyway? The bonfire starts at seven."

"Can't I come hang out with my big sis?"

I tilted my head and pursed my lips. "No."

"Well, shit. What if I told you I wanted to get the scoop on you and Colton before everyone got here?"

"No."

"I brought tequila. And I really want to know if his, you know, matches the size of his hands and feet. Because the man is large everywhere."

Damn. Alex knew that margaritas were my downfall. I sighed heavily, tilting my head back as I agreed.

"You always were an enabler," I joked as my phone rang.

Glancing down, I noted the unknown number. Usually, I didn't answer those and sent them to voicemail, but some sort of inclination had me pressing the green button. I silently gestured to Alex that I would join her in a minute, but she leaned her lean body against the doorjamb.

"Hello?"

"Yes, I'm looking for Autumn Easterly. This is Sandra from Elemental Design Events."

My heart jumped into my throat. It had been a couple of weeks since I applied for the job the weekend I had arrived in Ashfield. The posting hadn't crossed my mind again and I assumed my blacklist status had traveled all the way to Tennessee with me.

"Um. This is she. How can I help you?"

The woman on the other end of the line went into detail about how their hiring manager had attended a few of the events I'd put together in New York. When my name came across the list of applicants, she knew I would be the best person for the position.

"So, you're just offering me the job? What about an interview?" My eyes darted over to Alex, who had stiffened, her body rigid across the threshold of my room.

"Well, I mean, we can hold an interview if you'd like one, but she's pretty certain you're the event planner she wants. You came highly recommended and your resume is impeccable."

"Wow. I...ugh...don't know what to say."

"Say yes, of course."

"Can I have a few days to think about it?"

"Sure, I suppose you have many options available to you."

"Yes, thank you. I just need to adjust some plans, maybe."

"Will you be in touch by Monday?"

"Sure. Yes. That sounds fine. I will call you back at this number on Monday."

I couldn't see the woman on the other end of the line, but I imagined she was leaning over her desk as she quietly asked, "Is it true that you're dating Colton Crawford?"

My mouth hung agape as my fingers twitched.

"You can't always believe everything you read," I replied coldly, ending the conversation immediately.

Was this how it was always going to be now that I'd been tied to the sports superstar? My career blacklist nulled and voided with a single picture.

"I'm going to need that tequila. No margarita required."

Chapter Eighteen

Colton

Sunday had come and gone and I was still sitting in a luxury hotel in the outskirts of LA. My agent snuck in sponsorship deals during the trip, which required my time there to extend. Though I loved the weather and lifestyle of Hollywood, I missed Ashfield.

I missed the land, the mountains, and the smells. And, fuck, I missed Autumn fiercely. Everywhere I went, I swore that I saw her. Even at a local sushi place my agent and I dined at the night before, I stumbled over myself when I thought Autumn had walked through the doors. At second glance, it was clearly not her.

I'd reluctantly video called Autumn on Sunday when I learned my stay was going to be extended. She pretended to be okay with the change in plans, but I could tell by her eyes that she was disappointed. It was the same reason we hadn't put a label on our relationship or talked any further about our path. We went day by day.

She'd mentioned the job offer to a prestigious group that had an office in Knoxville, but she said she didn't think it was the right place for her. It was clear there was something she was hiding, but I had my own issues going on.

Sadie wanted to meet and I wasn't sure that was the best idea with the way the press was still buzzing about with the pictures of myself and Autumn. But she was persistent. And that left a bitter taste on my tongue. My fear of her trying to use me to get ahead in her life, whether that be money or status, seemed more plausible every day. I was going to have to nip this in the bud once and for all.

"Colton, my man," Lex, my agent, said as he strutted into my hotel room like he had zero cares that he had extended my trip by three days already. I was itching to get back to Ashfield. "We have another test spot today for-"

"For what, Lex?" I spun around, the vein at my temple bulging as I approached the agent that had been with me my entire career. "What is it for this time? A daytime talk show? A game show? Man, I don't want to be a part of any of this. We agreed to the cooking show because there was experience with other retired athletes hosting similar segments, but you know that none of this is me. When I decided to retire that was to take a step back and enjoy life, not find myself just as busy."

Lex held his hands up in defeat. "You're right, man. I was only trying to help you get your feet wet so you'd have options. Right now, everyone wants you. I already have contracts for multiple spots that you tested for the last few days."

My hand shot through my hair, leaving it in spikes as I sat on the edge of my hotel bed.

"Fuck, man. Look, how much longer do you need me here?"

Glancing down at his phone, he scrolled through what I assumed was his calendar before saying, "Another day or so? You have a magazine shoot after the test today and then the Hockey Network was hoping you'd be able to guest host the LA game tomorrow."

"Okay. Then after that, no more. I'm tired, Lex. One or two gigs every once in a while is fine. Sponsorships I'm okay with. Just. . .slow down. Alright?"

"Alright. I hear you. I'll let our contacts know."

"Also, I'm going to need a plane ticket to Knoxville on Friday. And I need you to help me coordinate a meeting."

Lex began typing away on his phone, arranging the items I needed. Looking up at me beneath his fuzzy furrowed brows, he asked, "Who is the meeting with?"

"Sadie."

"Who?" he asked as the pitter-patter of him touching the keys on his phone stopped.

I turned away from him and faced the windows. Off in the distance, there was a mountain range. Rocky and brown, they didn't look as resplendent as the ones in my backyard. I sighed, draping my arms over my thighs and hanging my head low.

"My sister."

The flight to Tennessee had been quick and painless, even though I'd flown commercial, which sometimes could be hard to do if someone recognized me. After the flight, I grabbed a rental and drove straight to the restaurant where I had agreed to meet Sadie.

"Sir, can I get you a glass of water while you wait?" the server asked as he stood at the end of my table. I'd kept my back to the room and tugged the brim of my cap down farther as news of my signing with the Hockey Network went worldwide. I'd be able to work mostly from wherever I decided to call home, so long as I had a green screen and power. They were willing to bend over backward to have me on the weekly show.

There was still talk of me co-hosting a baking show on the National Food Channel, but that would only require my commitment for a couple of weeks a year. It was still a gig that made zero sense to me, but the team behind it seemed excited.

But my face was all over the place, this time for my career, which was better than for my relationships, but I knew that people were still curious about Autumn. The paparazzi that stood outside my hotel in LA floundered around me, trying to get information. Originally, I had planned to ask her to come along with me, but I'd second-guessed myself. We hadn't defined our relationship and that would surely put us on another level.

But spending the week with her instead of having to text and video message would have been far better. God, I missed her. More so than I ever thought possible.

"No, thank you. I'll wait until my guest arrives."

"Okay. I'll check back with you." I couldn't see him, but based on the sudden breeze I felt at the base of my neck, I was certain the teen had scurried away at breakneck speed.

While I waited, I scrolled through my phone, my thumb hovering over Autumn's number. I had missed our call the night before because I was live at the hockey game. We'd messaged, but she seemed a bit distant, taking longer and longer to respond. Of course, I was to blame for her hesitancy. I still hadn't told her when I would return. A lot of that depended on how this meeting went.

If Sadie seemed as genuine as I hoped, then there was a good chance I'd want to stay in Knoxville and spend some time with her. If I had even the slightest inkling that she had something malicious or selfish in mind, I wasn't certain I could return to

Ashfield right away. I'd need another day or two to wrap my head around everything that had transpired. And that I was still an orphan with no family. As much as I wanted to see Autumn, I knew that she'd have questions. Ones I wasn't prepared to answer.

"Excuse me, Mr. Crawford? Your guest has arrived."

My breath shook as I turned in my seat and stood. I wasn't surprised at the girl's startled breath. What did take me aback was my own. The girl was clearly related to me, and I towered over her. From her olive skin tone to the mousy brown waves of hair, there was no mistaking us as anything else but siblings.

"Thank you. We'll order in a bit," I said to the host, who nodded as he left us alone, still staring at each other.

Finally, the girl chose to break up the silence.

"So. . .um. . .I'm Sadie," she said, holding out her hand in greeting. It quivered ever so slightly as she waited for me to return the greeting.

"Hi, Sadie. I'm Colton, but you already know that." I returned her impressively strong handshake and gestured for her to sit in the chair across from me.

We sat in silence. I had no idea what to say to this girl who seemed as lost as I was. Luckily, the server chose that moment to return to the table and take our drink order. We laughed as I ordered a light beer and her a soda to ease the tension.

"Sorry," Sadie said, squinting her eyes contritely. "Now that I'm here, I'm not quite sure what to say."

"Well, there isn't much about me that you can't find on the internet. I assume you Googled me before even sending me your first letter. Am I right?"

She shrugged her shoulders as petals of red scattered across her cheeks. "Guilty."

"So, tell me about you. What brought you to Knoxville?"

That seemed to be all the encouragement she needed as she launched into her childhood. Sadie had grown up living on the outskirts of the city with her mom. She had a stepfather for a short period of time, but he ran off with another woman when Sadie was only six. It amazed me when she said she had never been ice skating and couldn't believe when she found out that I spent the majority of my life on the ice.

"I'm studying environmental engineering at the University of Tennessee. I was so excited to get accepted. It had been my dream school my entire life."

While she had been speaking animatedly about her life, the server had come and taken our order. He quietly placed our burgers in front of us and I took a hefty bite of the large patty.

"What are you up to now?" Sadie asked as she snatched a fry off her plate and shoved it into her mouth.

"Not sure yet. I signed on to film a few spots on the Hockey Network and my agent is tossing around a few options."

"Nothing else? Because I'm pretty certain I saw a picture of you and a girl on the cover of a magazine at the grocery store this morning."

The bite of burger lodged in my throat and I covered my mouth with the napkin as I coughed.

"Sorry. That, um, girl's name is Autumn. "

"She's really pretty."

"I think so, too."

"Can I meet her?"

"Why?"

"I don't know. I mean, I don't have many girlfriends. Well, friends at all."

This was it. This was going to be the moment where she either asked for money or begged to live with me to gain some sort of celebrity status.

"Why is that?" I asked more sternly than I intended. It was clear that I hurt her feelings when her eyes grew to the size of saucers.

"Oh. . .I just mean. . .Money, er,"

The chair screeched against the floor as I shot up, slamming my fists on the table. Thank goodness the chain restaurant was mostly deserted.

"Of course. You came here wanting money."

"No! No," she cried out, shaking her hand in a stop motion. "No, please sit down, Colton, and let me explain." When I hesitated, she begged again. Slowly, I returned to my seat and pushed my burger aside. Any appetite I may have had early had quickly dissolved away.

"When my mom passed away, she left me a hefty inheritance from her life insurance policy. I had no idea it existed. When my so-called friends found out, they became leeches. Asking me for money, pretending they wanted me to join them for dinner only to leave before the check came and I was left to pay for it all. Just, not the kind of things friends do. So, when I started at the university, I kept to myself mostly."

"That really happened to you?" I asked the question, but I already knew the answer. It was clear with the way she flung her hands around, speaking so animatedly.

"Yes."

"I'm sorry I jumped to conclusions. I've just been burned before by people wanting something from me."

"I get it. I'd probably have done the same."

My appetite hadn't returned, so I sipped my beer while Sadie finished her meal.

"You'd like Autumn. She's funny and so fucking smart."

"Is she prettier than in the pictures?"

"They don't do her justice at all," I explained, tearing at the edge of the paper wrapped around the neck of the beer bottle.

"You really love her, don't you?"

"Love?" I asked, the bottle nearly falling over on the table as my hand jerked at the shocking accusation.

"It's clear as day. She sounds awesome. What does she do?"

Did I love Autumn? I mean, I knew I liked her and enjoyed the time we spent together, but what did I know of love? It was something I'd never experienced before.

"She's a...well, she was an event planner. She was fired by her douchebag ex and came back home. I actually met her the day I arrived in Ashfield."

"Aw, that's adorable."

"Thanks," I replied wryly, then gulped down the last sip of my beer.

The server brought the check and I grabbed the black folder before Sadie could attempt it. The girl even huffed with her arms crossed tightly against her chest. Like she was ever going to get to pay for this meal.

"Before you go, I have something for you. It's from our mom."

She dug around in a large bag dangling from the back of her chair, then she held out a well-worn letter.

My baby boy,

If you're reading this, then I can only hope that you have forgiven me. I spent many agonizing years wondering if I had done the right thing by giving you up. I was a baby myself when I had you and knew that I couldn't give you the life you deserved. I can't regret my decision, but I can regret not ever getting to hold you one last time. You were one of the best things that ever happened to me.

We all have tough choices to make and we can only hope that time heals the wounds left behind by our decisions.

I'm not sure what I intended with this letter as I know you'll never read it, but I just felt like you should know that I've thought of you every day of my life and will continue to do so when I pass along.

I love you, my sweet baby boy, and I hope you take the time to give your love to those who are important to you.

Sincerely,

Mom

"When—" I coughed, clearing my throat. "When did she write this?"

Sadie replied somberly, "I'm not sure. I found it stashed away with her things when I was cleaning out the house. I think she wrote it after you were born, though. It was nestled in a folder with some of your delivery items."

"Delivery items?"

"Yeah, like the hospital bracelet, cap, blanket. I think there is a copy of your footprint there too. After I did the genetics test, I became curious and dug through some of her boxes. I felt it was better to tell you in person than over a letter or text. There's more too, of her things, I mean."

"Can I see?"

"Yeah, of course. I actually still live in the house. It's not a long drive to the university and it made more sense to keep the house for now."

"Okay, I'll follow you there."

Standing from the table, I noted that Sadie was taller than most girls, and that drew a certain amount of attention as we exited together. Pulling the brim of my hat farther over my face and flipping the collar of my jacket over my neck, I did my best to duck out of everyone's watchful eyes.

Unfortunately, there were a few photographers lingering outside the restaurant who flashed their cameras at us as we dashed across the street. As if fate took pity on us, Sadie's car was parked only one spot over from my rental.

I'd told her to go straight home after she logged her address in my phone, and I did my best to drive around until I thought I was no longer being followed.

Thirty minutes later, I was sure no one was tailing me and I arrived at the small brick ranch-style house settled on a small lot in an older neighborhood. Sadie stood outside along a picket fence that needed a fresh coat of paint gnawing on one of her fingernails.

"Think anyone followed you?"

"Naw, I think we're safe," I replied as I followed her into the house. The living room looked clean and well lived in. It looked like a home that had been filled with love.

"I haven't said it yet, but I am sorry about your mom."

"Thank you. The cancer was fast and aggressive. It felt like one day we had a diagnosis and the next I was saying goodbye. The only positive is that the doctors said she didn't suffer much."

"That's good."

We stood awkwardly in the space, like we had at the restaurant when we initially met.

"I put her things on the kitchen table on the off-chance you wanted to come see them."

"Good, good. Show me the way."

Stacked plastic containers covered the wooden circle dining table. Despite being mismatched, the chairs complemented the space.

Sadie walked over to the refrigerator, leaving me at the table, and asked if I wanted a bottle of water while I sorted through some of the items. After agreeing, I lifted the top of the first box and got to work learning about a woman I never had a chance to meet.

"Wow," I said, holding up a framed picture of our mother with a tiny baby Sadie swaddled in a blanket while she rocked in a chair.

"Mom and her parents had a rocky relationship after you were born. They came around after she finished college all on her own merit, but they died in a car accident before I was born."

"Who took the picture?"

"A neighbor, I think. Mom wasn't sure who my father was. Someone she met at a work conference was all she ever told me."

Placing the picture back in the box, I turned my head toward Sadie. "I'm sorry you don't know who your father is."

"Thanks, but you can't miss what you never had," she said, the corners of her smile downturned.

"True. So, tell me what I'm going to find in the rest of these totes."

The sunlight of late afternoon was swallowed up by the darkness of night as it snuck in. The light over the table was the only illumination in the room as we went through the last box. It was cardboard, worn and weathered.

"This is the only one I didn't go through completely yet. Emotionally, I could only handle one a week or so. But just from opening the lid and finding the baby things, I knew it wasn't a box meant for me."

Folding back the lid, a musty scent overwhelmed my senses. As Sadie had mentioned, a few baby items rested on top, but what surprised us both were the newspaper articles about me when I accepted the hockey scholarship in college and following my career. We could tell that it hadn't been touched in years, but somebody had added to its contents.

"Do you think she knew?" I asked Sadie, who had earlier said that her mother had never mentioned having another child.

"Maybe. You bear a striking resemblance to our grandfather. If she wasn't certain, maybe she hoped that it was you. It maybe gave her hope that she had done the right thing by giving you up."

"Yeah," I said with a choked back cry.

"How about I give you a minute? I'll grab us a beer from the fridge in the garage."

Nodding my thanks, I crumbled onto the table and let the knowledge of what I'd spent the last three hours delving through wash through me. It was. . .overwhelming.

Minutes passed before I worked up the courage to lift my head, shoving the bottoms of my palms into my eye sockets to wipe them clean. I looked over and found Sadie sitting in a chair, quietly sipping on her beer.

"I brought you two. Figured you may need it."

Grabbing the still ice-cold bottle, I downed the first in four hearty gulps, then shoved my hand over my mouth as I belched loudly. "Sorry. Er, thanks for this."

"You're welcome. So, if you want to stay the night, I have a spare room and a fridge full of beer."

"I'm not going to ask how you were able to get the beer."

"Wow, turning into a big brother already?" she joked. "I have a fake ID, but I rarely get carded because of my height. People just assume I'm older."

"Well, I won't give you too hard of a time since I'm benefiting from it. And thanks for the room offer. I'll take you up on it."

"If you want to put something on the television, I can order us a pizza and make the bed up for you."

"You don't have to do that. I can sleep wherever."

"No, let me do this. Please," she pleaded as she stood from the table. Before a second passed, she wrapped her arms around my neck and I found myself returning her embrace.

"I always wanted a sibling."

Patting the back of her arm, I added, "Me too, kid. Me too."

I watched as she skipped away to a room down the hall and then I made my way to the living room with a flatscreen hoisted above the fireplace.

By default, I landed on a hockey game. It was the local pro hockey team out of Tennessee and at that moment, an idea popped into my head of taking both Autumn and Sadie to a game sounded like a great way to spend a night.

"Hockey?" Sadie asked ten minutes later as she plopped her body onto the recliner across from me.

"Well, it is my favorite thing to watch."

Groaning, she dramatically tossed her head back. "Ugh, I guess I'm going to need to learn all about it, aren't I?"

"It couldn't hurt."

The pizza arrived shortly after and it surprised me that Sadie and I both loved a fully loaded pie, but it didn't come close to the delicious concoction I had eaten with Autumn on our first date. It was a good substitute, though.

While eating the pizza, we lounged back and I explained the game on the screen. Sadie tried to grasp what was going on, but hockey and her didn't seem to mix. But it was clear she was trying to understand.

I felt a buzzing in my back pocket and I knew it was Autumn messaging me. Timidly, I pulled the phone out and read the message on the screen.

> **Autumn**
> Inspector came by today. He noted a few things and told your contractor. Will be back on Monday for final.

There was no warm greeting. No "Hey, I miss you." Nothing like our earlier messages. Instead, it felt more cold, impersonal. And I knew it was my fault. I'd been the one that was distant. In the last few days, I'd taken longer and longer to reply to her messages. I was an hour away from the woman that had thrown me for a loop and I was too chickenshit to do anything about it.

"That your girlfriend?"

Shaking my head, I shoved the phone back into my pocket. "Just finding out the inspector wants a few changes to my house in Ashfield."

"Kind of late for an inspector to reach out."

"It was my contractor."

Sadie pulled her gaze away from the television and bore it down on me. She may have been my little sister, but right now she made me feel like I was two feet tall.

"Anyone ever tell you that you're a shit liar?"

Settling back onto the couch, I crossed my arms against my chest and turned away from her, focusing back on the game on the television.

"You really are, just so you know."

"Am not," I sulked.

"Call her. I have no idea what's going on in this game anyway and to be honest, I'm whipped after this exciting day," she said sarcastically. "We can hang again tomorrow. Or do you need to head back?"

"I can stay, Sadie."

"Good. Now, let me show you your room and then you can call your sweetheart."

Following her to a room down the hall, I mumbled, "I'm going to regret this."

"Good night, big brother."

"Night, Sadie."

In the small room, I took note of the dresser and the full-sized bed that reminded me of Autumn's room and I immediately felt guilty for ignoring her message earlier. The bed screeched as I sat on the edge and pulled my phone from my back pocket.

I contemplated whether to call or message her, but I took the chance and pressed the dial button on her contact. It rang three times and I worried I was waking her up. With a quick glance at the clock on the nightstand, it read 10:00 p.m. so there was a chance this call could go either way.

"Colton?" Autumn yelled from the other line as if she was covering her opposite ear with her hand to hear better.

"Hey. I just wanted to call you back," I said. The telltale sign of music in the background became clear.

"What? Hey, hold on a second." Her breathing increased as the music settled down and then suddenly, there was complete silence.

"Autumn?"

"Shit. Sorry I dropped my phone. Hey. Hi. How are you?"

"Have you been drinking?" It was a stupid question to ask because after the few times Autumn and I had gone out, I knew she rarely drank more than one or two drinks. And it was very clear she was on the other side of tipsy.

"Maybe...Well, I was at the bar helping Alex and when I messaged you this afternoon, I was not drinking. And now I am because it's karaoke night."

"This afternoon? I just got your message like fifteen minutes ago."

"Really? Well, damn. I swear I sent it when the inspector left your house."

Curiosity got the best of me as I laid back on the bed. "What were you doing at the house, Princess?"

"Um. . .missing you?"

"Uh huh."

Off in the distance, I could hear a group of people calling Autumn's name and it warmed something deep inside me. Autumn claimed to not have any friends besides her sisters, but there were definitely more than three voices shouting at her to return to the fun.

"Hey, I'll let you get back," I said. "I should be home soon."

"Really?" she asked, her voice perking up.

"Really."

Her voice quieted as she asked, "For real this time?" and I felt like an ass.

"Yeah, baby. For real."

"Oh good. Because I have a surprise for you."

"Is it your pussy?"

"Colton!" she exclaimed and I caught myself laughing and feeling more carefree than I had in a long time.

"Sorry, I couldn't help myself."

"It's more than. . .that. Though she missed you, too."

"I'm going to fuck you until you can't walk when I see you again."

"Promises, promises. The book club is calling me," she paused before adding, "Don't be a stranger, Colton."

Before I could say more, she ended the call and I was left feeling better than I had in a long time.

For the first time, it seemed like my life was going down a path that I could follow and embrace.

As I got ready for bed, thankful for the toothbrush and toothpaste Sadie had left for me in the bathroom across the hall, I wondered if the woman that once owned this place was smiling down, knowing that her children had finally come together. Not that I knew her very well, but I suspected that our mom would have loved Autumn. She was strong, smart, and kind.

And I loved her.

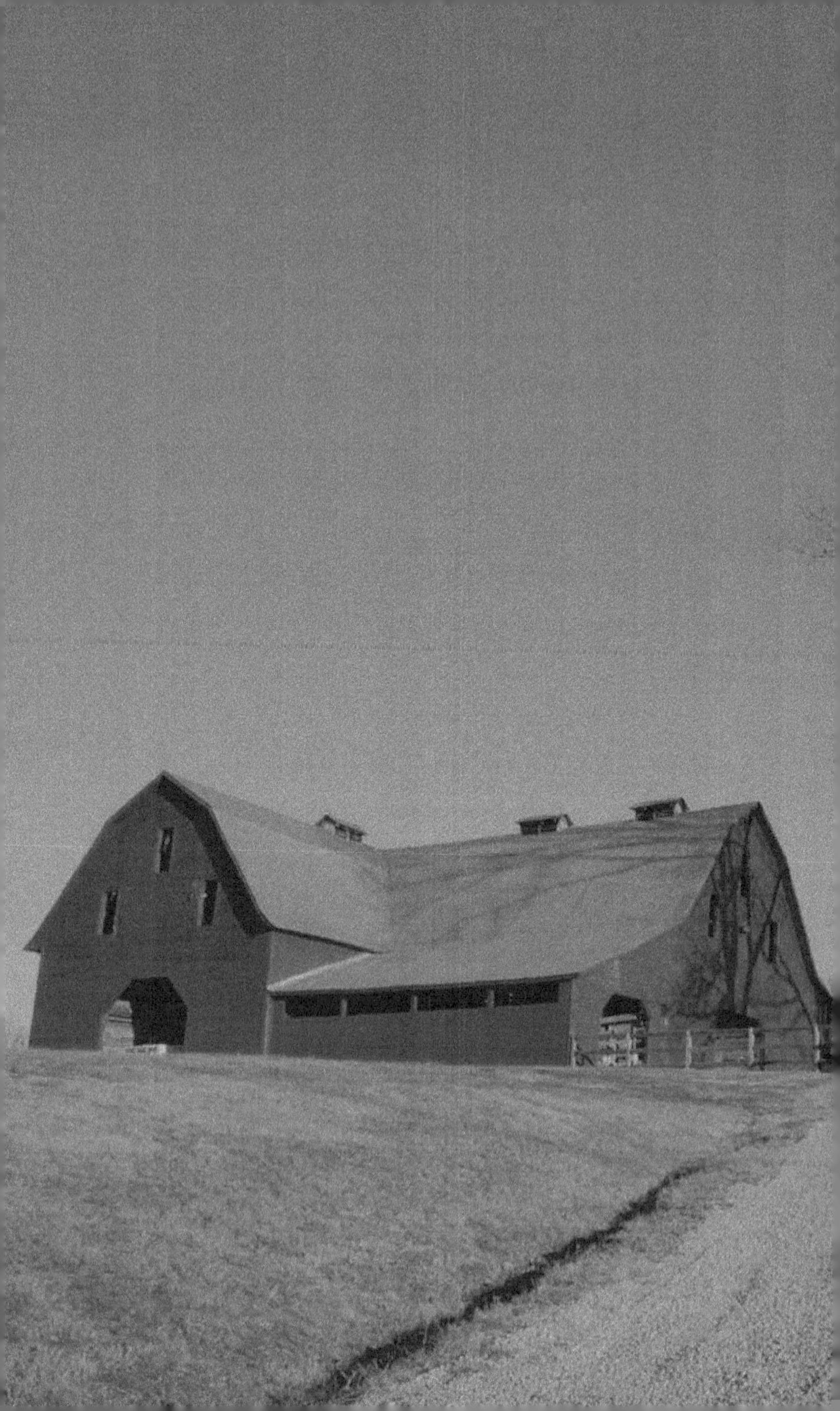

Chapter Nineteen

Autumn

Sawdust swirled around me like a tornado as I sanded the dresser in the attic of Colton's house. He had no idea I was tackling this project. Heck, I had surprised myself and the contractor when I said I wanted to turn it into his master suite.

With the last leg complete, I crawled off the floor and stared at the soon-to-be masterpiece. With the white paint on the newly drywalled walls and the light oak floors that had been freshly stained, the room seemed open and spacious even with the peaked ceilings. I suspected it was the last-minute skylights Colton requested to be installed.

So far, the upstairs was coming together as Colton had wished. Other than the few ventilation changes that needed to be made, the house was pretty much ready to live in. In thirty days, no less. I didn't know how much Colton spent to have the house remodeled so quickly, nor did I want to know, but his money sure made things happen faster than I'd ever seen.

When I chose to revamp the attic for Colton, I hadn't been completely selfless. I wanted the chance to scour through the walls to find any more goodies. Unfortunately, there wasn't anything of sentimental value besides some more newspaper articles. But I was devoted to renovating the space and a bit stubborn.

Instead of leaving the space completely open, I had the contractor set up a narrow hallway at the top of the stairs and divide the other half of the attic into three smaller bedrooms and a full-sized bathroom. Colton could use them for whatever he wanted, like an office or gym, but if he ended up deciding to rent out the rooms or the entire house, it would be great. Especially if I could get him to partner with me and the venue. If

Colton didn't like the new layout, he could easily take the walls down.

On the other side of the master bedroom was the master bathroom. I'd managed to get a modern oversized clawfoot tub into the room along with a standup shower that could accommodate Colton's height. All the colors were calm and serene and I tried to think of him when I picked out the items. I also kept the receipts because maybe I didn't know him as well as I thought I did.

Alex and Rory didn't know why I was spending so much time decorating a place for the man that had extended his trip out of Ashfield twice already. I tried not to think about any of the many reasons why he would want to stay away. I knew them all far too well. They were the same reasons I always struggled with returning. Now things had changed since I found a purpose here.

Colton had been part of that change. Somehow, even without the label, I'd fallen for the man. The man that I once thought had stolen my dream, but instead had helped me realize a new one.

Frustrated that it had been another two days since I'd so much as heard from Colton, I began to worry that all of this hard work was for nothing. He never did say exactly what day he would return, just soon. The ache in my heart had thought soon would be the next day.

Foolish of me.

Ripping the respirator off my face, I dusted off the antique dresser I'd found at a store in the next town over. I'd work on staining it the same rich walnut color Colton and I had chosen for the library later. But I needed to head over to dinner at my parents' house. I'd spent such little time with them recently and I felt guilty. Alex had also been pressuring me to tell them about the job offer from Friday. The one I'd turned down officially on Monday. I couldn't work at a place that potentially saw me as a one-way ticket to a celebrity of sorts. As much as it pained me to turn it down, I felt better about my decision afterward.

Placing my mask on top of the dresser, I took a last glance at the space and made my way down the steep stairs. The one thing I loved about this attic space was that it could be completely closed off from the rest of the house because of a door at the base.

The second floor was nothing more than white walls and freshly stained floors. But it looked exactly how I thought it may when it was first built. Rooms that had once housed children and family members and any guests passing through.

I took the back stairwell down to the kitchen area and smiled when I stepped into the space. The kitchen had all the modern fixtures of today but looked as if everything was still stuck in the past. Colton had taken the ideas I'd had in my binder and purchased it all.

I suppose he could have had an interior designer do the same, but it felt more special knowing that I had been the one to find these items to help keep the home's historic qualities.

Turning around, I stepped into my favorite room in the entire house. The library was now filled to perfection with thousands of books that Colton and I had scoured for in online bookstores and antique shops. Many of the shelves were still empty, but with all of the hardbacks, the room gave off that old book scent and I adored it.

I spent another minute in the space and then left the house, locking it up behind me. I'd been driving one of Dad's UTVs between the properties and made my way over to where I'd parked it close to the path connecting our two properties.

On the drive back I found myself laughing at how just a month prior my entire family had been distraught over the idea that someone bought the property I'd had my eyes on as a little girl. My parents probably could have figured out a way to buy the home on their own, but they had supported me and wanted to give me that chance to make it my own. We didn't know Colton Crawford or what his plans were for the place. Color us surprised when Dad brought him over and he claimed he wanted to restore the home.

To this day, it still seemed like a dream. But I wasn't naïve enough to realize that it could all slip away just as quickly. Colton could grow tired of the place or get a job back in New York or LA and decide to sell. It was getting harder and harder to vet the people buying up properties in town. Developers were already trying to swindle the ranch owners into selling their land for a hefty payout.

Sunny Brook Farms was going to hold steady, though, and I hoped my venue plans would help.

I parked the vehicle and walked into the house, inhaling deeply when the scent of homemade pasta sauce consumed me.

"Hey, Mom," I called out from the mudroom as I slid off my shoes and shook out my clothes one last time. Mom had already fussed at me for all the sawdust I'd been bringing into the house.

When I entered the kitchen, I found my sisters and brother fashioned around the table with a laptop between them. Mom and Dad sat on the couch with their gaze focused on whatever was playing on the screen, but it was clear they were listening in to my siblings.

"Hey, guys. I didn't expect to see all of you here. Especially you, Andrew. It's a weeknight after all."

"Well, sometimes we have to do things we don't want to," he said gruffly, slamming his index finger on the keyboard and then flipping it toward me.

"What's going on?" I asked in confusion as the group collectively stared at me as if it should be clear as day. Zoning in on the screen, there was a gossip page pulled up with Colton's name front and center. "What am I looking at?"

Unlike Alex's brash fashion, she calmly said, "We aren't really sure what's going on, but it looks like your boyfriend-"

Quickly I interrupted her and claimed that he was, in fact, not my boyfriend.

"Whatever he is, Autumn, there are pictures of Colton eating with another woman and then going back to her house. They finally saw him leaving with the woman earlier today."

I wasn't a jealous person by nature, but I couldn't ignore the adrenaline spike in my body or the way I felt the heat creep up my chest and onto my neck and cheeks.

"It's okay," Rory said calmly as she tried to reach for my hand, which I immediately darted out of her grasp. "We're all here for you."

"I don't believe he's a two-timing jackass like your ex," Aspen declared, only for our mom to shout, "Language," from the opposite side of the room.

"Can I see it, please?"

"It's okay if you need to take some time. I mean, you just got out of another bad relationship. Maybe you could give Colton a call and he could explain," Rory said, trying to placate me with her calm demeanor. It was doing the opposite as my fingers bit into my palms and my eye twitched.

"Give me the damn laptop so I can look at the pictures."

I knew from experience with some of the celebrity events I'd planned that you couldn't always believe everything in the tabloids, if ever. They'd got the relationship claims regarding Colton and myself correct, but that was because my sleaze of an ex had sold them the images just to hurt me. It did the opposite. Last I'd heard from rumblings of ex-coworkers was that Regent Events had been blacklisted by every celebrity in the vicinity.

"Autumn, maybe you should grab yourself some water and take a few minutes before you-"

"I don't want any damn water. Give me the freaking laptop!" I shouted, the room immediately growing silent.

Alex and Andrew released their grasps of the computer and I swiped it from the table, carrying it over to the kitchen island.

As I read the article, I noticed that Andrew and Alex had already pointed out what was written. Rolling my eyes, I clicked on the gallery of images, then held back my gasp.

Colton stared at me from the screen, that all-knowing smirk in place as the photographer captured the image. He pulled the brim of his hat down too low to see his eyes, but I knew him well enough to pick him out of a crowd. Whomever he was eating with in the picture had captured all of his devout attention.

I clicked on the arrow moving along to the next picture. It was of the back of Colton's head and the woman's he was with. She was tall and statuesque, with hair almost the same shade as Colton's. That's when things started clicking in place.

Sifting through the rest of the images, everything became clear to me, especially the last image of them leaving a smaller home with a clear view of their faces.

"You guys. You're blowing this out of proportion. He's not cheating."

A gentle hand landed on my shoulder and I turned to find my father standing behind me, offering his support.

"Autumn. It's okay to be upset," Rory said.

"He's not cheating!"

"Autumn. Are you blind? I mean, we want to believe he's not, as well, but these pictures are pretty damning," Aspen said, with Alex and Andrew agreeing with her statement.

"For goodness' sake. It's his sister, okay?"

"Psh, he doesn't have any family. You're seeing something that isn't there," Andrew replied, rolling his eyes in the process.

Slamming the laptop screen, I hopped down from the barstool and made my way toward the mudroom.

"Autumn!" they shouted.

Staring at them from over my shoulder, I narrowed my eyes. "Look at the pictures. Really look at them. If you can't believe those, then believe me. He's not cheating. Now, I want to be alone. I realize you all are just looking out for me and I love you for it, but I need a little bit of time," I announced, then stomped back out of the house.

Before I knew it, I was flying in the UTV toward the western field where I'd started planning the barn expansion for the venue.

I knew my family meant well, but they weren't giving Colton the benefit of the doubt. And as nice as they had been about finding the article, it meant they didn't trust my instincts either.

I may have been cheated on before, but Colton was not the same slimy coward as Max.

And I knew my eyes weren't deceiving me. That woman in the pictures had to be his sister. I believed that with every fiber of my being. And that meant that Colton had found his family.

Which left me both happy and confused. If he found some part of himself that he'd been searching for his entire life, then what place did he have for me?

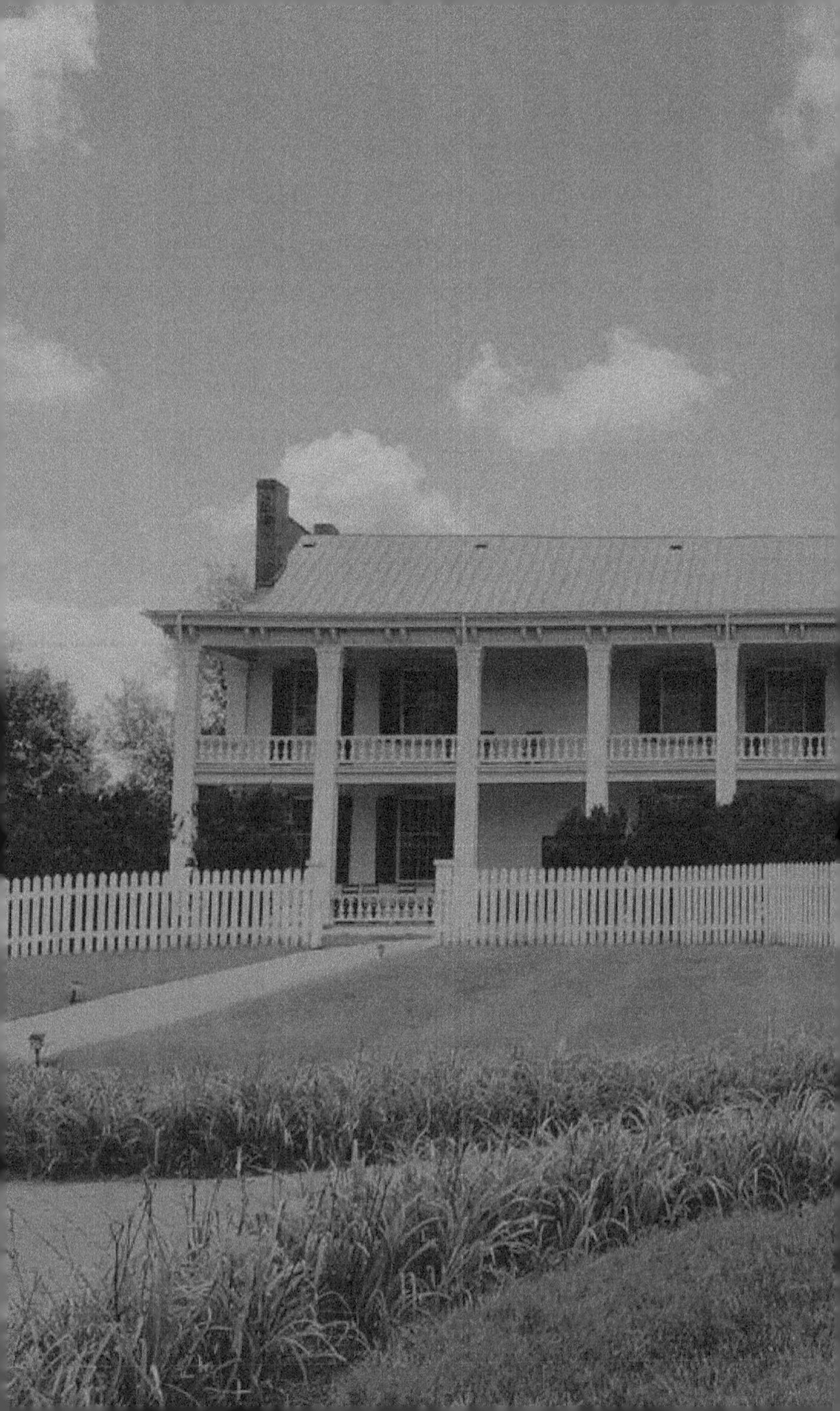

Chapter Twenty

Colton

The truck took the turn like it was nothing. Weeks of driving this path was paying off and I didn't need to creep around like a newbie, though I still felt like one.

"Is that it?" my passenger said as she leaned forward on the dashboard to get a closer look, because a foot was going to make a difference.

I chuckled as she continued to sway side to side to get a better view.

"Sit back, Sadie. We'll be there in a minute," I scolded but continued to laugh at her antics. The teen didn't listen to me at all.

She jumped from the truck before I even had it in park and ran toward the front door. The crew was gone for the day, which meant most of the work was complete except for what the inspector had noted during his recent walkthrough. Furnishings would start to go in next week.

It impressed me with how quickly the house had come together. The team I hired was superb and I planned to let the world know. Because while in LA, I somehow found myself agreeing to allow a popular home decorating show to come record the house during a walkthrough.

"Colton!" Sadie shouted from the threshold. "Get your ass out of the truck and show me around."

Succumbing to her demands, I jumped down from the truck and dashed to the porch to unlock the door for her.

"This place is going to be amazing. I can just imagine sitting on this porch in a rocking chair watching the sunrise in the morning."

Funny thing is, I had thought the exact same thing when I bought the house and already ordered two sets of rocking chairs for this porch and a swaying bed chair for the upper porch.

I held out my arm, gesturing for Sadie to enter before me, and said, "After you."

I wasn't surprised that in the time it took me to make it toward the kitchen, Sadie had already explored the first floor and was using the back stairwell to head toward the upper floors.

"Wow, Colton!" she shouted from the top of the stairs. "That attic space is amazing!"

"What do you mean?" I asked as I made my way toward her.

When I left, the attic was still mostly a barren space except for the skylights I'd had installed to get some more light in the rooms besides the two side windows. The contractor and I had tossed around the idea of dormer windows, but that was going to dig into our timeline and push out the date of the final inspection. The six skylights were a better option and I spared no expense for them. These had a lifetime warranty and claimed to be leakproof.

We would see.

"The attic was just stone and beams when I left."

"Oh, it's definitely not that any longer."

Sadie stepped aside as we approached the hidden third-floor staircase, which clearly wasn't that hidden if she had found it. I had to duck my head to pass through the threshold and then made my way up the almost completely vertical stairs. The contractor was surprised I didn't want to change them.

"Holy shit," I said on a gasp as I took the last step coming into a small hallway.

The doors were all open and I could see about three bedrooms to my right and a full bathroom. To my left was what I had described to Autumn as the master suite.

Autumn.

This must have been a secret project she had been working on.

I stepped into the room to find a metal bedframe and a newly sanded antique dresser. It was clear that it was from the correct period.

I hated that we couldn't salvage any of the furniture that was left in the space. Previous tenants or the weather had damaged most of it. But Autumn knew a good find when she saw it.

"This bathroom is killer."

Following my sister into the black and white penny-tiled bathroom, it amazed me to see a clawfoot tub that was large enough for my body on one end and a stand-up shower on the farthest wall that would accommodate my height.

"Who designed this? Because. . .wow," Sadie pointed out and I agreed with her sentiment.

"Autumn must have done this."

"Damn. Is she going to tackle the rest of the house?"

"I hope so."

"I can't believe this is the same woman you outbid for the property and then somehow her father tricked her into helping you restore it. Her dad must be freaking awesome."

"He really is. And his ranch is something else. I bet he'd love to pick your brain sometime." When she looked at me in confusion, I elaborated that it was because he was a farmer and she studied environmental engineering.

"When can I meet them and the other couple? Mr. and Mrs. Chisolm, right?"

"Yeah, my old coach and his wife. We are meeting up with them tomorrow. We can actually go next door to the Easterly's right now if you want."

"Really?" she said eagerly, but it was clear she didn't care for the actual answer as she dashed down the stairs, leaving me alone in the attic.

By the time I made it downstairs, Sadie was bouncing on her toes by the truck's passenger door.

"Behave," I scolded my sister as I turned around in my driveway. Or what would soon be my driveway. It was still a mud pit for now.

I drove the ten minutes to the entrance of Sunny Brook Farms and waited patiently for Sadie to get the full effect before I pulled through the gates.

"My goodness. It's so beautiful, Colton." Her face was basically pressed against the glass of her window.

"I had the same reaction when I came here for the first time. Wait until you see the house and farm."

We passed through the harvested corn fields until we crested the hill that pulled away like a theater's curtain as it showcased the Easterly's ranch.

Breathlessly, I could hear Sadie murmur, "Oh, wow."

Yeah, I know, kid.

"Now, before we go in there, I want you to be prepared that I haven't seen Autumn in over a week, so. . ."

"So, I need to make friends quickly so you can scurry off with your girlfriend?"

"Well, not exactly. I haven't spoken to her in like two days, so she may have my balls."

"What? Colton! Why haven't you spoken to her? What if she thinks you're dead?"

"She doesn't think I'm dead, but I've been hanging out with you. I even turned my phone off, remember?"

My agent was probably going nuts right now, but I'd enjoyed the reprieve from technology. I spent the last couple of days going with Sadie to all her favorite places and learning more things about our mom. But I'd completely ignored the thought that Autumn may have reached out to me.

"Probably not your smartest idea, big bro, but I guess you don't get paid for your brains, huh?"

"Man, not holding back with the punches, are you?"

"No way." As we exited the truck, Sadie asked who was going to be in the large modern farmhouse and I explained I had no idea, but Nash and Marisol were Autumn's parents.

Walking toward the house, I was used to seeing people milling about that worked the farm or at least

Nash hanging around the house. The man couldn't sit still to save his life.

I knocked on the large wooden door and waited, but when there was no answer, I twisted the knob and pushed the door open.

"Hello? Anyone home?" I called out, tilting my head for Sadie to follow me.

The sound of chatter grew as I approached the kitchen and living area, hoping Sadie was following behind me. When I crossed the entrance, I was surprised to find all of Autumn's siblings grouped over a computer that they were scrolling through, her dad leaning over the kitchen island with his phone in his hands, Marisol resting on the couch watching a decorating show on television. The same show that would be filming at my home in six months.

"Hey, everyone," I greeted, hoping to receive a warm welcome. I'd become good friends with the Easterly family. Instead, they greeted me with complete silence.

Autumn's sisters turned to face me in astonishment and her brother cracked his knuckles, a vein bulging in his neck.

"Well, don't you always seem to make a dramatic entrance," Alex said.

"What?" I whispered just as Sadie stepped up beside me.

"Hi, everyone! I'm Sadie Cartwright, Colton's half-sister." Leave it to my sister to stun the crowd further.

"So you're not cheating on Autumn with your sister?" Alex exclaimed as she stood at the table.

"What? No, don't be ridiculous, Alex."

"Ridiculous?" the tall blonde exclaimed as she approached me, her fists clenched at her waist. It was obvious she was itching for a fight and I got the feeling it wasn't on Autumn's behalf, but maybe something going on in her own life. "I'll show you ridiculous, you two-timing-"

A domineering shout masked the room as Marisol stood from her spot on the couch. "Hush, Alexandra. I told you from the beginning that you and your siblings jumped to conclusions. Look at her. This young lady has so nicely come to meet our family and you all haven't even welcomed her and Colton. I am ashamed of you all."

"We didn't know, Ma. There were pictures and stories," Alex tried to explain, but my focus had zoomed into the laptop screen on the kitchen table. There was a zoomed-in picture of me leaving Sadie's house with her at my side. The headline accused me of having multiple women since my breakup with Nina.

"Did Autumn see this?" I asked, interrupting Mrs. Easterly and the growing noise in the room. "Hey! Did Autumn see this?" I shouted again. Finally, that seemed to get the room's attention.

Nash approached me with his eyes open and brows relaxed. "She did, but she defended you tooth and nail. She immediately knew this young woman was your sister. And so did I."

"Where is she?" I asked frantically, grabbing Nash's forearm. "Was she okay? Did she seem upset?"

"She was frustrated. Not with you, but with her siblings. I'm pretty sure you know where you can find her."

Glancing over my shoulder, I searched for Sadie who had planted herself on the couch with Marisol, talking animatedly with her hands as I'd learned she seemed to when she was excited.

"Yeah, I do. Think you can watch my sister for a bit?"

"She's in good hands."

Nodding at my friend, I turned and headed toward the mudroom, grabbing a set of UTV keys along the way. Just as I found the collective of off-road vehicles, Alex came running toward me.

"Colton! Colton! I'm so sorry. We all are. We should have trusted you and Autumn. You both knew your relationship better than we did."

Grabbing her shoulders, I shook her until she silenced. "Alex, I need to find Autumn."

"Oh, yes. Sorry. Go get her. I'll do my best to keep everyone from the west field for a while." I appreciated her hint as to where I could find my girl.

"Thanks."

I tucked my body into the UTV and made my way over to the west fields, trying to remember the path Autumn had taken after I came and enjoyed dinner with her and her family. I felt numb as the wind whipped across my skin, but it wasn't from the growing chill in the air. It was from the knowledge of Autumn trusting me. That had to mean something more.

The drive was agonizingly slow, but when the roof of the barn came into view, my heart started racing. There were things I wanted to tell Autumn, things that I needed to say so it was clear where I stood with her.

"Autumn!" I yelled, tossing the vehicle into park and grabbing the keys from the ignition.

I ran around the exterior of the barn, calling out her name, but I couldn't locate her anywhere. Was there a chance that there was a similar barn on this side of the property? Luckily, as I approached the backside of the barn, I saw another UTV parked along the along the hay bales.

"Autumn," I shouted, just as I trampled over a small figure in my haste to turn the corner.

"Oomph."

"Autumn, are you okay?" I said, hovering over her as she lay flat on the ground. My hand shook as I checked her over for any injuries from the fall.

"We've got to stop meeting like this," she replied with a giggle. It took me a moment, but I recalled that the first time we met, she had nearly run me over at the grocery store.

"Probably a good idea." Standing, I held out my hand and held her to her feet.

When she finally seemed steady on her feet, I took a step back.

"Hi," I said. Autumn surprised me as she launched herself into my arms.

"I missed you." Her breath was warm and affectionate as it wrapped around my neck.

"I missed you, too, baby."

I held her like she would disappear the second I unraveled my arms from around her waist. Unwillingly, I settled her back on her feet.

"What are you doing here?" she asked and I explained I came straight from her family's house where they accused me of cheating.

"I kept trying to tell them, Colton." Her hands flung around spiritedly as she spoke. "They already had their minds made up and wouldn't listen."

"I brought her with me."

"Who?"

"Sadie. My sister."

"She's here?" Autumn's eyes began scanning the area excitedly.

"She's not *here* here. She's at your parents' house. I left her with your mom."

"Well, that's probably better than leaving her with my siblings."

My fingers caressed her arm as I reached for her hand, intertwining our fingers.

"They apologized. They were only looking after you because they love you."

"Yeah, I know," she said begrudgingly, the toe of her boot kicking at the grass.

I was too nervous to outright tell her I loved her, too. Something about speaking the words I'd never said before locked them deep in my chest. Instead, I found myself thanking her for what she did with the attic at my house and for believing in me when no one else had, especially when the pictures of us had surfaced. Autumn had no desire to be in the public eye under everyone's scrutiny. It was why she detested small town living.

I'd already come up with backup plans if she found a job somewhere else because I couldn't be without her.

"You know, if you take a job in Knoxville, or anywhere else, I've thought about renting out the place as a vacation home when I'm not using it."

"I'm not going anywhere, Colton. At least not for a while. I turned down a job offer last Friday."

"What? Why?"

"I could never be sure if they would hire me for my merit or because I was connected to you." Quickly, she added, "And that's not your fault, Colton."

"So, you turned down a job because of me?"

"No, I turned down a job because of *me*. I'm good at what I do and I think the best use of my talent is going to be here, running our own venue. I'll be able to make my own decisions and not worry about someone stealing my idea because they own the company.

"But, while it may not have been for *you*, there was a part of me that was hoping we could see where this goes."

The smile that grew on my face was contagious as Autumn's spread to match.

"That's really good because I turned down almost all of the gigs my agent set up for me. I'll only do a few of them that don't require a lot of time away from Ashfield. Time away from you."

"Really?"

"Yeah. I love you, Autumn Easterly."

Her eyes shimmered in the light of the setting sun. "I love you too, Colton," she whispered before launching herself into my arms, her legs wrapping around either side of my waist.

Our lips met in a hungry kiss. Too much time had gone by and we were starved for each other. Tongues danced and hands roamed.

I growled her name as her center rubbed against my jean-clad erection. "I'm famished for you."

Sliding down my body, my cock practically whimpered as she pulled away.

"I know just where to go," the vixen replied, tugging me inside the barn. I followed her like a bewitched sap. I was completely under her spell.

She took us to an old office in the back corner and in lightning-fast time she had me stripped down and an equal amount of her own clothing removed.

There was no holding back when she pushed me to lean against the old desk, which I prayed would hold our weight, and straddled my hips. Autumn rode out both of our orgasms at an agonizingly slow pace.

Cradled against my body, the desk squeaked, but neither of us moved or cared. I'd take the brunt of the fall anyway. She would be protected so long as she was with me.

"They're probably wondering where we are." My fingers trailed up and down her spine and I loved the way her body shivered with each pass.

"Most likely," she replied but made no hint of moving.

"I should go save Sadie."

That information perked Autumn up and she bounced down from the desk. I groaned at the loss of contact and my unabashed stare at her swaying breasts.

"Get dressed, Colton. I want to meet your sister."

"She's not going anywhere," I joked, only for Autumn to throw my hoodie at my chest.

"Yes, but she's your family. This is huge."

Grasping her arm, I waited for Autumn's rush to change to stop.

"Autumn, you're my family. You, Brett, and Lily, and the rest of the Easterlys are more family than I ever thought I deserved. It took meeting Sadie to realize that."

"Oh, Colton. They all love you just as much as I do."

"Hopefully in a different kind of way," I teased as I finished tugging on my shoes.

"It's definitely different. You didn't steal their house from them."

"You're never going to let that go, are you?" I draped my arm across her shoulder.

"Not in a million years."

I walked Autumn to her vehicle and then we caravanned back to the house. Upon entering, I kissed Autumn one more time because I knew once she met Sadie the two women were going to spend the rest of the night together.

"Look who finally arrived," my annoyingly sweet sister said from her perch at the kitchen island where she swirled a piece of bread in a dish. She shoved the starchy goodness in her mouth and made her way over to us. "You must be Autumn," she said with a mouth full of food.

"Yes, and you're Sadie. I'm so excited to meet you." In true Autumn fashion, she wrapped my sister in a tight embrace and I wasn't surprised when Sadie returned it.

"You made it back just in time for dinner. Everyone have a seat," Mrs. Easterly called out to the room as she poured noodles into a dish.

Autumn's hand trailed against mine as she went to take a seat at the table, making sure my sister had the open chair between her and Nash. I watched in fascination as the Easterlys welcomed us at their table as if we were old friends, not mere acquaintances.

"You going to join us, son?"

Nodding, I made my way over to the table and the open seat on the other side of Autumn. I glanced around the table, watching everyone interact. This was all I'd ever wanted growing up, and by the look on Autumn's face, she did too. All we needed was to take the time to find it.

Epilogue

Autumn

I hung the last of the decorations for the open house event we were hosting at The Easterly Barn. It was a chance for the town to see what we created and drum up some word-of-mouth marketing.

Not that we needed much. After Colton had allowed cameras in his fully furnished 1800s home, he not so slyly mentioned that the now bed-and-breakfast was available for those booking events at The Easterly Barn. Our calendar was booked up for the next two years from the single mention.

In the last six months, we'd completely overhauled the space and instead of looking like a rustic wasteland, it now appeared like a well-loved space with exposed wood and stone. It was romantic.

"Hey, Sadie, can you hand me that string of twinkle lights, please?" Colton's sister was here on spring break and was helping us with the event tonight. It seemed like everyone was chipping in. Vendors from across the state were interested in contracting with us and we now boasted a slew of options for our guests.

All of our hard work was coming to fruition.

The girl, who just celebrated her twenty first birthday held out the thin strand and I casually draped it around one of the beams that ran across the three-story roof. Apparently, I was the only Easterly sister that wasn't terrified of heights as I stood on scaffolding just to reach the beams.

"You're making me nervous. Can you get down from there?" It seemed it wasn't just the Easterly sisters affected.

"Yeah. I need to get the crew to tear this all down, Alex," I called out. "What time will the catering staff arrive?"

"In thirty minutes. Plenty of time."

The caterers we partnered with in Knoxville had been so gracious when we reached out. They were another family-owned business and had been looking for a new venture. The timing had been perfect.

The father was a bit of a hockey fan, too, so he was thrilled to potentially work with Colton, who took the recognition in stride.

When I descended the last ladder, I asked Alex where everyone had scurried off to, but she shrugged and assumed everyone was getting ready for the event back at the house. We'd converted most of the rooms in the barn into spaces for bridal parties to get ready and relax.

"Why are they at the house?" I asked, confused. We'd brought everyone's clothes over to the barn this morning.

"Um. . .I don't know? Something about Mom's forgetting a pie."

It didn't make sense, but I'd been frantically trying to get the space perfect that I must have missed everyone getting ready earlier.

"I'll be back," Alex declared and then dashed away before I could question her further.

"Hey, Colton," I said as my boyfriend walked into the barn. He was dressed to the nines in a tuxedo that fit like a glove. As he got closer, I reached out and adjusted the bow tie, whispering how I hoped he wanted to play with it later.

"We'll see," he said as he took my hand and asked for me to show him all the final touches. He'd been in Knoxville most of the day for something his agent had set up with the hockey team. It was a game I still didn't understand fully, but I'd learned that Colton was one of the best players in the league.

As we walked around the space, I rambled on about the last-minute changes, like swapping the pub tables for seated round tables instead and how we moved some of the food stations to the other side of the main floor.

Just as I was about to go into detail regarding the twinkle lights on the beams, Colton tugged at my hand.

"Hey."

"Hey," I said as I nestled up against him. This was my favorite spot in the entire barn. Dad had hung three oversized chandeliers that lit up the entire space. But this one in particular would be where the wedding arch would stand. It was at the opposite end of the entrance to the barn and we'd installed glass paned windows that climbed from the floor to the third-floor ceiling, giving an outstanding view of the fields and mountains. The windows weren't originally in our budget, but Colton surprised us with them one day.

All I knew was that the man had a great financial advisor.

Colton released my hand and slid it up my arm to cup my face. "I want to have you here one day."

"Have me where?"

"Here. Where the ceremony takes place." My brows furrowed as I titled my head. Colton was spewing riddles I didn't understand.

"I'm confused," I told him.

Filling his chest with air, Colton slowly bent down to one knee and then everything made sense.

"Autumn Easterly, you are the best thing that has ever knocked into me," he began and I found myself giggling as I remembered the day we met and I crashed into him while he was looking for flowers. "We had a rocky start in the beginning, but there isn't a single person I would have wanted to spend the last seven months with. Be my wife and we can share the next seventy years together. Will you marry me?"

He opened up a black box with shaking hands, but I couldn't pull my gaze away from his eyes. The same eyes that hypnotized me the first time we met.

There was no one else for me in this world. Colton was not just my best friend; he was my soulmate.

"Yes!" I exclaimed as I sunk down to my knees and wrapped my arms around his neck.

My family scurried out from their hiding places in the barn when he placed the ring on my finger, but I was too focused on my now fiancé to acknowledge them right away.

Pressing a kiss to my lips, I found my cheeks aching from how hard I was smiling.

"You know what this means, right?" Colton asked as we stood in unison.

"No, what?" I replied, finally taking a chance to admire the large diamond ring now sitting perfectly on my finger.

"What's mine is yours. Once we're married, the house will belong to your family again."

Laughing as our family and friends approached us with congratulatory wishes, I said, "Maybe that was my plan all along."

Without skipping a beat, Colton replied, "Ha, you love me and you know it."

Reaching down for his hand, knowing that I would get forever to do so, I said, "I do. I really do."

THE END

Stay in Touch

Newsletter: http://bit.ly/2WokAjS

Author Page: www.facebook.com/authorreneeharless

Reader Group: http://bit.ly/31AGa3B

Instagram: www.instagram.com/renee_harless

Bookbub: www.bookbub.com/authors/renee-harless

Goodreads: http://bit.ly/2TDagOn

Amazon: http://bit.ly/2WsHhPq

Website: www.reneeharless.com

Acknowledgments

First, I want to thank the readers, bloggers, and influencers that took a chance on me, Time For You, and this new series. I agonized over wanting you all to love Autumn and Colton as much as I did.

Patricia, without you I'd never be able to finish a single book. You are there whenever I need to hash something out and I truly appreciate you.

To my editing team. Your late nights and quick turnarounds helped make sure this book was the best it could be. Thank you for loving Colton and Autumn's story.

To Carolina, my life would crumble to pieces without you. Thank you for pushing me to be the best that I can be and knowing when I just needed you to listen to me vent. You are truly a diamond and I treasure you.

To my family, I do all of this for you. Thank you for your patience, love, and support. It means far more than anything else in this world.

About the Author

Renee Harless is a *USA TODAY* bestselling romance writer with an affinity for wine and a passion for telling a good story.

Renee Harless, her husband, and children live in Blue Ridge Mountains of Virginia. She studied Communication, specifically Public Relations, at Radford University.

Growing up, Renee always found a way to pursue her creativity. It began by watching endless runs of White Christmas- yes even in the summer – and learning every word and dance from the movie. She could still sing "Sister Sister" if requested. In high school, she joined the show choir and a community theatre group, The Troubadours. After marrying the man of her dreams and moving from her hometown she sought out a different artistic outlet – writing.

To say that Renee is a romance addict would be an understatement. When she isn't chasing her kids around the house, working her day job, or writing, she jumps head first into a romance novel.